FIRE
IN THE
SNOW

FIRE
IN THE
SNOW

JOHN McRAE

Deseret Book Company
Salt Lake City, Utah

Library of Congress Cataloging-in-Publication Data

McRae, John, 1927–
    Fire in the snow / John McRae.
        p.   cm.
    ISBN 0–87579–752–0
    1. Frontier and pioneer life—Utah—Fiction. 2. Mormons—Utah—Fiction. 3. Utah—History—Fiction. I. Title.
PS3563.C69F57   1993
813'.54—dc20   93–27311
                                           CIP

Printed in the United States of America

10 9 8 7 6 5 4 3 2

To my family,
with grateful appreciation and love
for those who showed their special affection

CONTENTS

CHAPTER ONE

PENWYTHE, CORNWALL

JANUARY 1856

Rain fell on the little village of Penwythe in a cold, slashing torrent. For seventeen days the villagers had seen incessant rain, and though it was not yet three in the afternoon, the sky was near-black. Grey and unassuming even in sunshine, Penwythe's small cluster of drab stone buildings was almost obliterated by the misty gusts. The entire length and breadth of Cornwall, the narrow boot protruding into the Atlantic at the southwestern tip of England, had been engulfed by the stubborn, howling storm.

Rain cascaded from the steep slate roof of the two-storied stone house of Jacob and Jennie Boyle near the village center. This house had been the only shop in Penwythe for over two hundred years, the Boyle family its only shopkeepers. It served as grocery, greengrocery, chemist shop, and social center to the villagers, who at last count numbered one hundred and sixty-four persons.

A somber group of men had gathered in the shop on this blustery January afternoon. They sat at the back near the hot stove, arguing among themselves as they had throughout most of the afternoon.

Ed Simpson, a thin, seedy-looking man with a straggling moustache, poured some tea from his cup into the saucer and blew on it. The tea was already cold, but Ed always blew before he slurped. He peered over the saucer out the shop's front windows, seeing the rain hammering into the street.

1

"A proper guts of rain, that is," he muttered. He blew on the cold tea again, then drank noisily from the saucer.

"Well, what are we going to do about it?" The shopkeeper, Jacob Boyle, a large, pallid man in his late forties who was wearing a shopkeeper's apron, looked about the room as he asked the question.

"Can't do nuthin'," Simpson answered, still staring at the rain. "Won't stop 'til it's a mind to."

"Not the rain," Boyle said irritably. "This evil foreigner what's living right here among us—it's time we made up our minds what we're doing about it."

"I agree," Charlie Rudd said, nodding. Charlie was a fisherman, and his ruddy, weather-beaten cheeks contrasted sharply with the white pallor of the shopkeeper. "It's been four days now—I say we heave him out of Penwythe."

Jennie Boyle, a short, heavyset woman in a long, black dress with a knitted shawl drawn about her shoulders, came out of a back room, carrying a teapot. She made a round of the men, filling the cups held out to her.

"That's the last of it," she said tartly. "I'm making no more. Go home to your families. You've stewed enough over a young lad of a preacher."

"This lad, as you call him, came all the way from America just to find young girls like our Gertie," her husband growled.

John Connell, also a fisherman, who worked his uncle Nat's boat out of St. Ives, angrily banged a fist against his knee. "Let's run him out and be done with it. The vicar's made it plain this American Mormon, or whatever he is, is up to the devil's work."

"What John says is right," another of the men, Leslie Farr, grunted. "The vicar knows right enough what these Mormon preachers are up to. Give the girls some fancy talk and turn their heads, then whisk them off to America—where who knows what happens to them."

"I don't want the likes of that heathen around my daughter

2

Mary, I tell you straight," Charlie Rudd said heavily. He glanced across at Leslie Farr and frowned. "I'm not too happy 'bout the way your boy Fred keeps coming around, neither," he added. "There's been too much giggling going on between them two—"

"The question is," Jacob Boyle interrupted, "what do we intend to do about this Mormon preacher?"

"The same thing they done to that one up in Devon last month," Farr growled. "Baste him good with tar and feathers—send him up the road like a bloody chicken."

Harry Coombs, a mild-mannered farmer with a soft, flowing white beard, who seldom said anything to anybody, took his pipe out of his mouth. "We've not heard the foreigner speak his piece—"

"And we won't," Leslie Farr snapped. "Not if I can help it. He knocked on our door the other day and my Lucy slammed it right in his face. He's lucky I wasn't to home, I tell you that. Give the devil a tongue and no telling what harm will come."

"Why don't someone just tell this preacher to leave," Coombs said quietly. "Seems better to me than stirring up trouble we don't need."

"There'll be no trouble," Connell retorted. "We give him a tarring, and that's the end of it. Won't none of his kind be back. That's the only way we can be sure God's work is done right and proper."

"I hope God explains it to the constable," Coombs muttered, putting the pipe back in his mouth.

"Won't be no constable in this, Harry, unless one of us puts him in it," Boyle said firmly. "This Mormon won't stop running 'til he's in Sussex."

Jennie Boyle, who had been leaning with folded arms against the wall in a corner of the room, listening to the conversation, cleared her throat with an angry noise. "You men better stop all this foolish talk—"

"We'll have no interference in this, mother," her husband warned sternly, pointing his pipe at her.

Jennie paid no attention to the threatening pipe. "What about the Tregales? Elsie's with child, you know. Carn won't take kindly to you upsetting her. Don't forget he'll be back from hospital soon—with a big hook where he lost his arm in the Crimea. I doubt if any of you wants to stand up to that."

"They had no business taking that heathen into their home," Charlie Rudd said angrily. "Vera knowed it were wrong, even if Elsie hadn't the brains. It were sinful, taking a stranger like that under their roof, especially with Carn up in London. Who knows what's been going on in that house—"

"That's an evil thing to say, Charlie Rudd," Jennie said sharply. "You'd better hope Carn Tregale never finds out you've held thoughts like that about his wife. He'll take that hook to you for sure."

"All I'm saying is, it doesn't look right," Rudd muttered, obviously shaken by the warning.

John Connell shoved his chair noisily back as he stood up. "And I'm saying, let's get on with it. Tar him good and send him packing out of Penwythe. No need to fuss about Carn Tregale nor his hook—he'll thank us for getting that heathen away from his womenfolk."

About a half mile down the hill from the Boyles' shop, set back from the main road on a narrow lane, the Tregale cottage looked as if it was in the middle of a lake formed by rainwater trapped inside the hedged gardens front and back. Like the other buildings in Penwythe, the cottage looked forlorn in the grey, gusting rain.

Inside was cheery enough, however. The fireplace was stoked high with glowing coals, making the tiny front room warm and cozy. This room served as sitting room and kitchen, the worn shabbiness of the furnishings concealed by bright knitted throws. Despite the deepening gloom outside, the lamp on the small, polished table remained unlit. The three people in the room gathered close about the hearth, enjoying the heat and the flickering light of the flames. The whole afternoon had been so dark and dreary that no one paid any attention to the gathering of nightfall; it was hard to tell one from the other.

Elsie Tregale was a pretty woman barely turned twenty, with glistening dark hair. She had rosy cheeks and a natural glow of health that came from Cornish wind and sun, accentuated now by the child forming inside her. Elsie was four months pregnant and was just beginning to show.

Without being consciously aware of it, Elsie let her hands stray to her stomach, feeling the bulge of life. A little smile of pleasure lifted the corners of her mouth. This child would always be a reminder of the day her husband had finally come home from the dreadful horror of the Crimea. She could still see how pinched and pale he had looked, his left arm, or what was left of it, heavily bandaged and hanging in a sling. Lines were etched on her husband's face that he had not had when he left a year before to fight in a foreign land she still could not place easily in her mind.

Carn had returned to London four weeks ago to have the smooth leather sheath on his arm fitted with a hook. Carn had insisted on having it, for it would mean he could use the arm again in earning a livelihood. Other than the hook, there was no other compensation from the government; it was a price some paid for serving their country. Carn was grateful he was alive. Many others, good Cornishmen among them, had paid a far greater price.

Elsie had not allowed herself to picture the hook fully in her mind—a cold, cruel curve of steel forever replacing the soft touch of loving fingers. She had expected her husband home several days ago, but he must have been delayed in the fitting. Elsie comforted herself that each day now might be the one that would see her husband trudging up the lane and back into her life.

She realized guiltily that her thoughts had slipped away from the conversation when she heard her mother asking a question rather sharply, apparently for the second time.

"I said, you're not really serious about this talk of going to America, are you?"

Elsie glanced quickly at the young man they had opened their home to several days ago, saw him watching her intently. She nodded. "I think I am, mother."

"Nonsense," her mother snorted. "If you must be one of these Mormons, you can be one here in Penwythe, where you belong. No need to go clear around the world to tell God you love him. He can hear you just as good right here in your own home."

"But America, mother—doesn't it stir something exciting in your heart?"

"England is what's in my heart, child. England—and Cornwall. Our home. You can be sure Carn won't want to go traipsing off again—he's had his fill of foreign places."

"I'll not go without him—"

"Then it's settled, isn't it. You'll be staying here and raising your babies in a proper fashion."

Vera Thomas, a thin woman with a stern face that showed the hardships of years spent struggling to raise a daughter alone, fussed her fingers nervously over the tight, grey bun of hair at the back of her head. Elsie had been a baby when her father's fishing boat capsized in a storm and sank off Land's End. Vera had thought she was lucky to have had one husband; she knew there would be no second chance, not with her plainness and a baby. So she had put her life into her child.

What little happiness and pleasure Vera had enjoyed these past twenty years had all been linked to Elsie. Thoughts of her daughter going off to the Americas to join some strange religion were devastating, although she tried hard not to show it too much. Better to let Elsie use her own head to sort things through. She had grown into a fine, intelligent young woman, well able to tell what was nonsense and what was not. The tales of this young preacher from America made no sense at all to Vera.

Not that he wasn't a perfect gentleman, give him his due. He was dressed in a black suit badly in need of pressing, but clean. He wore a white shirt that Vera had washed just yesterday, starching the high collar. He was wearing a billowy black tie and looked all the part of a traveling preacher except for the boyish face barely used to the touch, or the need, of a razor. He was more boy than man, Vera thought, a couple of years younger than Elsie. What on earth were his parents thinking about, letting a young lad take off around the world with hardly a shilling in his pocket. Gone for at least two or three years, the boy had said. That told her something about these Mormons; they had to be a strange lot.

Much of what the lad said had a ring of common sense to it, but there were things that defied reason unless you plain believed in miracles, which Vera didn't. Hadn't been any in her life, nor in anyone else's that she knew about. Miracles had stopped happening a long time ago. Still, there was no doubting the Mormon lad had tugged a string inside her daughter. Vera felt very uncomfortable about that.

The young man sensed that Mrs. Thomas was thinking about him, though she was trying not to show it. "You've both been very kind to me," he said, looking directly at the mother, "and I'm sure it was God's will that brought me to this door. I've told you what God has revealed in these latter days, but it would be painful to think the words of the new and everlasting gospel have come between mother and daughter—"

"I know you have no malice," Mrs. Thomas said quickly, "but it's not easy for me to believe some of these stories. Goodness gracious—you've told some tall ones, haven't you. God coming down and having a chat with a fourteen-year-old boy. Angels coming down from heaven and digging up gold plates buried for a thousand years. Dead prophets from the Bible popping up all over the place. It's a bit hard to swallow, isn't it."

"Not when the words touch your heart, mother," Elsie murmured. "Not when you feel a burning inside, a joy you cannot explain."

"Well, I'm sorry, and no offense intended," Mrs. Thomas said, her mouth pulling into a tight line as she stared at the young missionary, "but it sounds to me like your Mr. Smith has been having hallucinations, not heavenly visions."

All three of them jumped at a sudden, crashing sound against the front door. They looked at each other, then Elsie sprang from her chair and rushed to the window. She wiped her hand across the fog of moisture on the glass and peered outside. "There are men out by the gate," she gasped, turning back to her mother.

Vera Thomas crossed quickly to the window, squinting outside as she wiped a bigger hole. She studied the crowd of dark shapes bunched just outside the front hedge. "Why, that's Jacob Boyle," Vera snapped, "and there's Charlie Rudd and John Connell. What on earth are they doing at our—"

Another loud crash came from the front door. Vera turned to look at her daughter in disbelief.

"John Connell—he heaved a rock at our front door!" she exclaimed, an incredulous expression on her face. "I saw him do it—"

Jacob Boyle shouted from outside, the words battered by the the storm but clear enough to be heard by the three people inside the house. "We don't mean no harm to you, Vera Thomas, or your daughter. It's that heathen preacher we want. We'll have no Mormons in Penwythe. You just send him out, and we'll have done with this."

The young missionary sprang to the window and peered out over the two women. His face paled, but he did not hesitate. Turning back toward the chair where he had been sitting, he picked up two small books of scripture from the floor, pulled his jacket together, and straightened his shoulders. There was a resolute set to his mouth.

"God works in strange ways," he told the two women. "I've been trying to talk to these people—perhaps this is the time chosen for me to do it."

"More like the devil's time," Vera snorted. "Those men are going to give you a beating, lad, not listen to a sermon. If you've a scatter of sense, you'll sneak out the back door and lift your heels.

No time to gather your things—better to have a whole skin than a second shirt. You'd best be off, lad."

There was another shouted warning from Boyle. "Send that heathen out, Vera, or we'll come in and get him."

The missionary gave the women a wan smile, his shoulders lifting in a helpless gesture. "Wouldn't do any good for me to run, Mrs. Thomas—I'm shaking so much inside, they'd have me in no time. But one person here in Penwythe has seen the truth of the gospel, and if I were to lose my life this night, that makes my coming here worthwhile." He stretched out his hand toward Elsie. She grasped it, and he could see the tears welling up in her eyes. "Sister Tregale, I'll tell you the truth of it. I've spent eight months already here in England, and you are the first to accept the gospel from me. I want to thank you for that. It's the truth, Sister Tregale, all that I've told you. Now I'd better go out there. Don't worry. God is with me. Whatever happens will be his will, I am sure of that."

Tears flowed freely down Elsie Tregale's cheeks. She looked angrily out of the window, then stepped in front of the missionary, putting her hand on the door latch. "If it's Mormons they want," she said, "they shall have both of us."

Even as Vera Thomas protested, Elsie flung open the door. Wind and rain blasted into the room as she stepped outside, but she took no more than one step before a shrill cry broke from her. Her knees sagged, and a few drops of blood splattered the doorpost. She had stepped directly into the path of a large rock thrown from the gate. It struck her on the forehead with a horrible cracking sound. There was only that one cry, then Elsie Tregale collapsed in a heap in the open doorway. An ugly line of blood welled across her forehead and ran down into her hair. Elsie's mother and the young missionary stared at her, horrified.

Now there was a rush of feet up the path. Jacob Boyle reached the doorway first and he quickly knelt beside Elsie's still form. As the other men crowded around, Boyle's fingers held the woman's wrist, seeking for a pulse. The look on his face confirmed the fears of those around him.

"Somebody fetch the vicar," Boyle muttered, "and the doctor in St. Ives. Tell him to hurry—Elsie's hurt bad."

John Connell groaned in agony as he clutched both hands to his face. Charlie Rudd looked up at Vera Thomas, whose eyes were still transfixed on her daughter's silent body. "It were not meant for Elsie," he told her. "We didn't know it was her opening the door— it were an accident, Vera."

Words finally pushed out from Vera Thomas's constricted throat. "You've killed my baby—you've killed her baby too."

"Nobody's dead, Vera," Jacob Boyle said. "Elsie's had a bad blow and she's unconscious, but she's not dead."

Vera fell to her knees and threw her arms about the limp form of her daughter, great, heaving sobs shaking her bony frame.

Jacob Boyle stood up, not wanting to be in the way of a mother's grief. He glared over at the young missionary, who was staring down at the fallen Elsie with anguish on his face.

"You're the cause of this, you heathen," Boyle hissed.

Charlie Rudd motioned to the other men beside him. "Let's get her inside." He pulled the sobbing Vera away from her daughter. "We'll put her on the bed, Vera. You'd better get those wet clothes off her. The doctor will be here afore long to tend to her."

Elsie was carried unconscious into her bedroom, her mother holding her hand. The door closed and Jacob Boyle reached out and seized the young missionary's arm in a vicious grip.

"See what you've done. This wouldn't have happened if it weren't for you. It's evil you are and evil you've brought to this house."

Connell pushed forward into the room, the rain streaming from head and clothing. Pain and fear were on his face. He slammed his fist hard into the face of the missionary. Blood spurted from the youth's nose. "It should have been you, Mormon, who took that stone, not Elsie—"

"Let's get out of here," Charlie Rudd muttered. He looked at Jacob Boyle. "You know Vera better than the rest of us, Jacob. Should be you who waits 'til the vicar comes. I'll send over my wife and your Jennie to help." He surveyed the group of men. "None of this changes what were going to happen, do it?"

The men in the room growled agreement. Connell grabbed the missionary by his coat and dragged him outside. The other men followed and Boyle shut the door.

In the darkness and the driving rain, the young Mormon preacher felt the hate of the men holding him and tried not to let terror overcome him. He could not shake the image of Elsie Tregale slumped on the ground, blood smearing her face. That man Jacob was right—it was his fault Sister Tregale had been struck down. Tears stung his eyes, mixing with the rain.

It was full dark by the time the men entered the barn at the back of Jacob Boyle's shop, dragging the beaten and nearly unconscious missionary by his legs. An oil lamp was lit in the center of the barn, old Harry Coombs sitting on a rickety chair beside it. Coombs had declined to accompany the men to the Tregales, claiming arthritis and an inability to walk such a long distance in the storm. They all knew Harry was not in favor of this night's doings, but he had agreed to wait for them in the barn.

Coombs came to his feet as they hauled the missionary's limp body into the lamplight and dropped him unceremoniously on the ground. The youth did not move. Coombs leaned forward, peering anxiously down at him.

"Haven't killed him, have 'e?"

"He'll wish he were dead 'fore we get through with him," John Connell growled. "Elsie Tregale lies near death up at cottage because of him. He's the devil's messenger, for sure."

"What happened to Elsie?" Coombs asked fearfully.

They told him, placing the blame on the youth at their feet but seeing in Harry Coombs's face that, no matter how they told it, the truth was plain as to who was responsible for striking down Elsie

Tregale. It gave each man a shiver. The rock had struck squarely, cracking Elsie's skull, and they knew there was a real probability Vera's fears would come true. Each man could clearly hear Vera repeating the charge of murder before a magistrate.

The missionary's suit coat and most of his shirt had been torn away in the beating given him after they took him from the cottage. The starched collar was still around his neck, and strangely, the billowy black tie also was in place. Connell reached down and ripped off the collar and tie. Others stripped off the remainder of the youth's clothing, including shoes and stockings, until he was sprawled naked on the hard dirt of the barn.

The young missionary groaned and tried to push up onto his knees but a booted foot smashed into his buttocks and knocked him back flat on the ground. The missionary rolled onto his side and raised himself on one elbow, shaking his head and staring dazedly around the grim circle of faces. His voice came as a frightened croak.

"What are you going to do——?"

John Connell stooped down, leaning belligerently toward him. "What do you think, you heathen?"

The young man met Connell's angry stare evenly. "If you intend to kill me, sir, I would ask one small favor."

"A favor is it," Connell snorted. "You've got gall, I'll give you that. What favor would you be asking?"

"To write a final word to my mother, sir. And to have someone post it to her."

Harry Coombs spoke up. "No one is going to kill you, lad. You'll not be needing last words to your mother, though I for one think the more of you for making such a request."

"Don't you go soft, Harry Coombs," Connell snarled, straightening. "The devil guides the tongue on this one."

Coombs looked around at the other men, saw their fears, their anger. "I'm having no more part of this," he stated quietly. He fastened his stare full on John Connell. "And when it comes to the

12

devil, it may be you he's guiding this night." Harry Coombs turned and walked out of the barn, favoring the left leg where the arthritis troubled him most. He did not look back.

Connell saw the rest of the men gazing uncertainly after the limping figure. "None of this would have happened if it weren't for this Mormon," Connell told them angrily. "Les, fetch that bucket of tar over there by the heater. Looks as though Harry has it all ready even if he hasn't the stomach for what has to be done. Just remember, all of you—we're about God's work in running this heathen out of Penwythe."

The Mormon missionary looked up at them, a difficult thing to do now that both eyes were purplish and swelling shut. "I preach only the gospel of Jesus Christ, sirs, restored in these latter days. I wish no harm to anyone—"

"You tell Elsie Tregale that," Connell spat at him. "You tell her mother about no harm coming to anyone. But I warn you, heathen, you keep your bloody mouth shut around me." Connell squatted beside the youth and clubbed his head with a clenched fist. The missionary fell back.

"What's your name, preacher?" Simpson asked.

The missionary pushed his tongue out between battered lips, trying to wet them so as to get out the words. "Williams—Elder Williams," he whispered.

"Elder, is it?" Simpson said, smirking. "You look more like a baby to me, lying naked to the world."

Leslie Farr brought the bucket of black tar and set it down beside Connell. The tar was hot enough to be steaming. The other men gripped the missionary tightly and Connell lifted the bucket over the head of the now thoroughly terrified youth.

"Hear me good, Mormon," he said. "If you or any other Mormon preacher ever sets foot in Penwythe again, you'll get more than tar and feathers."

The youth's eyes, even swollen as they were, widened in fear as Connell tipped the tar bucket toward his face. At the last minute,

Connell moved the bucket, and the thick tar spilled onto the youth's chest. The missionary gave a hoarse screech and started to struggle violently. The men held him firmly and Edwards clapped a hand over the youth's mouth to silence any further outcries.

Connell grabbed a length of wood and used it to spread the steaming ooze. He poured more tar into the missionary's hair and black rivulets oozed down around forehead and cheek. The missionary lifted his head, desperately trying to keep the tar from pooling into his eyes and mouth.

When the front of his body was completely covered, Ed Simpson upended a sack of chicken feathers over the tarred lad. The other men sputtered and coughed and backed away. Hands loosed from the victim, but there was no fight left now to escape. Connell shook his head to escape the flying mass of feathers.

"Watch it!" he yelled, spitting out feathers. "Those bloody things are up my nose. Roll him over and let's do the other side."

The young missionary was rolled over onto his stomach. Again Connell poured steaming tar over quivering flesh. As the youth cried out in pain, Simpson shoved his face into the dirt, smothering the cries. There were more feathers and more cursing. When they finished, the men backed away. The missionary lay unmoving.

Ed Simpson looked about the barn nervously. "Let's get him out of here. We'll have doctors and constables poking about soon, asking questions about him and Elsie." He reached out and kicked the youth on the ground. "On your feet, heathen. You head north and don't look back."

Connell leaned over and spat on the huddled shape. "It's the devil's word you've been preaching, Mormon, but God has had the better of it this night."

The young man tried to push himself up off the ground, groaned, and fell back. Connell kicked him hard in the stomach.

"On your feet, heathen, or we'll tie you behind a cart and drag you to London."

The missionary agonizingly got onto his knees. He knew he

14

couldn't make it to his feet, so he started to crawl toward the barn door. Once there, he grasped the post of the doorway and slowly pulled himself upright, gasping from the pain of the tar and feathers coating his body. In the flickering light of the oil lamp, he was a grotesque and pitiful sight.

Then something else loomed in the doorway—a sight bringing fear to every man in the barn. Standing in the entrance was Carn Tregale, his face twisted into a mask of pain and anger. In the flickering light, Tregale could not have struck more terror if he had been the angel of death. He took in the pitiful sight of the tarred and feathered youth clinging to the doorpost, then the empty bucket still in Connell's hand. John Connell saw Tregale staring at him and dropped the bucket to the ground. The other men could not move.

Tregale was tall for an Englishman, taller than any of the other men in the barn. He was lean and muscular, all fat lost in the hardships of the Crimea and the long months in hospitals. His face too was long and lean, clean-shaven, with a strong jaw and a rather hawkish nose. He lifted his arm to point at Connell, and everyone shrank as the lamplight glinted on the shiny new metal hook.

"It was you, John Connell," Tregale said, his voice quivering with rage. "It was you who threw the rock at my Elsie—"

"It were an accident, Carn," Connell said, the words tumbling out fearfully. "I didn't know it were Elsie coming out the door. I thought it were him," he said, pointing at the missionary. "It were his fault—"

"If my Elsie dies," Tregale said grimly, "so will you."

Tregale looked over at the grotesque figure clinging to the doorpost, swaying as if ready to fall. He crossed to the missionary and put out a hand to steady him. Tregale turned back to the men, his glare settling on them with heavy intensity. "Get this lad to hospital in Penzance. Put him in Boyle's carriage there." He could see their looks of uncertainty. "Get about it—that tar won't hurt the carriage as much as it has this poor lad."

Elsie Tregale died two days later, never regaining consciousness. The doctor put the cause down as concussion and internal bleeding resulting from a cracked skull. Elsie's unborn baby died with her.

John Connell left Penwythe that same day, telling no one where he was going. It was rumored he had crossed the channel and gone to France, but no one knew for sure, not even his wife.

The coroner ruled Elsie's death to be accidental and the charges Vera Thomas brought against the men of the village were dismissed. A bitter, unending loneliness settled into Vera's life.

Elder Williams spent two weeks in the hospital in Penzance, then church authorities transferred him to London. The church decided not to pursue the matter, and no one in Cornwall wanted to be seen taking the part of the Mormons over their own kind.

Officially, the cruel incident had not happened.

CHAPTER TWO

LONDON
MARCH

Two months later, Carn Tregale put Penwythe and its memories behind him. No family held him there now, except a mother-in-law he did not feel particularly close to. He could not avoid the men responsible for his wife's death and therefore he found no way to let the anger inside him subside. The constant rage he felt was not healthy for mind or body, so he finally decided to leave the surroundings that had become cold and unfriendly, a place that no longer held a promise he could share with his wife and child. He deeded the house, which had been in his family for generations, to Vera. It would become a lonely shrine for a mother who would never stop grieving for her daughter.

Tregale went off to London. The city, he felt, offered the best opportunity for a man with a hook to find a new life. He moved into a tiny flat and was fortunate to get odd jobs on the docks to keep at least some money coming in. These were bad times for England, and thousands could find no work at all. It was the hook that helped, Tregale knew, and the sympathy it roused for a veteran who had suffered more than others in the tragedy of the Crimea.

After several weeks, Tregale felt driven to look up the Mormon preacher who had been so brutally treated by the men of Penwythe, the young man who had so affected his wife. He wanted to know everything he could about the events that had led up to that black night, the night the train had broken down in the storm, the night he had walked nine miles in the driving rain, eagerly anticipating the reunion with his wife, only to find her unconscious and dying.

Elsie's mother had given him her account, of course, many times—but it left no satisfaction. It gave him no insight into what had touched Elsie's life so deeply or how she had come to be so affected. Whatever Elsie had felt had not been shared by Vera Thomas, and the mother was incapable of explaining it.

Finally, Tregale visited the London headquarters of the Mormon church and found the people there understanding and helpful.

"Of course we remember, sir," the older man to whom he had been referred said sadly. "We were so sorry to hear about your wife and baby. Truly unfortunate."

"It was Williams, wasn't it?" Carn asked hesitantly. "The name of the young preacher—"

"Elder Williams, yes," the older man said, nodding. "He went through quite an ordeal himself. He's said many times, and meant it, I know, that he wished his life had been taken instead of Sister Tregale's."

"My wife hadn't joined your church, had she?"

"No, but she had expressed her desire to be baptized as soon as she'd had a chance to share the gospel with you. It was her wish, and unless you oppose it, we'll see that her work gets done."

"What does that mean?"

"Baptism for the dead. It's a part of our belief. Life doesn't end with death—we just return to our Father in Heaven and resume our existence where we left off when we came down for this earthly experience."

Carn frowned. "Well, that's a little over my head, I'm afraid. What I really want is to talk to this Elder Williams. He obviously had a great influence over my wife and I'd like to hear from him how she felt about your religion."

The other nodded. "That can be arranged, of course. Elder

Williams is laboring here in London—if you give me your address, I'll have him get in touch with you. I'm sure he'll be most anxious to talk to you. Your wife was his first convert, you know—that's always special to these young missionaries."

They chatted for a few minutes more, Carn struck by the caring the man expressed. It was difficult to lay some of the terrible things he had heard about Mormons at the feet of people like these at the Church offices.

A few days later, the young missionary showed up at his flat.

"Mr. Tregale, sir?"

Carn nodded.

"I'm Elder Williams. I was told you wished to talk to me about—about the terrible thing that happened to your wife." Carn was startled to see tears suddenly well up in the eyes of the young man in front of him. "She was very kind to me, sir. I'd be more than happy to answer any questions you may have."

Carn invited him in, studying the young man as he settled in one of the straight-backed chairs beside the table. The flat contained only one battered and worn overstuffed chair, so Carn took a seat at the table across from him.

Williams still showed clear signs of the harsh treatment he had received in Penwythe. Carn could see red blotches on the missionary's forehead and left cheek where the tar apparently had burned deeply. There was no telling how badly the rest of his body was scarred, for he was wearing the traditional black suit and high collar the other Mormons at their headquarters wore. Another very evident sign was the short stubble of hair that had begun to grow back on the young man's head, which obviously had been completely shaved to get rid of the tar. More red scars could be seen on his scalp.

Elder Williams noticed Carn's scrutiny, smiled, and shrugged his shoulders. "It looks worse than it is, really. Doesn't hurt anymore—although it gave me fits for the first few weeks."

"They had no right to do that to you—to do it to any human being."

The missionary shrugged again. "They thought they were doing the right thing. I don't hold it against them, for my own good as much as theirs. Won't do any good to harbor ill feelings."

"Well, there's no forgiveness in me," Tregale grated, "not for what they did to you, and not for what they did to my Elsie."

"That was an accident," the missionary said quickly. "Your wife stepped in front of me—told us if those men wanted Mormons, they would have the both of us. The stone that struck her was meant for me. I can't find forgiveness within myself for not stopping—"

"Elsie considered herself a Mormon?"

"We talked of the whole gospel plan, Mr. Tregale. It struck a chord in her—she had a witness in her heart to the truth of it all. She could hardly wait for you to get home so she could tell you how she wanted both of you to go to America—"

"My wife was planning on going to America?" Carn was startled to hear that his wife's conversion had been so deep. Vera had given no indication that Elsie had taken this Mormon gospel so seriously. She had made her daughter's feelings appear vague and undecided, nothing more than a passing sympathy for the words of a traveling preacher.

"Sister Tregale was my first convert to the gospel," young Williams said quietly. "It thrilled me to see the Spirit working in her."

"What was it that drew her to your faith?" Carn asked.

Williams smiled. "I wish I could answer that, Mr. Tregale, but the truth is I really don't know. I know she was struck by our belief in a life before and after this mortality, and she seemed to feel real joy and understanding in the relationship we have with our Father in Heaven. Are you a God-fearing man, Mr. Tregale?"

"I suppose you could say I am," Tregale answered thoughtfully. He had never really considered himself in exactly that light. "As a child, I went to church regularly with my parents, but I can't honestly say I felt any real religious stirrings. It seems to me to all boil down to a goodness and morality and righteous living that should be a part of any person whether he goes to church or not."

That plunged the young missionary into a long discussion about the way he felt concerning such things. It was interesting to hear Elder Williams talk of beliefs and doctrines he had never heard before. Though many of them sounded strange to him, he quickly understood why Elsie, good and honest and sincere as she was, had been struck so deeply by what she had heard.

In the days that followed, Carn and the young missionary met often, sometimes at the flat, sometimes just for a walk about the park, sometimes with other elders and members of the Church. There was no doubt they believed the stories they told, believed them with all their hearts. This new gospel had become a plan of life for them, a purpose, a goal. Yet Carn felt a little uncomfortable to see people so eager to let the heavens dictate what course their lives should take. He knew he never could submit so completely to a spirit in the sky that he could not see or prove to exist.

Carn Tregale also found something else among the Mormons he did not expect: true, caring friendship. It went beyond trying to make a convert of him. He could not doubt Elder Williams's sincerity, his pain for what had happened to Elsie. While he never tried to push religion onto Carn, he was always ready with an answer to a question, always able to explain the peculiar relationship Mormons had with their God in so many aspects of their lives.

One of the other Mormons Carn met through Elder Williams was Edward Martin. Elder Martin had nearly completed his mission in England and planned to return to America in a couple of months, in company with a large body of converts from the British Isles and several European countries. Elder Martin was a few years older, but Carn liked the open honesty of the man and a strong friendship soon developed between them.

Edward Martin was a stocky, weather-beaten man who looked

out of place in his tight-fitting black suit, high starched collar, and black ribbon tie. The outdoors had taken this man and marked him. It showed in keen blue eyes, in dry, unruly hair that hung long at his neck, in sun-coated cheeks circled by a black, close-cropped rim of beard. Wind and sun had roughed Martin's thirty-seven years into the appearance of at least ten more. Yet though he looked the part, the man was not, strangely enough, a product of the American frontier.

Carn found that out one afternoon when Martin was visiting at his flat. The men were sitting at the small table. "You sound like an Englishman," Carn told him. "One could believe you were born in England."

"I was," Martin laughed. "In Lancashire—Preston, to be exact."

"I was there once. Grimy little city, as I remember."

"It is. Hardly have any family there now."

"How did you get to be a Mormon missionary?"

"Became converted to the gospel in Preston. Heard it preached one Sunday, and something about it touched me. One thing led to another, and I was baptized and went rushing off to America."

"How long ago was that?"

"Twelve years."

"Where did you go in America?"

"To Nauvoo. Beautiful city. The Saints built it out of the Mississippi swamps. We made it the largest, finest city in Illinois—had over twenty thousand people at one point."

"So you came back from Nauvoo to be a missionary—"

"Took a little military stint first," Martin said with a quick shake of his head. "Volunteered to join the Mormon Battalion."

"The Mormons have their own army?" Tregale asked, surprised.

"Not really," Martin explained. "Things weren't going so well in the war with Mexico, so President Polk asked the Church authorities to form a battalion of five hundred men to march to the relief of General Kearney. Anyway, I volunteered. The Saints had just been driven out of Illinois by the mobs, out into the wild frontier plains of Iowa. The Church was destitute. Brigham Young figured the pay and supplies would help the Saints survive and move west.

"We marched down from Iowa to Kansas and on down to Santa Fe, then cut across to southern California. After the war was over, the men in the Battalion marched back to Utah Territory. Wasn't much of a war, but it was a march I'll never forget."

Carn grinned. "So you left on a mission from Salt Lake City—"

"That's right. In the past three-and-a-half years I've served in Glasgow, Newcastle-on-Tyne, Hull, and the Carlisle Conferences. A month ago I was assigned to the emigration office in Liverpool."

"So what have you been doing in London these past few weeks?"

"Taking care of a few things for the emigration group I've been given, mostly getting papers signed and making ship arrangements. It'll be a large group going all the way to the Salt Lake valley."

Carn rubbed his chin thoughtfully. "Sounds like a long way from London."

"Five thousand miles, give or take a few yards. Which brings me to the main reason for this visit. Have you thought about that proposition I made you?"

"I didn't think you were serious about it."

"Never more serious," Ed said firmly. "I talked to President Richards about it again today. He approves—thinks we'll be getting the best of the deal. How about it? I'm leaving for Liverpool in a few days and I'd feel a lot better if I knew I could count on you."

"I'm not a Mormon, Ed, probably never will be. I have no bad feelings about your church, as you know, but whatever it takes to be a Mormon just isn't inside me."

"I'm not asking you to be a Mormon. I'm asking you to come with me to America, to help me with all those folk who have no idea what they're getting into. For that, the Church will pay your passage all the way to Salt Lake City. You'll owe nothing when you get there and you'll be free to go or stay. If it's California that calls you, I'll see you have the means to get there. I've talked this over with President Richards and he agrees to it all. So what do you say?"

Carn shook his head. "Don't feel right about it, Ed. Not being a Mormon, having free passage."

"I'm offering a straight business deal. I need someone strong like yourself to help me get these people to Salt Lake. Just moving them to the frontier is challenge enough, with a company that has more than its share of eighty-year-olds and babies who must be carried. Once there, they'll have to walk another thousand miles across desert and plains and through rivers and over mountains. It's a hard-enough journey in a wagon, but these folk will be walking and dragging handcarts. None of them have any notion of the hardships they'll encounter. I need your help—and you need a new start. Seems like we both come out ahead by accepting my offer."

Carn Tregale pursed his lips thoughtfully, staring off into space. "I have nothing to hold me here, and I admit to liking the idea of going to America—seems like that's the place of opportunity. But I don't have the fare, and it doesn't seem right to take a gift when I know how hard it is for your church to raise all the funds needed for emigration."

"It's no gift," Ed insisted, leaning toward him. "It's wages paid for a job done—and not very good wages, considering how long and hard you'll be working. If that still troubles you, you can pay back the passage when you've made your mark. There's no handout here, Carn."

Carn thought about that a few moments longer, then quickly reached a hand across the table to Ed Martin. "Put that way, seems like there're no obstacles left. I'd be more than happy to accompany you to Utah Territory, Ed Martin."

Ed grasped his hand, smiling his pleasure. "I hope you feel the same after we get there, my friend."

After Martin left, Carn sat at the table for a long while, looking out the window over a smoky, grey world of chimneys and slate roofs. His thoughts were not in London, not even in Penwythe. Perhaps the idea of once again being aboard a ship, carried to an unknown world, set thoughts to drifting. Suddenly, he was once again in that terrible world of the Crimea.

Sevastopol.

Inkerman Ridge.

It was all incredibly sharp in his memory, as if it were happening all over again. He could feel the frozen, snow-packed ground beneath his body as he waited. How many times had they waited, he and the other men of his company. Dirty and miserable, most sick with fever and dysentery, grim-faced men feeling forgotten and alone in an unfriendly country filled with foreigners and death. Little sounds carried clearly on the air, the memory as real as the moment. Bill Hutchins chipping a bayonet into the hard pack of frozen mud clogging the instep of his boot. Thad Turner belching. Turner could belch even when they went a day or more without food, which they frequently did. The metallic tap of the lieutenant's sword on the shoulder button of Carn's greatcoat. Carn clearly remembered how muddy and torn that coat was. He could see the great flakes of mud that almost completely obliterated sight of the cloth. He felt how damp and stiff it was from the rain that had fallen in the evening and then frozen in the night. For some reason, he couldn't remember the lieutenant's voice. Only the words. Strange not to remember a person's voice but to hear the words so clearly in your mind.

"All right, sergeant. Get your men on their feet. We'll be taking that ridge with the bugle."

Take the ridge with the bugle.

That was funny. He could hear Corporal Stratton, sitting next to him on a little cushion of snow he had scraped together, sneering mockingly at the lieutenant behind his back.

"Taking it with a bugle, is he. Well then, he won't be needing me—I don't play the bloody bugle."

That was Stratton in his mind, Stratton's real voice he was hearing. Stratton was dead less than five minutes later, while the bugles were still sounding, his body shattered by a direct hit from a cannon shot. Around him, Tregale could see all that red snow.

Again Tregale felt the tension, heard the confusion of a thousand different sounds blending together yet each distinct. Once again he was part of it, sweating cold sweat. The hoarse cries, the shrieks of agony, the smoking flames. Bayonets waving fiercely in the grip of wild-eyed men. Pounding feet. Snow crusted hard and ungiving underneath. Panting men. Whistling shot. Turner giving his last belch as his life gurgled from the gaping hole in his throat. Splinters of mud stinging his own face. His hand lifting to brush at his eyes, then feeling the shocking touch of hot blood. His blood. He was still running, gasping for a lungful of bitterly cold Crimean air, looking in stupefied disbelief as the rich, red blood spurted from a mangled stump of flesh where fingers and palm and wrist should have been.

Sevastopol.

Inkerman Ridge.

Sitting there in his tiny flat in London, Carn Tregale could feel the fingers on his left hand flexing. It was real, despite the fact that he no longer had any hand, only a curved hook of steel. Just like the image of his wife was real, smiling up at him as she drew him into her arms. Only she was gone now too, just like his hand. Tregale roused himself from the window, forcing himself back to the now. Sevastopol was done, marked into unfeeling pages of history at a table in Paris. His life with Elsie was done, marked by a small headstone in the graveyard of a tiny village in Cornwall. His unborn baby was done, buried in the cold womb of its mother.

All of the yesterdays were done.

It was tomorrow that must be dealt with now.

Tomorrow—and America.

CHAPTER THREE

LIVERPOOL

FRIDAY, MAY 23

I t was a cold, unpleasant morning in Liverpool. Fog wreathed thin fingers across the smooth glass of the Mersey river, reaching into the maze of docks and warehouses that stretched unending along the river's edges. The chill was deep, and Carn Tregale, leaning on the polished rail of the packet ship *Horizon* tied alongside Bramley Moore pier, remembered how much he disliked cold, unpleasant mornings.

The ship's bell clanged sharply. A grey gull striding along the dock was startled into sudden flight. Four bells, two each in quick succession. Six o'clock. The gull flapped a few feet into the air, took a cautious swoop over the stern of the *Horizon*, then settled again on the dock, resuming a sharp-eyed watch for the morning garbage.

A carriage turned onto the dock, wheels rattling on the wood planking as a pair of matched mares clopped toward the ship. The seagull screeched in annoyance and flew away.

The carriage halted before the gangplank. One of the horses pawed nervously, giving a shivering jingle of harness. The driver, a thin-faced man muffled in an upturned overcoat, sniffled and wiped a finger across his nose. He clambered down and opened the carriage door.

A young woman appeared from the coach, standing for a moment on the step. She was slender, almost willowy, with a height that set her above the average. About twenty-three, he guessed, perhaps a year or two older. Her features might have tended to plainness, yet they did not. It was something in the way her chin tilted, in the way well-spaced eyes held steady yet without boldness. Her face had a proud set to it, softened by gentleness and a natural graciousness. He could see excitement on her face as she studied the long, bulky outline of the *Horizon*.

The sailing vessel was large, built for long runs across the Atlantic and the stormy hauls across the bottom of the world to India and Australia. There was a sleekness about it, though, that breathed of wind and bulging sails, of smooth slicing through white-capped waters. The woman's glance took in the orderly brass work and mahogany of the decks, lifting toward the topmost height of the mainmast. She suddenly became aware of the man watching her from the ship's railing, of her dress held above black-stock-inged ankles. She stepped quickly to the ground, eyes lowered.

The driver wrestled two travel bags to the dock. At the same time, a pudgy, heavily bundled man with a florid face and grey moustache climbed from the carriage, which responded with a bouncy squeaking of springs. Clearing his throat noisily, the man crooked a finger at Carn's overcoated figure by the gangway.

"You there—the bags, if you please." His manner was imperious, the tone commanding. After a moment's hesitation, Tregale moved down the plank.

The driver straightened to help an older woman from the carriage. Once on the dock, this woman took one look at the sailing vessel and buried her face into a handkerchief, beginning to sob loudly. The pudgy man spoke sharply to her, then turned to glare at Tregale as he came down the gangway. His bluish lips pursed into a tight little funnel.

"You one of these Mormons, sir?"

Tregale nodded curtly and reached for the bags. He wasn't about to go into any family history for this obnoxious stranger. The pudgy man rapped him on the shoulder with his fingers. Tregale came erect, holding the bags, frowning. The man, obviously the young woman's father, stabbed a fat little finger at him.

"Take care my daughter isn't harmed. That goes for all of you. No nonsense, do you hear." The blue lips twitched as deeper color worked into the man's cheeks. "What I'm saying is, you bloody Mormons better keep your hands off her."

"Father—" There was a desperate plea in the young woman's voice.

On the *Horizon*, orders were shouted. Striped-shirted sailors could suddenly be seen moving about on deck. Dock workers drifted from the grey sheds to take up positions near the huge bollards that held the lines fastening the *Horizon*.

Tregale started up the gangway with the bags, holding one with his good right hand and pushing the metal hook through the handles of the other. The eyes of the pudgy man widened as he saw the hook.

Tregale turned at the head of the gangway. "We're catching the morning tide, sir. You have only a few minutes." He turned and carried the bags to one of the open doors leading into the cabin area.

The mother was sobbing unrestrainedly and the young woman's attempts to calm her had no effect. The father took his daughter by the arm and led her around to the other side of the carriage. Through the windows, the black beaver hat on his head could be seen waggling emphasis to his last-minute, and undoubtedly oft-repeated, advice.

The young woman came back and gave her mother a long embrace. Fumbling at a brooch on her coat, the woman removed it and pressed it into her daughter's hand. She hugged her daughter again, tears streaming down her face, her whole body shaking with sobs. The daughter broke away and ran up the gangway. She was now sobbing almost as hard as her mother.

The noise and the activity increased as the *Horizon* made ready for departure. A bos'n's whistle blasted shrilly. On the quarterdeck, the first mate bellowed angrily at the crew. He was a tall, dark-complexioned man on whose countenance scowling seemed a natural state.

Beside him, the captain scrubbed a hand across a bristling white beard and leaned over the outer rail. He watched with eagle eyes as the steam tug *Great Conquest* nosed carefully alongside. The captain was a much shorter man than the first mate, with the fair, ruddy complexion of a seagoing Scandinavian.

Rope splashed into the water, curses lifting at someone's slowness of hand. Then men were tugging and hauling, grunting in unison. The captain nodded and raised a hand, and again the mate's nasal Yankee twang lashed out at the crew.

"Let go for'ard!"

A caustic stream of oaths accompanied the order as there was more scrambling and tugging and hauling of the heavy ropes.

"Haul in!"

"Let go aft!"

"Look to it—"

The sea churned and frothed under the twin paddles of the tug, and the sailing vessel eased slowly away from Bramley-Moore pier. A steam whistle blew, and one of the horses on the dock shied in the traces. The mother of the young woman continued to sob, even harder now that she saw the gap widening between her and her daughter. She leaned on the arm of her husband, whose eyes were also red and moist as he watched the ships pull away. The driver of the carriage jerked the bridle of the nervous mare, wiped the scarf across his nose, then wiggled the fingers of one hand in farewell.

A dockhand, with no more ropes to worry about, hunched on a mooring bollard and spat into the river, then tipped a steaming mug of tea to his lips. Far out on the river, a ship's bell sounded the half hour, echoed almost instantly by the *Horizon's* bell.

While the packet ship suffered the ignominy of a rope leash, wallowing in the wake of the *Great Conquest* as it threshed a path downriver, the entire company of emigrants was mustered on deck.

British inspectors passed from section to section, examining papers and medical clearances, and checking off names.

Carn Tregale, known by all now as the first assistant to Edward Martin, was the man to whom all the watch captains reported. He had accompanied the inspection party headed by the second mate, Mr. Stahl, a pleasant man who hailed from Devon. Excusing himself, Tregale left to check on the company captains making their rounds of the passenger quarters.

Tregale was aware of the curious stares that followed him. The attention, he knew, was partly because of the metal hook curving from his left arm. Carn tried not to be impatient, knowing he would show the same curiosity himself. He was grateful the other leaders of the company had accepted him as well as they had, despite the little they knew about him. They accepted the authority Edward Martin had given Tregale, even if Carn wasn't a baptized member of the Church.

Climbing the ladderway to the cabins in the rear section of the ship, Tregale stooped his head slightly as he entered the doorway of one of the tiny port cabins. Ed Martin was sitting at a desk, frowning over the stack of papers in front of him.

"Don't ask me to sort it out," Carn said, smiling, "although you look like a man who needs help."

"That I do," Ed sighed. He riffled a thumb along the edges of the stack. "All this paperwork drives me crazy. You seen Captain Reed?"

"Up on deck at the muster, last time I saw him."

Ed sighed and picked up some papers. "You know what I'd do with this out on the trail?"

"Look for a strong wind?"

"You got that right."

Voices in the companionway announced the arrival of Captain Reed and the chief government inspector. They crowded into the cramped cabin.

Tregale stifled a grin as the government inspector, bustling and

31

efficient, placed another sheaf of documents on the desk in front of
Ed Martin.

"That's the last of them, Mr. Martin, all in good order." Taking
off his cap, he ran a handkerchief around the inner band. With a
quick wipe at his mustard-colored moustache, he replaced the cap
and stuffed the handkerchief back in his pocket. "My compliments,
Mr. Martin. It all moved very quickly, very quickly indeed. You
have a well-organized company, sir."

Captain Reed spoke up testily. "All compliments aside, the
inspector here says we have too many passengers aboard."

Martin looked surprised. "All according to posted regulations,
sir. I assure you we have not exceeded them."

The inspector shook his head, a sad look coming to his face.
"I'm afraid you have, Mr. Martin." He consulted a little notebook
he withdrew from his pocket. "I'm sure my numbers are accurate,
Mr. Martin. I tally seven cabin class passengers and eight hundred
and sixty-nine steerage."

"That's too many?"

"Yes sir. Regulations are clear on that." The inspector expelled
air up through the bushy moustache, shaking his head as he riffled
through more pages. "Here it is: *Horizon*. Berthed for a maximum
of eight hundred and fifty steerage."

Ed Martin showed his relief. He glanced over at Tregale. "Only
nineteen over. Better take off twenty, Carn, just to be sure. Ask for
volunteers. They could still sail this season with President Richards's
company. Tell them the inspector here is firm on the matter."

The inspector nodded. "That I am, that I am."

The second mate, Mr. Stahl, stuck his head in the doorway. "All
clear below, Cap'n."

Captain Reed acknowledged the report. "Stand by, Mister Stahl.
The tug will be shoving off presently."

The mate disappeared up the companionway. From his position near the door, Tregale saw a sailor slip from one of the star-
board cabins and start for the deck. The man's furtiveness caused

Tregale to call out to him. The sailor looked back, then bolted down the companionway.

Tregale burst after him, catching him just as he started out on deck. Carn grabbed the sailor and slammed him against the bulkhead. The man cursed and wrenched free, smashing a fist into Carn's stomach. As he tried to lunge past, Tregale grabbed him once more. Ducking under the sailor's roundhouse swing, Tregale chopped the metal end of his left arm hard across the bridge of the sailor's nose, careful not to use the point of the hook.

Blood squirted and the sailor howled in pain, clutching both hands to his face. Two more sailors standing near the companionway charged toward Tregale. Whirling, Tregale shoved the first one back into the other. Both went to the deck in a melee of arms and legs. Tregale pounced forward.

Passengers close by pushed back in startled alarm as Tregale pulled one sailor to his feet and rapped the man's skull hard with the steel cap. The man dropped, eyes glassy. The other passengers, lined up at muster stations, strained to see what was happening.

Now more sailors came leaping into the fight and Tregale went down under a smothering pile of them. Smacking and kicking his way free, Tregale saw the first mate charge down from the quarterdeck, dark features contorted with anger. Swinging a Colt revolver by the barrel, the mate hammered out ruthlessly. In moments, the fight was over.

Breathing heavily, Tregale pulled at a coat sleeve that had almost been ripped off his shoulder. The mate confronted him, feet planted apart.

"What in tarnation was that about, sir?" he demanded harshly.

The sailor Tregale had caught was crouched on his knees by the doorway, clutching a red-soaked cloth over his nose. Grabbing the man by the hair, Tregale hauled him to his feet, shoving him toward the ship's officer. "I saw this man sneak out of a cabin. He ran when I called to him. Those two over there—" he said motioning to the two sailors who had first attacked him, "were obviously helping him."

The accused sailor glared at Tregale over the cloth, then looked at the first mate. "Bloody well smashed my nose—"

The mate lifted the Colt threateningly and held out his other hand. "Hand it over, you plundering blackleg."

Another threatening gesture with the Colt brought quick response. The sailor reached into his pocket and handed a woman's brooch to the officer.

"And the rest of it—" the first mate demanded.

"That's the lot," the sailor muttered.

The first mate turned and held up the brooch so the passengers could see it. "Any of you passengers recognize this brooch?"

There was an exclamation from the young woman Tregale had helped with her baggage. She pushed forward to take the brooch from the mate's hand. "It's mine," she said. "My mother gave it to me this morning just before we left."

The mate touched the barrel of the Colt to his cap. "Sorry this happened, miss. A few bad ones get in a crew now and then." He swung on the group of sailors watching the proceedings. "Put these three bilge rats in irons and send them back with the tug. From now on, any crew member who enters a passenger's quarters for any unlawful purpose will hang. Now back to your stations."

Captain Reed, who was going ashore with the tug for final clearance papers, requested a report of the incident. As Tregale was leaving the captain's cabin, he almost bumped into the young woman whose brooch was stolen. Both started to speak at the same time, then lapsed into awkward silence. Edward Martin stepped into the passageway as they were looking hesitantly at each other.

"Don't believe you two have met. Sister Heather Lee, from London. Carn Tregale, a Cornishman."

Tregale nodded. "My pleasure, Miss Lee."

Heather Lee extended her hand. "May I offer you my gratitude, Brother Tregale. My mother's brooch means a lot to me."

"I'm not your brother—" Tregale stopped, awkwardly glancing at Ed Martin for help in finishing the sentence.

"What he means, Sister Lee, is he's not a baptized member of the Church. Carn has agreed to go all the way to Salt Lake City with us as my assistant, for which I'm grateful."

Heather Lee smiled at Tregale. "It seems we are all in your debt, sir. I also want to thank you for your assistance this morning on the dock. I apologize for my father—he's not usually that rude. He was worried about his little girl going off to America—I suppose I'll always be that to him."

She noticed the torn sleeve on his coat and hesitated slightly before asking, "Is there someone to mend that for you, Brother Tregale?" She gave a quick smile. "I'm sorry. I hope it doesn't offend you when I call you that. It seems so natural—"

He shook his head. "The answer is no—to both questions."

"Perhaps you would let me mend it for you. I feel responsible, since it happened while saving my property."

"I'd be grateful. I'm not much with a needle. I'll send it to your cabin."

They nodded again, then Tregale continued on down the passageway.

Heather Lee watched him for a brief moment, trying not to be obvious in front of Elder Martin. She hoped Tregale had understood her intentions and not thought she was being forward. She felt a slight flush of color. There was something unsettling about the man. She would mend the coat quickly, then she could feel the debt paid and put him from her mind.

Towed to mid-river, the *Horizon* dropped anchor with a rattle of chain. The captain, the team of inspectors, the three sailors in manacles, and twenty disappointed passengers returned to Liverpool aboard the tug.

That was the morning of Friday, May 23, 1856.

CHAPTER FOUR

IRISH SEA

SUNDAY, MAY 25

A modern Israel—a new Zion in the mountaintops!"

The booming voice carried firm conviction. Franklin Richards held one hand to the rail of the *Horizon*'s quarterdeck, steadying himself against the rough swells of the Irish Sea. A breeze swept the vessel, fluttering the pages of his Bible, billowing the tails of his black frock coat. Full cheeks nipped with color, hair blowing in disarray, he commanded the attention of the passengers crowded topside.

"Hardships will test your last ounce of strength," President Richards warned them solemnly. "Even with fully outfitted wagon trains, crossing the plains and the high country of the Rockies is no easy task. The graves of many good men, women, and children testify to that."

President of the European Mission the past two years and the man responsible for directing the huge emigration movement that had swollen this season into thousands, Franklin Richards had earned the affection and esteem of the passengers on board the *Horizon*. Most would not be making the voyage if not for the aid the Church had given them through its Perpetual Emigration Fund. The converts aboard the ship were mostly those who had not enough savings or possessions to sell to raise the price of passage, but they had the determination to join the other Saints of their new religion in faraway Utah Territory. The P.E. Fund had been created to help such people fulfill their dream.

The *Horizon* plunged headlong into a rolling comber, splitting it and showering spray over many of the emigrants near the railings. Once more the hawser, stretching across the water from the *Horizon*'s bow to the stern of the steam tug *Great Conquest,* snapped taut, the tug's paddles foaming the sea furiously as it towed the sailing vessel in search of a friendly wind.

Franklin Richards braced his feet farther apart, tapping a finger on the open Bible. "You Saints are fleeing to a promised land, just as the Israelites did. They traveled on foot, husbands, wives, and children together. Now the Lord is calling on you, modern Israel, to do the same."

To make the resources of the emigration fund help as many as needed it, the emigrants this year who could not afford full passage were required to walk from the frontier—though few of these eager converts had any idea where that was or how far it was from the Salt Lake valley.

"No wagon trains are waiting in Iowa City," Richards told them. "You will pull handcarts that you probably will make yourselves. You'll pull them over thirteen hundred miles of deserts, rivers, and mountains. I doubt if any of you have known a sun so hot as the prairie sun. You'll eat dust one day and be knee deep in mud the next. You'll be tired down to your bones. It will be hard, your only joy that of knowing every step, every hour, brings you closer to Zion."

President Richards closed the Bible with solemn finality. He brushed futilely at his blowing hair. Smiling at the congregation, Richards motioned to Edward Martin, in the crowd below, to come up and join him. When Martin finally stood beside him, the president put an arm affectionately about Martin's shoulders.

"This company is fortunate to have Elder Martin as their captain. Ed is no stranger to the march. He walked from Iowa to California with the Mormon Battalion—and back to Zion. He knows well enough how to nurse a sore toe." Laughter rippled through the assemblage. "Listen to Captain Martin and do what he tells you. He knows the trail, and he'll get you safely to the Salt Lake valley."

A broad smile broke over Franklin Richards's face. "They tell me we have some young folk to join in holy wedlock. If they'll come forward, we'll be happy to do that now."

Two young couples pushed through the crowd to join President Richards on the quarterdeck, embarrassed yet thrilled by the attention and congratulations showered on them. The simple ceremonies that followed on the quarterdeck of the *Horizon* could not have been more exciting or romantic or joyful for the newlyweds if the weddings had been solemnized in St. Paul's Cathedral.

The meeting over, people crowded along the rails, watching the shoreline slip away. In each heart were emotions and thoughts to be carefully stored away, to be hoarded through the years, mellowed and flavored by the passage of time into precious memories.

On the quarterdeck, Captain Reed approached Franklin Richards and the small group with him, and they exchanged pleasantries. The captain looked every inch the seafarer, from immaculate blue suit and brass buttons to the squared peaked cap.

"Please get your party together, Mr. Richards," he said. "We'll be dropping the river pilot soon." He glanced up at the top gallants, waving from the slender stem of mast. "It's a contrary wind, but it appears we'll get no better."

The bos'n piped all hands. The first mate bellowed orders that sent sailors scrambling into the rigging, unfurling more sail. Others manned the windlass, and the towline was let go. The tug swung in a circle and returned alongside the *Horizon,* paddles barely turning, its crew holding to tossed lines. A hemp ladder, twined and brined to hardness, was lowered to the tug's sponson deck, protruding behind the paddle casing. The river pilot clambered downward. The departing mission officials and several missionaries who had been closely associated with the emigrants received many tearful embraces. Burdened with letters thrust into their hands, they clambered down the ladder one by one.

Franklin Richards was the last to leave. He turned to Edward Martin, clasping his hand firmly. "Take care of them, Ed," he muttered in a choked voice. "You've got a late start, remember. Don't waste any time getting to the valley." With a final wave of his hand, President Richards disappeared over the side.

The space between the two vessels widened amid a chorus of farewells. The paddles picked up speed, and the tug's skipper stepped from the housing, a megaphone to his mouth.

"Fair winds, Captain!"

Captain Reed waved acknowledgment. The *Great Conquest* began to churn water and came about, heading for the distant shoreline. For those on the *Horizon,* the last tie with England and home was broken.

Tregale spent an hour topside walking and adjusting stomach and legs to the roll and pitch of the ship, having learned in his travel to and from Crimea that fresh air and exercise combatted seasickness best. He finally decided to look up Edward Martin and found him in his cabin still poring over stacks of affidavits and documents.

"Come in," Martin said, pushing back from the desk with a sigh of relief. "I need a break from this confounded paperwork."

The door of the outer companionway burst open and two boys came squealing down the passageway in what appeared to be a game of tag. There were a scrambling collision down the corridor, a thud, and a gleeful screech of victory, then another flash of flaming cheeks and flaming red hair as the boys raced back out on deck. Tregale waited for the door to slam again, but it didn't.

"Those are the Tate boys. If they don't fall overboard, we'll be lucky," Carn said, grinning. "Is it true we have nearly two hundred children on board?"

"One hundred and sixty-odd."

Tregale eyed the man across from him thoughtfully. "Thirteen hundred miles is a long stretch for a child to walk—"

"That it is," Martin agreed.

"Do you think the children can do it?"

"I'm more worried about the older folks," Martin replied. "Give a youngster a good meal and some sleep, and he's ready to go again. For those in their fifties and sixties, it won't be so easy. It gets hard to breathe up in the high country. Then there're the eighty-year-olds—almost no stretch left in a body at that age."

"Yet you're still going to drive them thirteen hundred miles like mules in harness—"

"It's the only way, Carn."

"How long do you figure it will take us?"

Martin peered pensively at the ceiling. "Well, this is the twenty-fifth, almost the last of May—and that's three weeks later than it ought to be." His eyes squinted under the dark line of eyebrows. "If we don't sit here in the Atlantic for weeks waiting for a wind, and if we're lucky enough to get booking right away on the trains, we might reach Iowa City about the first of July. Then if our luck holds, we could get started on the trail the next few days—but I doubt it. That would mean all the handcarts are built and all the supplies are bought and ready. I don't put much stock in that happening. If everything goes as well as it can, we could reach the Salt Lake valley about the end of September—but most likely later." He slid a serious glance over at Tregale. "That's not counting, of course, sickness, broken equipment, heat prostration, storms, or any one of a hundred other things that could delay us—including Indians."

"How many can we expect to die?"

"Considering the high numbers of young and old, probably as many as fifty."

"Fifty—?"

"It's a tough journey no matter how you make it," Ed muttered, "especially this late in the season. Winter will be hard on our heels."

An impromptu wedding party was held on deck that afternoon for the two newlywed couples. The day being the Sabbath curtailed the merriment somewhat, but there was singing and a shower of small, hastily gathered gifts. The outpouring of good wishes left everyone feeling cheerful.

The evening gathered, and Ed Martin and Tregale conducted an inspection of the lower decks. They expected wind at nightfall and ordered pots and bedpans placed in readiness despite the high spirits of everyone they talked to. Seasickness was the last concern of these hungry, lighthearted passengers, but in these stuffy, cramped quarters it was sure to come.

Everything below seemed well organized and in good order. Both steerage decks contained double-tiered rows of bunks, each wide enough for two persons, protruding like teeth from each bulkhead. Additional berths ran down the center isle. Martin and Tregale felt satisfied when they completed their rounds that the company was in as good a state of organization as could be expected.

After the evening prayer service on each deck, all the men went up to the main deck while the women prepared themselves and the children for bed. A bugle call announced that all was clear, and the men filed below. The ship quieted, rolling gently in the calm sea.

Carn Tregale remained on the almost-deserted deck, looking out across the expanse of black, moonlit water. Stars were thick in the sky overhead, dark masses of clouds banked to the east. Tregale let his gaze fasten on the clouds, imagining them as the rocky cliffs of his native Cornwall rising from the sea. A wisping formation became the bay of St. Ives, with the moors reaching from Clodgy toward the lonesome tip of Land's End.

In memory, those moors stretched wild and forlorn. In his mind he could see the waves collide on the jutting fingers of rock, tossing sheets of spray high against the strong, incessant Atlantic breeze. Gulls screeched and wheeled overhead, playing in the wind streams. A boy strolled along paths almost lost in the tangled growth of knee-high ferns, turning as the collie at his side began barking a challenge at a far-off, jangling cowbell. Strangely, the boy had no face, though Tregale knew the boy was himself. Perhaps that was because he had hardly been a boy—one moment a child with few recollections, the next a man with man's work and a man's burdens.

The memories shifted and this time there was a face, a young, innocent girlish face that smiled radiantly. Tregale felt the tingling that Elsie had stirred inside him that first day he had seen her at a fair in Penzance. He had fallen in love from that first moment, and six months later they had married. A wash of soft pictures rushed through his mind as Tregale let the warmth and wonder of their months together course through his memory. The brightest image was Elsie's face shining up at him as she breathlessly told him of their child inside her. The parade of their life together was sadly short—the summons to fight in a war that had no meaning for them had taken away their time. The imprint of memories was so quickly reviewed, it left Tregale with a sad hunger, a deep sense of frustration. Elsie had brightened his life for so short a time, and now she was gone. Staring out over the railing of the *Horizon,* Tregale wondered for a fleeting moment if any of it had really happened. He knew it had because of the hurt inside him, the crushing sadness, the despairing sense of loneliness.

The companionway door opened behind him, interrupting the moody depths of his thoughts. Glancing back, Carn saw Heather Lee emerge. She came to the railing, standing a few feet from him, holding a shawl over her shoulders. She seemed not to notice him as she gazed out across the dark sea. Tregale could see her shiver, then she looked directly at him, giving a polite nod of recognition.

"Good evening, Mr. Tregale."

The firm manner in which she said his name made it plain she no longer had any difficulty recognizing the fact he was not a member of the Church.

"Good evening, Miss Lee. I'm afraid there is no sight of England—"

"I have made my farewells," she murmured. "There are no regrets."

She drew the shawl closer about her shoulders. Her eyes roved the horizon again, studying the clouds. "The captain says we are expecting a wind."

"I have every confidence in the captain," Tregale replied. "I doubt that the weather will disappoint him."

"You don't have that much confidence in many people, do you, Mr. Tregale?"

Her frankness caught him by surprise. Her eyes were still fastened on the sea, so Tregale took the moment to study her more closely. Even in the moonlight he could see the proud tilt of her chin that he had first noticed on the dock. Her hair, which fell in dark curls held loosely back by a wisp of ribbon, was longer than he remembered it. Perhaps the moonlight silvering the sky behind her was tricking him, or perhaps her hair had been caught in a bun before, and he had not noticed.

He suddenly felt vaguely annoyed at himself. What reason did he have to remember details about this woman? He had spoken to her but once, seen her only twice. She obviously was of high station, undoubtedly knew little of the England most of her fellow passengers came from. She would not know of dingy, crowded flats, nor the constant companionship of cold and hunger, the dismal world of street urchins and smelly fish markets and noisy pubs where dreams were etched in the froth of ale. The phantoms of despair that stalked the streets of an England depressed and without work for teeming thousands were undoubtedly far removed from her experience. This woman belonged in dignified drawing rooms and afternoon teas, open carriages in the park, and fancy gowns at society balls. She was crystal and violins, silverware and servants, sweet smiles and polite conversations.

"You are staring, Mr. Tregale." She had turned to face him.

He shifted uncomfortably. "Forgive my rudeness—"

"No, Mr. Tregale. I have had men stare at me rudely before. You were merely curious. In fact, your look was almost condemning. Do you find something strange about me?"

Crystal shattered and violin strings snapped in his mind. This woman possessed an unnerving directness that pinned a man squarely. He hesitated. "My apologies, Miss Lee."

"I would rather have an answer than an apology." Her manner was determined. "Please speak frankly, Mr. Tregale."

He was staring again, then caught himself. "Very well, Miss Lee," he said finally. "I was wondering why a person like yourself was making this voyage."

"I thought we were all making it for the same reason—converts going to America because of our faith, our belief in a better world here and in the hereafter."

He shrugged. "A better world, perhaps. I hope it's better than most of us are leaving."

"You sound a trifle bitter, Mr. Tregale."

"Just not as sure of my reasons as you are. There is no religious belief in my decision to make this journey."

"I'd have thought you sure of everything you did, Mr. Tregale."

He gave a short, hard laugh. "Frankly, Miss Lee, I'm not even sure if I'm looking for a new world or simply trying to escape from the old one."

"You still haven't answered my question," she insisted. "Why do you think me different from the others?"

He could feel her intense scrutiny. A trace of annoyance edged into his voice. "Miss Lee, I have hardly had an opportunity to form any opinion about you. But since you ask, I might point out that over eight hundred passengers are crammed together in the bowels of this ship. For the next four or five weeks, they'll eat together, sleep together, wash together, and undoubtedly be sick together. Only half a dozen will be fortunate enough to do those things in the privacy of their own cabins."

"So the fact that my father paid sixty pounds for my passage is what bothers you. Is that quite fair?"

Now he was plainly exasperated. "Miss Lee, I was rude and I apologize. I've spoken more plainly and hastily than I should. I assure you, however, I'm not trying to condemn you for anything."

Carn was standing straight now, confronting her almost belligerently. Heather judged that he was nearly six feet tall. He looked thin, even underfed, but that was deceptive. She knew this man was strong, commanded respect. His hair was unruly; he had deep sideburns, but the rest of his face was clean-shaven. It was sternly hewn, attractive in a rough, masculine way, she noted, though the lines about his eyes made a person wonder what storms had left them there. Here was a difficult man to know, she thought, a man of many moods who rarely displayed inner thoughts. Suddenly she realized with dismay that this man was a total stranger and that she had demanded from him things that were irrational even to herself.

Heather realized she had allowed her own thoughts to spill out, sharing them with a strange man simply because they were simmering fiercely within her and because the loneliness of her cabin on this first night had brought an urgency to talk to anyone.

What an utterly ridiculous thing to do. Of course he could not have answered her questions. She had not sought his opinions anyway—she simply felt a need to express her own feelings. She had not the vaguest idea what his thoughts were or what kind of a man he was, other than the few strong impressions he had made upon her earlier. Poor man, he must think her completely mad.

Forcibly controlling her flood of embarrassment, Heather Lee ended the conversation by saying crisply, "Your coat is mended, Mr. Tregale. You may pick it up any time. Good night."

She turned and was gone, the companionway door closing behind her. Tregale was more than a little confused. He tried to bring his thoughts back to Elsie, but it was no use. She had faded into the darkness of the past again, along with the boy who had no face.

CHAPTER FIVE

ATLANTIC CROSSING
JUNE

The wind freshened in the night, though remaining unfavorable, and the *Horizon* began tacking to squeeze distance out of the choppy, blustery Irish Sea.

With morning, the wind blew harder. The vessel rolled and lifted and sank headlong between the combers. Pallid faces replaced the grins and rosy cheeks of the day before, and the rapidly increasing sourness and stuffiness below decks caused even the few healthy stomachs to churn.

Carn Tregale fed the seagulls early. Stomach emptied, he kept on his rounds but took frequent turns up on deck in the fresh air to accustom himself to the ship's heaving pitch and calm the churning in his head. Though pale and fighting nausea, he forced himself to descend below again.

Carn found only two of the ten men on watch to be on their feet. Three others sat at their stations with head in hands; the rest could not rouse themselves from their bunks. After doubling up duties on the healthier ones, Tregale made his way forward between the rows of bunks on the upper steerage deck.

The company of emigrants had been divided into nine wards, these again divided into smaller sections of about twenty passengers each. In addition to his duties as captain of the watch, Tregale had charge of one of these sections, and he was concerned as to how its members were faring.

George and Annie Kimberley, a gentle, soft-spoken couple in their seventies, were both bedridden.

"How are you feeling?" he asked, knowing full well exactly how they felt.

"Stomach's a bit upset," Annie murmured, gamely trying to smile. "George isn't feeling well at all, though."

"I'm as well as the next one," George protested weakly. "I'll be up and about as soon as my head steadies."

"Both of you stay down and rest for a while," Carn told them. "I'll check back later this morning. If you're up to it, I'll arrange for a place on the deck for you to sit so you can get a breath of fresh air. It's pretty stuffy down here."

Carn noted that the bunk above them was empty. That meant the young Hilliger sisters, Harriet and Lydia, were up and about. Both young women were in their late teens and were traveling alone. Their family had disowned them when they joined the Mormon church, but no one was more excited about making this journey west to America.

In the next bunk, his head drooping over the side, was Alfred Cunningham. A sickly pallor in his cheeks, he showed no interest in Tregale or in anything else for that matter. Carn passed him with merely a nod. Cunningham had a surly way about him that did not invite friendship, but he was an expert carpenter from the Midlands and undoubtedly would be a great help on the journey. His wife, Esther, a pleasant woman by contrast, was nowhere in sight, nor was the couple's nineteen-year-old son, Aaron. Find the Hilliger sisters, Tregale thought fleetingly, and Aaron wouldn't be far away.

Mopping up energetically between the next two tiers of bunks was Agatha Harbon, a tall, sparse woman in her fifties. Dressed severely in a long black dress, her grey hair pulled back into a tight bun, she looked stern and unsmiling as usual. A widow for many years, she rarely spoke with anything but a sharp tongue, so people were cautious in engaging her in conversation. But Carn liked her, saw the strength and depth behind the gruff facade.

47

"You look well, Sister Harbon," he greeted her.

Tregale had quickly fallen into using the familiar Mormon greeting of "Brother" and "Sister" with this smaller group because, Church member or not, he felt a special kinship to most of them. The twenty had bonded into what amounted to an expanded family, even in these few hours at sea.

"Takes more than a little wind to upset my stomach," Agatha Harbon snapped. She stooped over a pail, bony fingers wringing clabber from the mop. Watching, Tregale felt the saliva thicken in his mouth. Shaking out the strings without paying attention to the vomit clinging to her fingers, Agatha wiped a hand down the faded half-apron tied about her waist, then resumed mopping the deck. She cast a glance over her shoulder toward Carn. "If you're going to throw up, go somewhere else and do it."

"There nothing left," Tregale said, smiling wanly. He moved in closer to one of the bunks. The young woman huddled between the covers was biting her lip in pain, her eyes shadowed darkly. She looked up at him with a weary expression.

"Jim's up on deck, Brother Tregale," she murmured. "He'll be back shortly."

Elizabeth Wilson was twenty-four, from Preston, the same town as Ed Martin. She was within hours of giving birth to her first child and Tregale felt sorry for the extra suffering she must be enduring.

"Anything I can do, Sister Wilson?" Carn asked.

She shook her head. Her eyes slid over to Agatha, who for the moment had stopped mopping and was watching her. "Agatha's taking good care of me."

Agatha grunted, and began mopping again. "No need to make a fuss over babies being born. Had four myself. When they're ready, they come."

Elizabeth looked surprised. "I didn't know you had children, Agatha—"

"Put them all in the grave, and a good husband too." Agatha

glanced up, saw the look on their faces. "Don't need pity—got better memories than most my age."

A moaning from the next bunk caused Agatha Harbon to drop the mop and hurry past Tregale. Grabbing a pot from under the bed, she held it in front of the man who had raised up on one elbow, his mouth working spasmodically. "Use this, Willie Tate. I'll not be wiping up any more of your mess."

The man groaned, leaned his face over the pot. He retched, the sound tearing painfully from deep inside. When he had finished, he spat disgustedly and wiped a hand across his mouth. "Where's Maude?" he croaked.

"She's not lying about in bed," Agatha told him tartly, "no matter how sick she feels."

"And the boys?"

"Up to mischief, probably."

There was no argument against that assumption, Carn thought wryly. He'd wager that Ted and Fred Tate, twin sons who at thirteen were fiercely competitive with each other, were responsible for a large share of the grey that streaked their father's closely cropped, carrot-red hair. All five of the Tate children had inherited that flaming red top.

Willie Tate swung hairy legs over the side of the bunk, tugging a woolen nightshirt lower over his knees. He slid the pot out of sight under the bunk as he nodded weakly at Tregale. In his late forties, Willie was short and solidly built, with deep lines etched into his face by years of worry and work. Usually bluff and jovial, he looked pale as death now as he stood up, cautiously holding to the upper bunk for support.

A freckled, five-year-old face surrounded by a shock of red hair poked out from the bunk above. Maggie Tate was smiling happily. "Beryl's sick, daddy. But not me and Dolly."

Carn saw a flailing of arms and legs from behind her. "Get your legs off my stomach, Maggie!"

Willie lifted the moppet down, glancing at his eldest daughter still in the bunk. Beryl, a scrawny fourteen-year-old, was a mass of untidy hair and sad, dark eyes showing out from the covers.

"That's a good girl, Beryl," Willie told her, giving her a pat on the head. "You need to get up and give your mother a hand with things."

"I'm too sick, Daddy—"

"So am I, girl," Willie grunted. He sat down on the edge of the bunk, wiping at the sweat beading on his forehead.

Maggie leaned over, peering under the bunk. "The pot's full, Daddy—and it smells awful!"

Willie hauled her back by a handful of her nightshirt. Agatha gave him a flinty stare.

"The child's right," she said. "The pot's ripe—and then some. And there are a whole lot more that need emptying."

"I'm sick, Agatha," Willie protested, probing tenderly at his stomach. "I'm not steady enough to carry a po—"

Agatha snorted. "Lie abed and you'll get sicker, Willie Tate. A body coddled is a brain addled, I say." She moved back to her mop, muttering.

Tregale grinned as he gave Willie a sympathetic shrug of his shoulders. He turned to move back down the line, exchanging words with those of his group still in their beds. They were miserable but no worse than could be expected.

Returning to the deck, he let his gaze wander in search of Heather Lee, but she apparently was remaining in her cabin. With a slight sense of disappointment, he set himself to other tasks at hand.

Tregale was approached by the stern-faced first mate. The man touched a hand deferentially to the tip of his cap.

"If I might have a minute, Mr. Tregale—"

They moved behind the protection of a bulkhead, for the wind was whipping salt spray from the bow down the length of the *Horizon.*

"I want to report the crew has been mustered and organized

into their watches," the mate clipped in his hard nasal twang. "And I made it clear that any of them as goes below decks into steerage without being accompanied by an officer will hang."

"That's rather severe, isn't it," Tregale murmured, not knowing for sure if he should take the officer at his word.

"The law of the sea, sir," the mate retorted. "Would you pass the word to your people, Mr. Tregale. I want a report of any crew member seen in passenger quarters. Take him into custody, if that can be accomplished without harm. And believe me, any such blackguard will hang, sir."

"I'll see to it our people know of your orders, sir. But I might add, we have found the crew most respectful. No trouble at all, except for that one incident."

"And that's the way we'll keep it, Mr. Tregale."

"Thank you for your concern, sir."

The next day the wind decreased, bringing some relief. Elizabeth Wilson gave birth to a healthy baby girl, the first slap on its bottom delivered by a beaming Agatha Harbon. The parents, ignoring a well-meaning stream of suggestions for a name connected to either the ship or its voyage, named their new daughter Nancy.

It was Thursday morning before Tregale saw Heather Lee again. He was on his way to confer with Edward Martin when he met her in the passageway. She was carrying a heavy travel bag, and several items of clothing were thrown over one arm.

"Good morning, Miss Lee." He almost called her Sister Lee, but too much formality still existed between them. His gaze went to the travel bag. "May I help you with that?"

She shook her head. "I'm just moving down to the lower deck for a few days." She saw his surprise, and her manner became defensive. "Several children have come down with measles. They should be kept away from the others."

"That's very considerate, Miss Lee."

"I'm not being noble, Mr. Tregale. I have very selfish reasons for doing this."

He studied the resolute set of her mouth. "The quarters below are very crowded."

"That's why the children need to be moved."

"There isn't much light, and the smell is quite bad at times." He tried to pick his words carefully. "There is very little privacy."

"I am not a child, Mr. Tregale." She made a move to pass him. "Now, if you will excuse me—"

He took the bag from her hand. "The stairways are dark and steep. A broken leg won't help anyone. Let me carry this down for you."

Heather followed him to the lower steerage level without speaking. Tregale glanced at her as they walked between the rows of bunks, detecting only an absorbing interest in what she saw. This wouldn't be easy for her, he thought. The crudeness and familiarity forced upon people by such cramped living conditions were not designed for delicate natures. Obviously, however, nothing would change her mind. Besides, he understood why she was doing this, and he admired her for it. She no doubt had a genuine concern for the sick children, but he knew she was testing herself, forcing herself out of the protective bubble in which she had spent most of her life. Again the streak of strength and determination in this willowy young woman impressed him.

Heather insisted on the top bunk vacated by the two sick children, despite the urgings of the grateful parents that she take their lower berth. Tregale chatted with them for a few moments, then returned to the weather deck.

It was a beautiful day, the sun shining, the deck crowded with emigrants. When Tregale emerged from the companionway, a fishing smack was alongside the *Horizon,* waiting to take off the channel pilot, who was busily gathering letters from the passengers into a small sack. At sixpence apiece, they made a profitable enterprise for him and no one complained at the price of sending this last word home.

Tregale found himself standing at the railing beside Aaron Cunningham. Tall and thin-faced, healthy looking, with curly blond hair, Aaron had fastened his attention on the girl next to him. She was Lydia Hilliger, younger of the two sisters, barely five feet tall, rosy complexioned, with a pleasant, lithe figure. Her sister, Harriet, was nowhere in sight.

"Quite a trim little craft, isn't she," Tregale said, catching Aaron's attention. Aaron's eyes swerved guiltily toward Lydia. Carn smiled. "I mean the fishing smack."

Aaron grinned. "To tell you the truth, I hadn't much noticed it."

Tregale leaned forward to look over at Lydia. "Good morning, Lydia. You're looking well."

"Feeling marvelous, Brother Tregale." She gave him a happy smile, coyly including Aaron. Suddenly she spread her arms wide, held her face up to the wind and sun, and leaned against the ship's railing. "Isn't this exciting! We're going to America. I still can't believe it."

Carn smiled at her. "Well, don't go falling overboard or Aaron will have to jump in and rescue you."

Her eyes fastened on the young man. "Would you do that for me, Aaron?"

"I'd do anything for you, Lydia," Aaron blurted. The intensity of his reply revealed more of his feelings than he had intended, and color rushed into his cheeks.

Lydia placed a hand lightly against his face. "You're so sweet, Aaron. I'll tell Harriet how you offered to jump in and save me."

The channel pilot left the ship, and the fishing smack pulled away. The *Horizon* was set under full sail, and a sudden onslaught of wind plunged her through the waves with quickening speed, showering the decks with spray and sending many of the emigrants scurrying below.

With Ireland behind and the open Atlantic ahead, the sea roughened steadily. Passengers took to their bunks, and again the air below decks became sour.

On Saturday, one of the women in the lower steerage gave birth prematurely, the infant living for only a few minutes. This sadness was followed by a second death that afternoon, an elderly sister who had been poorly since the start of the voyage.

The next day, Sunday, saw yet another death. The three deaths, coming so quickly together, made most of the adults come to grips with the reality that they had not embarked on a holiday trip but on a long and difficult journey that could claim any one of them as a casualty.

After almost four weeks at sea, the lookout sighted a fishing boat amid the fog banks off Newfoundland. Captain Reed traded the fishermen some kegs of nails for a supply of huge codfish that provided a welcome relief from the prolonged diet of salt pork and beef.

Six days later, while the sailing vessel lay becalmed in a glassy sea, the British mail packet *Asia* passed astern, steam paddles churning a furious wake toward America. It was a stirring sight for those who lined the railings, waving as the two ships exchanged salutes. Seasoned seafarers and passengers alike seemed to sense the brush of history, the final numbering of the days of sail.

Saturday, the twenty-eighth of June, was a day all would remember.

"Land-ho!"

The cry rang out from the sailor standing watch in the crow's nest, high up on the mast. The deck had been unusually crowded all morning, for the rumors had flown that today might be the magic day when they sighted America for the first time. Heads craned and eyes strained to the west, and there it was, a smudge along the western horizon.

Maggie Tate, held in her father's arms, squeezed his neck. They had crowded with scores of other passengers onto the fo'c'sle deck. "Is that America, Daddy?" Maggie asked excitedly.

"That it is, lass," Willie said, giving her a big hug. His eyes were glistening. He looked around for his wife, saw her pushing toward him with young Dolly in her arms.

"It's America, Willie!" Maude cried. Tears streamed unashamedly down her cheeks. "It's America!"

Cheers and shouts rose on all sides as eyes stayed fastened on the mass of land ahead. Captain Reed used a bullhorn to make an announcement from the quarterdeck.

"That's Cape Cod on the horizon. We'll be casting anchor in Boston harbor this evening. Once we pass the cape and enter the river mouth, I must ask all passengers to remain below decks." A chorus of disappointed groans rippled along the decks. "The crew will be busy tacking upriver to the harbor," the captain explained, "so the decks must be kept clear."

Eager emigrants lined the rails for the next few hours until the time came for all passengers to go below. Packing proceeded feverishly, though the word passed through steerage that they would not debark for another two or three days.

Later that evening, after the huge anchor had splashed into Boston harbor, the rails were filled again with passengers straining to catch every detail that could be seen in the glow of the lights of Boston. This was the New World, the land of opportunity, the land of new beginning, the start of a better life.

CHAPTER SIX

EASTERN STATES

EARLY JULY

Everything Tregale owned he quickly packed into one worn traveling bag. He decided to make another round to check those directly in his charge.

Harriet and Lydia Hilliger were sitting on their bunk, folding clothes. Harriet was a year older than her sister and held little resemblance to Lydia. Harriet was several inches taller and had a larger, bonier frame. While she was attractive, she did not possess the fresh beauty or quick, vivacious flair of her sister. The two were close and they obviously relied on each other. Carn found them talking rapidly and excitedly to Aaron Cunningham, standing in the aisle beside their bunk. Aaron ostensibly was helping his mother stack their family belongings into the sturdy wooden cases Alfred had built specially for the journey, but his attention was not on family matters.

Esther Cunningham smilingly returned Tregale's greeting. "We need no help, Brother Tregale," she told him, "or at least, we won't if I can get this young son of mine to pay attention to what he's doing. We're almost all packed."

Passing along, Tregale saw Agatha Harbon holding the Wilson baby, Nancy, in her arms while the parents busily washed diapers and strung them on a line between two rows of bunks. Agatha's face had the merest break of a smile as she looked down at the baby, but the familiar, unsmiling sternness quickly returned as she caught Tregale's eye.

"There are more diapers to wash if you've nothing better to do," Agatha told him.

Jim Wilson, short and stocky, looked up quickly from his chore of wringing out his daughter's diapers in a bowl of soapy suds. "That's not true, Agatha," he protested. "Sister Harbon's giving you a bad time, Brother Tregale. Everything is just fine with Beth and me—and little Nancy."

Tregale nodded and moved on. Across from the Wilsons, Maude and Willie Tate and their daughters milled about the aisle between their bunks in noisy confusion. Teddie and Freddie were up in their bunk, squabbling over whose shirt they were stretching and tugging between them.

George Kimberley sat on the edge of his bunk, his wife, Annie, lying down with the covers pulled up snugly about her shoulders. Both smiled at Tregale as he stopped.

"You two feeling all right?" Tregale asked.

"Annie's a little tired," George answered. "It's been an exciting day. Will we be starting for the frontier tomorrow?"

Tregale shook his head. "Lots to do before that. There's no rush—plenty of time to gather your things together."

"I was looking at our diary this evening," George said. "It's taken thirty-nine days to cross, according to my record."

"Have we far to go on the train?" Annie asked.

"Far enough to get a good rest," Tregale assured her. He let it go at that. After all, what sense was there for a woman who had probably never been, until now, more than a hundred miles from home in her whole life, trying to imagine traveling twelve hundred miles on a train. Or for that matter, himself trying to imagine this tired old couple walking thirteen hundred miles beyond the railhead, pulling a loaded handcart.

The only other couple in his company were Derek and Gwen Pitts, one of the four couples who had married aboard the *Horizon*.

They had kept mostly wrapped up in each other for the whole voyage and Tregale had seen little of them. They were young, Derek eighteen and Gwen seventeen, and they had met aboard ship. Their families were berthed close to each other on the lower steerage level. The couple had wanted to get away from their parents, understandably, so Ed Martin had assigned them to Tregale's group on the upper steerage. Their bunk was empty, so Carn assumed they were wandering together on deck. In these cramped quarters, privacy was a rare commodity for young newlyweds. Tregale completed his inspections, received reports from the other captains, and satisfied himself that all was in order. He went back up on deck.

It was now past eleven o'clock and most of the passengers had gone below. Carn was leaning on a railing, staring at the lights on shore, too much churning inside him to think of retiring to his own bunk just yet. For some reason, he had started to think of Elsie. Perhaps it was watching the families so eagerly preparing for the future, seeing the excited embraces, the happy faces. It all made him aware of the lonely emptiness inside him. The aches and memories he had kept buried the past months were suddenly again on the surface of his mind, tender moments coming hauntingly from the past.

Someone crossed the deck to stand near him at the railing. He turned, surprised to see Heather Lee. A coat was draped about her shoulders and the light breeze was blowing her hair. She gave him a quick smile, a little awkward, he thought, but with more warmth and friendliness than usual.

"It's a wonderful evening, isn't it," she murmured, her eyes roving over the harbor lights. "America is so beautiful."

"Lights are a welcome sight after six weeks at sea," Tregale agreed.

"Some say we'll be disembarking in the morning. Is that true?"

"I'm afraid not. We must wait a couple of days at least before leaving the ship. The medical inspectors will board tomorrow and examine everyone. Then on Monday, providing there's no quarantine, we'll be towed to the dock—Constitution Wharf, according to Captain Reed. Then we'll have two more days to disembark from the *Horizon* and board the railroad cars—which Ed Martin has been assured will be waiting for us. If that's so, the train will leave Wednesday for Chicago."

She nodded. "It will be good to set foot on solid land again."

"That it will," Tregale agreed.

Heather half-turned and stared at him quizzically. She said nothing for a long moment and Carn finally broke into the silence.

"Is there something I can do for you, Miss Lee?"

She continued to look at him without saying anything, then finally drew in a deep breath and expelled it. "Can we talk for a few minutes," she asked, "about some personal things that have been troubling me?"

"Of course. I'd be happy to."

Heather Lee turned away and leaned both arms on the railing. When she started to speak, she carefully avoided looking at Carn, seeming to be concentrating on the activities barely discernable on shore.

"I think you have the wrong impression of me, Mr. Tregale," she said.

"I have no bad impressions, if that's what you mean," Carn said quickly.

"But I fear you also have few good impressions of me—"

"You're wrong in that, Miss Lee. I'm aware of many good qualities about you."

"Like what?"

"Just that, for one. You're direct. You ask for the truth, and I'm sure you give it."

"You didn't answer my question. Directness may be a fault as much as an asset."

"It's difficult to put into plain words—"

"I'd be interested in anything you might say."

"Why is that, Miss Lee?"

She hesitated, then turned to look squarely at him. "Because I've been thinking about you, Mr. Tregale. There, you see, I'm being direct again."

"Then I can be as honest in my reply," Carn said quietly. "I've thought about you, Miss Lee. I've even gone out of my way in hopes of striking up a conversation with you. It seldom worked, of course. You've kept yourself busy these past weeks—"

"No busier than you, Mr. Tregale. I appreciate you telling me that, though. I've seen you from a distance several times and wondered if you had come to talk to me."

"To tell you the truth, for some reason I find it difficult to do that—talk to you, I mean. I suppose it's because every time I've made a mess of it."

"No," she said quickly, "if there's fault, it's mine. I've been cold and unfriendly—and I have no idea why. I certainly don't feel that way toward you."

"I'm happy to hear that, Miss Lee. I really am."

She smiled at him and suddenly held out her hand. "Shall we pretend we're meeting for the first time?"

He took her hand, giving her a friendly smile in return. "It's a pleasure, Miss Lee. But I can hardly pretend this is the first time I've seen you. You've been in my thoughts too much for that." He let go of her hand awkwardly, shaking his head. "I'm sorry, Miss Lee. I hope you don't think me presumptuous. I know our worlds are far apart—"

"Are they?" she interrupted. "In what way?"

"I'm a simple Cornishman, Miss Lee, from a small village with fewer people than live on one London street. You obviously have fine upbringing, come from a family I assume is well-to-do—and I don't find any fault with that," he added hastily.

"You're a finer man than most I've met in my world, as you put it. And don't try to tell me you're a village clod. I imagine you are comfortable in any surroundings—you have the assurance of a man who knows himself and is content with who he is. But it's not the worlds we've left that are important now, is it—it's the new world we all face together. I can tell you honestly, Mr. Tregale, I face it with more trepidation than you do."

"You give no sign of it."

"It's there, believe me," she murmured. She looked questioningly at him again. "Why do you think we've been at such odds?"

"Perhaps because we haven't let ourselves be friends," Carn said quietly. "Like yourself, I have no idea why, other than the fact that I naturally hold back these days. I've found myself doing that ever since I got this." He held up the hook capping his left arm.

"Why is that?" she asked, genuine curiosity in her voice.

"It's a bit shocking, isn't it. Everyone notices it."

"Does that bother you?"

"Of course not—well, perhaps a little. It's a constant reminder I'm not the same as other people."

"I can't imagine you being bothered by what other people think," she said, "and I mean that as a compliment. You lost a hand in the Crimea. There's nothing but honor in that. And besides, you seem to do as well with that hook as most men do with fingers."

"I still feel a little like a freak on occasion."

"A handsome man like you—you should be ashamed of such thoughts." She stopped, suddenly feeling color rush into her cheeks. She hoped the night gloom was sufficient so that he could not see it. "I—I mean," she stammered, "I watched you fighting those sailors. You handled yourself better than any of those two-fisted ruffians."

"Well, there is a certain intimidation in tackling a man with a steel hook," he said, grinning.

Heather Lee studied him. "You're an interesting man, Mr. Tregale. I think I'd like to know you better. There, how's that for being direct."

"Perhaps we can start by you calling me Carn."

"And Heather—"

"Heather, it is. I like that name—it fits you."

Heather inhaled deeply, seeming to savor the freshness of the salt air, feeling a strange lightness inside, as if a burden had been lifted. "I'm happy we've had this chat, Mr. Treg—Carn. I've been upset with myself for acting the way I have around you. It really wasn't me."

"I look forward to our friendship." Carn smiled at her. "I hope you'll call on me for help whenever you need it."

"I will, Carn," she told him evenly. "I most certainly will."

The train that sped the emigrants westward through a sweltering, humid night trailed a streamer of smoke and sparks across the lush Ohio countryside. Moonlight washed rich greens with a pale suds, throwing passing hamlets into shadowy relief.

The awed company of over eight hundred emigrants had taken almost the full forty-eight hours granted by the ship's agents to disembark and straggle through the streets of Boston to the train station. The special railroad cars were waiting as promised, and early Wednesday, as soon as the last baggage and people were aboard, the trainload of new arrivals huffed and puffed out of Boston on the long journey west to the railhead.

Tregale's twenty kept together as a group in one of the railcars. The friendly and familiar faces were reassuring, and the emigrants did not mind the noise, smoke, and uncomfortable wooden bench seats so much. The Tate boys moved about constantly, day and night, chasing each other, craning out the open windows to point at some unusual sight, once even climbing onto the roof of one of the swaying cars. Bringing them down took a screaming, frightened Maude, a white-faced Willie, and the firm grip of Carn's hook. Beth Wilson felt so much better, now that the heaving decks were behind her. She frequently broke into song, either a hymn of praise or a cheerful ditty from English lore, and within minutes the whole car would join in lustily.

For four days and nights, the company of emigrants clickety-clacked their way through Albany, Buffalo, and Cleveland. They were now racing through night-shrouded countryside toward Chicago, bodies sprawled and twisted in uneasy slumber. Tregale had just made his rounds and found himself in the end car of the long train.

Carn tugged open the door and stepped out onto the small rear platform. Smoke and cinders wreathed around the edge of the car, causing him to cough and reach for a handkerchief. He was startled for a moment to see a man standing in the shadows behind him. It was Edward Martin, who offered a quick word of advice.

"Better close the door. Bad enough inside without all that smoke."

Tregale pulled the door shut, pressing back against the rear of the platform, wiping tears and cinders from his eyes. "This wasn't such a good idea," he grunted.

"It comes and goes, depending on the wind."

Tregale stuffed his handkerchief back into his pocket and squinted at the scenery rushing past them, the whole panorama brightly illuminated with moonlight. "Looks like good country."

Martin nodded. "Put in some hedges and you've almost got England."

"You used to live in these parts, didn't you?"

"Farther west, beyond Chicago, in Nauvoo." Martin stared somberly across the rolling hillsides. "Those were happy days, in a happy city, before the mobs and the violence. Nauvoo was bigger than Chicago in those days."

Carn had heard the story of Nauvoo several times from Mormons, how they had built a model city on the swamps of the Mississippi, only to be driven out in the dead of winter, after a mob had murdered the Church's leader and prophet, Joseph Smith. "Must have been hard, driven out of your homes like that, with no place to go."

"There was a lot of hate," Martin muttered. "The Mississippi ice saw a lot of blood that winter."

"Does it make you bitter? It would me, I think."

Martin shrugged. "You remember the good things, like how proud you felt of the city, how beautiful the temple looked with the sun shining on its spire. I worked on the Nauvoo temple, you know—helped paint it when I first came over from England. The Prophet himself came to meet us that first day. Memories like that blot out a lot of ugliness." His voice dropped, took on a warm softness. "Three years and seventy-five days—that's how long I knew the Prophet Joseph before they killed him at Carthage."

Tregale gripped the iron rail of the platform to steady himself. "Perhaps if I had known him, I'd understand why you people feel so deeply about your religion."

"Are you having any second thoughts about going West?"

"No," Tregale answered firmly, "although I'm just beginning to realize how far it is."

Martin nodded understandingly. "You can't describe how big this country is to someone who hasn't seen it. We're less than halfway to the railhead. It's as far again to the Salt Lake valley as it is from Boston to Iowa City. The people on this train, most of whom have never walked farther than the corner greengrocer, can't comprehend such distances. You see why I'm counting on your help."

"I'm pleased to be here, Ed. You were right—nothing was left for me in England."

"Which reminds me—how are you and Sister Lee getting along? You two seem on friendlier terms these days."

Tregale shrugged. "Just friends. She's from a different world. Besides, Heather has her standards—she'll not be interested in any man who isn't a Mormon."

"She could plan on having you become one," Ed said, smiling.

"I'm afraid that won't happen. As much as I admire the lot of you, I don't understand how you can have such blind faith in things. I need to see and touch."

The train arrived at the Chicago terminus on Sunday evening, hissing great clouds of steam and grinding and jerking its wheels noisily to a halt. Emigrants clambered stiffly from the coaches, and a weary chorus of sighs and groans lifted as muscles stretched in unaccustomed exercise. A mixture of relief and disappointment greeted the news that they could not leave for Rock Island, the railhead on the eastern bank of the Mississippi, until early morning. The announcement also precipitated a rush for benches and mail sacks and any sheltered corner in which to spend the night. The station restaurant sold out its sandwiches and pastries, latecomers finding only empty shelves and coffee that had been watered to stretch. Those few who could afford it— those who had paid full fare and were due to cross the plains in wagons—took accommodations at nearby hotels.

The people in Tregale's group were early in line for breakfast the next morning, but few bought more than hard rolls after they saw the prices. By seven o'clock, the emigrants had again boarded the special train, which was soon whistling and puffing its way through a patchwork of small Illinois farming communities.

That evening the train chugged into the eastern terminus at Rock Island. There was no bridge over the Mississippi, so the emigrants would have to take the ferryboat in the morning across the river to Davenport. They spent the night aboard the train or in nearby buildings and early the next day ferried the Mississippi. Again they boarded railcars for the journey to the final western railhead at Iowa City.

They reached Iowa City that evening amid a heavy thunderstorm. Sheet lightning lit up the entire sky in ragged intervals as thunder crashed through the darkened clouds. Stinging rain turned the ground underfoot into a quagmire. A tired, frightened stream of emigrants poured out of the cars and sloshed through the rain and mud, desperately seeking any kind of shelter. Some found it in the station itself, although the building was much smaller than the grand terminal of Chicago. Others huddled in the many outbuildings and roundhouses used for switching the train engines back into an easterly direction.

Tregale's group had become scattered and he felt obligated to search the various buildings to locate each family and make sure all was well with them. In one of the roundhouses, he came across Heather Lee, who had joined up with Jim and Elizabeth Wilson. Heather was holding little Nancy while Beth Wilson slept soundly on her husband's shoulder. Jim was also asleep, snoring softly.

"Just giving Beth a break," Heather said, looking up at him. "You look tired."

Tregale sighed and squatted down beside Heather, glancing at the baby barely visible in the blankets. "That's the life," he grunted. "Carried and coddled. She'll probably never appreciate how lucky she was, getting to the Salt Lake valley without walking a step."

"I've been meaning to talk to you about that," Heather said, glancing quickly at the Wilsons. They both continued to sleep soundly. "I know my fare is paid to travel with one of the wagon trains, but I wonder if I might change and join the handcart companies instead—"

"Why would you want to do that? It's twelve or thirteen hundred miles from here to the valley. Why would you want to pull a handcart when you could ride the whole way?"

"I don't have a profound explanation. I just want to do it. Can you arrange it?"

"All it would take is a word to Ed Martin, but think about it, Heather—"

"My mind is made up. If the old people I've seen can walk to Utah Territory, I'm sure I can too."

"I'm not sure those people will make it," Carn said grimly. "Some of them will die before getting to Utah—"

"I'll not be discouraged, Carn."

Tregale stared at her, saw the resolute set to her face. He realized she would not change her decision. Despite his concerns, he was glad she would be traveling with the handcarts. He had felt increasingly saddened these past few days as they approached the railhead, knowing he might never see Heather Lee again once she joined the wagon train.

"If you are not to be dissuaded, would you consider joining my company," he found himself saying. "I would feel better if I could be around to help."

"I would like that very much," she said, looking directly into his eyes. She could tell that made him uncomfortable, so she glanced quickly away. "That is very thoughtful of you."

He stood up, afraid she might see something in his face he could not allow. He didn't want her to know how happy he felt about sharing her company. "I'll talk to Ed in the morning," he told her. "I've told my group to meet at the northwest corner of the station house as soon as the bugle sounds."

"I'll be there," she said. She glanced down at the baby and began to rock her gently.

CHAPTER SEVEN

IOWA HILL

MID-JULY

B y morning the storm had passed, but the ground underfoot was still muddy and slippery. The company of emigrants formed into a long, straggling column and began the march to the campsite at Iowa Hill, three-and-a-half miles northwest of the city. For the first time, many realized how much baggage and possessions they had brought with them, for every box and suitcase had to be carried or dragged along the trail, strapped to backs or tugged by rope. Suddenly those families who had overburdened themselves saw very clearly that things would have to change before three miles could stretch into thirteen hundred.

It was well into the afternoon before all of the newcomers arrived at the sprawling, bustling encampment. Several hundred people had already arrived, all converts to the Church who had emigrated on various ships from Europe over the past several weeks. The passengers from the *Horizon* were the last large body of converts scheduled to arrive this season, or at least, the last of the Perpetual Emigration Fund emigrants.

Some tents were already set up for the new arrivals, though not nearly enough. A cluster of buildings stood near the middle of the sprawling encampment, several of them housing supplies and equipment, one serving as a central headquarters. An hour after arriving, Ed Martin summoned his captains to a meeting. Tregale was there, along with the eight men who had been placed in charge of groups of one hundred. The office was too small for all the men to crowd into, so they gathered outside.

"Well, men," Martin began, "you saw what happened this morning on the way up from the city. Granted, it was the first stretching of muscles that have been cramped for the past ten days on trains, but you saw how people suffered. You saw all the baggage—baggage they were told not to bring, of course. Now you must get serious about the rules. Each person is allowed seventeen pounds of clothing, bedding, and personal belongings on the trail—no more. They must sell the surplus or give it away to the Iowans. They won't be able to haul more, and neither will the handcarts. So pass the word—be firm with everyone."

"What about organization?" one of the captains asked. "Do we keep it the same as on the *Horizon*?"

"Generally, yes. As soon as we're outfitted and ready to leave— hopefully that won't take more than a week or so—we'll be moving on to the frontier, to Winter Quarters at Florence. We'll be traveling to Florence in two groups, but once in Nebraska, we'll join together as a single company again before striking out across the plains.

"I've gone through the rosters and taken out the two or three hundred we'll be losing to the wagon trains. That means your lists of hundreds will have some changes, but for the most part, those who are leaving were already grouped together. Check your names closely and make any replacements of sub-captains as needed.

"Some of you captains also will be leaving us for the wagons— you need to check in with Captain Hodgett or Captain Hunt for your assignments. Those captains remaining will report to Brother Tregale, who will be in overall command on the trail, under me. You should know the people in your groups fairly well by now— who can be relied on and who will need special attention. If changes are needed, make them and let me know."

"When do we get the handcarts?" another of the captains asked.

Martin frowned. "There's bad news, I'm afraid. More P.E. emigrants have come this year than anticipated, and since we're the last to arrive, we get the short end. Chauncey Webb, who's in charge of constructing the handcarts, tells me they're short on timber and wheels. More carts have been made than originally intended, but the demand has still been greater than the supply. We'll need to give Elder Webb all the help we can in getting enough made—that's the most important assignment for all groups. We have the same problem with tents—not enough of them. All the men must go to work making handcarts, and all the women must start sewing tents. The large tents must accommodate twenty people, with ten in the smaller ones."

"My people are asking about food," another captain called out. "How do we handle meals and other supplies?"

"Food will be distributed to each group from the main supply cabin, next to this one. Elder McAllister is in charge of supplies and outfitting. Bring all requests to his attention. Each group will prepare its own meals and be responsible for its own firewood. Might as well get used to trail conditions from the start."

There were more questions, few answers. The meeting broke up, and Tregale followed Martin inside.

"Did the request for Heather Lee to join my group meet with your approval?" Carn asked.

"Of course," Ed nodded. "I think she's crazy, but I'm grateful. We can use every able-bodied person we can get. By the way, I'm adding two men to your twenty." He sorted through some papers on the desk, leaning closer to read from one of the lists. "Sam Williams—a widower in his early sixties, but he looks like a tough old bird. And Arthur Smith—I knew Art in Newcastle-on-Tyne. A confirmed bachelor, sort of an odd fellow, a loner, but he's healthy and can pull his weight."

Tregale found his group sitting almost forlornly on their baggage at the edge of camp. They were all there, even Sam Williams and Art Smith, who had already learned of their assignment to the

Tregale group. Both men had been in lower steerage on the
Horizon. Williams indeed looked tough and spry, his hair grey and
cropped close to his head, his cheeks ruddy with color. He looked
muscular and fit, and Tregale was instantly grateful to have him
join the group. The other man, Art Smith, was difficult to assess.
He was taller than most Englishmen, thin, though not frail by any
means. Sandy-haired, he wore a small moustache, and he avoided
making direct eye contact when introduced. Tregale was willing to
take Martin at his word that the man would pull his weight. Any
additional man was to be appreciated.

Tregale's glance flitted over the rest of his group. Agatha
Harbon, standing unsmiling and arms folded. Jim and Beth Wilson
and little Nancy. Heather Lee, a little off to one side near the
Wilsons. Carn knew she had already told the group she was joining them. He was aware of her glance fixed on him but tried not to
show it. Then there were the Hilliger sisters, Harriet and Lydia,
looking happy and eager. The Cunningham family, Alfred and
Esther sober and frowning, and Aaron, who was standing near
Lydia. The Tate family, Willie and Maude, the twins Ted and Fred,
and Beryl, Dolly, and little Maggie. For the moment, at least, the
twins were standing silently, not even wiggling. George and Annie
Kimberley sat quietly on some boxes, and near them stood Derek
and Gwen Pitts, holding hands. Twenty-four souls in all, counting
himself and the children.

Fred and Ted Tate finally erupted into motion, both raising and
shaking an arm in the air.

"You have a question, boys?" Tregale asked.

"We're hungry," they said in unison. "When do we eat?"

The others laughingly voiced sympathy with the boys. Tregale
pointed across the camp toward the supply buildings. "There's food
waiting. Someone will have to pick up the rations for the group—
just give them my name. It won't be a banquet, but it should suf-
fice. I've been told each person will receive half a pound of meat,
along with a pound of flour. Also potatoes, and other things like

71

sugar and molasses. Don't know much about molasses myself, but I'm told it's nourishing and tastes sweet—sort of like our English treacle."

Maude spoke up. "What about cooking?"

"We'll have to do our own—we can cook as a group, or as individual families. That will be up to each group to decide for itself. You can get utensils from the supply wagon—Elder McAllister is in charge of that—but we'll have to forage for our own firewood."

He could tell that food was on all of their minds, but he raised a hand to hold them for a few moments longer.

"Alfred, I wonder if you and Aaron would offer to give Elder Chauncey Webb a hand with the handcarts. You're both journeyman carpenters, and we need all the skilled help we can get. You won't even have to wait for dinner—Webb has food cooked special for the woodworkers. You other men are needed too. You'll be given tools and told what to do, so don't worry about not being skilled like Alfred here and Aaron. As for you women, there's a need to help sew tents. All of our group will share one of the large tents, but the company needs to make a lot more tents before we can start for Florence."

As soon as Tregale left, Alfred and Aaron crossed the confusion of the campsite and joined the rest of the men gathered to construct the handcarts. Alfred was shocked as he took in the scattered array of parts and partially built handcarts.

"They don't need carpenters to put that lot together," he muttered to his son. "They need a bunch of angels who can work bloody miracles."

They soon found Chauncey Webb, a tall, burly man, harried and tired, who obviously knew as well as the Cunninghams that miracles were needed. He was grateful to learn that Alfred and his son were skilled carpenters and assigned them to assembly work. After a hasty but satisfying meal of stew, the Cunninghams bent to the task of putting the handcarts together. Seeing how poorly constructed and inadequate the carts were brought a scowl to Alfred's face that deepened as the work progressed. He worked side by side with Aaron, muttering complaints almost continuously.

Assembling the carts was a simple enough task. Alfred and Aaron started by nailing together the main box of the cart, consisting of two parallel sticks about five feet in length and roughly two inches square, then laying four more sticks across them to form the bed. They fitted a single crossbar into one end, allowing space between it and the bed for one or two persons to get inside for pulling the contraption. Alfred fastened an axletree under the middle of the bed, noting with disgust that it was untreated and had no metal covering the ends. Aaron helped him attach two of the lightest wheels Alfred had ever seen. The wheels were made of three-inch-wide uncured oak, less than an inch thick, spaced apart about the width of a normal wagon. It was painfully obvious to Alfred, seeing the poorly crafted spokes and the thin metal outer covering on the wheels, that this was where the greatest concentration of miracles was needed.

When they finished assembling the first handcart, Alfred stepped back and stared at it with a look of complete dismay. He sought out Chauncey Webb, pointing back at the handcart. "Elder Webb, is that the way those carts are supposed to be put together?"

Webb crossed with him and examined the handcart. He gave the bed a couple of tugs, waggled one of the wheels, then nodded. "That's it, Brother Cunningham. You've done all you could."

"Are there no sides to the box?" Alfred asked.

Webb shook his head. "There were on the first ones, last spring," he replied, "and canvas to protect the goods. But we've barely enough wood to make what is needed now, and all the canvas must go for the tents."

"What about the wheels?" Alfred persisted. "They'll be smoking and binding before they get out of camp. There's no metal on the axles, nor grease—"

Webb showed weariness and irritation. "I know the problems, Brother Cunningham, but we have to make do with what we have.

The demand for carts has been twice as great as expected when we ordered supplies early last spring. There's no more metal, no more seasoned wood, no more canvas to be had. I appreciate your concerns and respect your craftsmanship, but we can't do more. You and your boy are doing fine work. Just put them together as well as you can, as fast as you can. It will be up to the Lord after that—I'm sure he knows we're in trouble."

It was dusk before Tregale returned to his group. He was pleased to see that they had acquired a tent and had already set it up. They had also nearly finished the evening meal, but Agatha produced a plate of boiled potatoes and meat that had been cut into strips and fried in a skillet. He thanked her and was just about to sit and eat when Alfred and Aaron Cunningham came into sight, pulling one of the new handcarts. It brought everyone to their feet and the group crowded excitedly around the cart and the two men.

The handcart seemed to Tregale to be much more frail than he had anticipated. His concerns were mirrored on the face of Alfred Cunningham as the carpenter pointed at the handcart.

"We're in trouble," Cunningham said, disgust and concern plain in his voice. "I tell you that right off. I've never seen such a poorly made thing. It's all green wood—not even the axletree is seasoned. There's oak on the wheels, but everything else is ash or hickory. And there's not even iron skeins on the axles—no grease either. The dust will wear out those axles before we've gone a hundred miles, let alone a thousand."

"They can't be as bad as you're saying, Alfred," his wife chided. "Hundreds have made it to the Salt Lake valley already—"

"Not like these," Alfred snorted. "I've seen one of the handcarts that went with the earlier companies—seasoned oak, iron skeins on the axles, iron tires more than a thumbnail thick, milled and shaved wheels, boarded sides, even a canvas topping. Those are the carts you're talking about, not these skimpy things."

"Well, the elders know the trail better than you," his wife

74

replied defensively. "They wouldn't let us go if they didn't think we'd make it."

"We won't be going very far with these," Alfred said flatly. "I know my trade, mother, and I know wood. We've got problems."

Tregale saw that people had been affected by Cunningham's condemnation of the handcart. "Thank goodness we'll have people like you and Aaron along," he said, "to fix whatever breaks."

"We'll have almost a hundred and fifty of these things in our company," Cunningham pointed out. "It'll take more than craftsmanship to keep them on the trail. The only good thing you can say about these handcarts is that they're light. Even at that, they crowd sixty pounds."

"Well, speaking for those of us women who'll have to pull them," Agatha snapped, "that's a big point in their favor. The wood will get seasoned quick enough on the trail, I suspect."

"Oh, it'll season, that's for sure," Cunningham growled. "You'll be able to tell by the warping, and cracking, and splitting."

"I for one am thankful we have them—and we can do without more of your complaints, Alfred Cunningham," Agatha told him sharply. "Just be grateful for what the Lord provides."

The meal was finished without much more discussion of the carts and soon the bugle sounded the call to evening prayers. The group knelt in a circle about the fire and Sam Williams led them in prayer. Tregale knelt with them, feeling awkward and not really a part of the activity but not wanting to separate himself so far as to stand off by himself. Besides, he thought grimly, after what Cunningham had told them, they would probably need all the divine help they could get.

After prayers, the women and younger children retired to the tent to prepare for bed. After a while, Agatha Harbon stuck her head out of the door flap and announced that the men could enter. Tregale was concerned about how crowded the tent would be, but amazingly, it did not appear crowded at all. Everyone seemed comfortable, wrapped in blankets, with heads at the outer circumference and feet pointed toward the middle.

Agatha pointed to an open space near the door. "That's for you," she said, looking at Carn. "If someone has to fetch you in the middle of the night, I'll not be wanting you tramping over me or anyone else."

Tregale lay down and pulled his blanket about him. It wasn't exactly comfortable, but it felt good. Falling asleep took only minutes and one of his last conscious thoughts was that Heather Lee was positioned almost directly across from him on the other side of the tent. Agatha probably had something to do with that too.

CHAPTER EIGHT

IOWA FRONTIER
AUGUST

W e're losing too much time," Ed Martin said, frowning at the two men standing in his office. "It's been eight days since we arrived at Iowa Hill and we're still not ready to start for Florence."

One of the men was Carn Tregale, the other Chauncey Webb. A returned missionary like Martin, Webb was wearing a work shirt faded with sweat from working dawn to dusk alongside the scores of volunteers helping to assemble the carts. His wide, thin mouth now was pulled into a tight line, his brow drawn into deep furrows.

"We can't make them faster than we are, Ed. I feel sorry about the shortages, but we had no idea so many handcarts would be needed when we ordered supplies last April. I've got every mill in Iowa City working on parts, but everything is in short supply."

"I know you're doing the best you can, Chauncey," Martin told him. "The pressing question now is, will the carts hold up?"

"The axles worry me the most," Webb replied. "Wood on wood—they'll wear, no doubt about it. But there's no iron or tin available. It's either stop altogether, or keep going with what we've got."

"We'll just have to make do, I suppose," Martin said, scratching worriedly at his beard.

"At least the Fourth Company is on the trail," Webb added. "It's been easier these past two days with them gone."

"How soon can the first two hundred get started?" Martin asked.

"We'll finish their handcarts today," Webb replied. "The mill in Iowa City delivered the last load of wheels this morning."

"When can we get the other four hundred on the trail?"

"Today's the seventeenth—all handcarts should be completed in another six days, at the outside. Assembly will go fast now that we have the wheels."

"That puts us at the twenty-sixth for moving out—almost the end of August. We're slicing the bacon thin." He glanced searchingly at Carn Tregale. "Any problem being ready to march by the twenty-sixth, Carn?"

"The whole company is packed and ready to go now," Tregale answered. "Only problem for some is making the seventeen-pound limit."

"Stay firm on that," Martin cautioned, "especially with the handcarts in such poor shape. We need to keep that weight down."

"Some are cheating on the weigh-in by wearing half a dozen dresses and two or three sweaters, just so they can beat the limit."

Martin frowned. "I suppose it's all right to be a little lenient with clothing—they may need it before they reach the valley. But no allowances for other things."

"Will the wagon trains be ready?"

Martin nodded. "Hunt and Hodgett assure me they're ready to start any day we are. They'll be following hard on our heels the whole way."

"That's a comfort," Carn grunted. "We can always draw on them for help."

Webb frowned. "I'm not so sure. I've heard more than one say they didn't pay full fare to baby-sit the P.E. companies."

"Things will change on the trail," Ed murmured. "Are you clear on the order of march? The Fourth Company, under Captain Willie, will be seven or eight days ahead of us. That could be as much as a hundred and fifty miles, so I doubt that we'll have contact with them. The first two hundred of our group also will be about a week ahead of the main company, until we form a single company again at Florence. Captain Hunt's train of about fifty wagons will stay close behind, no more than ten or fifteen miles. Hunt's train has about two hundred emigrants, along with some three hundred oxen, cows, and beef cattle. Behind them will be Captain Hodgett's company of thirty-three wagons, almost two hundred passengers, and about as many oxen, cows, and beef."

Martin gave the two men a worried look. "Let's not lose a day we don't have to. Carn, you need to draw up schedules for guard duty. Everyone will be tired to their toenails, so I suggest you try to keep the watch to two-hour stints. We'll need guards posted every night on the trail. We have enough rifles for those on guard duty, but the guns will have to be turned over to each new shift, then returned to the supply wagon every morning. Not as much fire-power as I'd like, but then, we're not expecting to need any."

Two days later, the first two hundred emigrants moved out of the encampment at Iowa Hill. Everyone stopped what they were doing to watch them, a long line of beaming families pulling hand-carts piled high with belongings and cooking utensils. Above the shouting and farewells, the squeaking of handcart wheels could be heard for miles.

Alfred Cunningham took back the frail handcart and ex-changed it for five new, unfinished carts. Alfred and Aaron worked on them by the light of the campfire, after returning from their long shifts with Chauncey Webb's crew. Before long, those five carts began to meet Alfred's standards of quality. They used tin plates and cups to fashion metal skeins for each axletree, put more cross-bars on the beds for greater strength, and added sideboards. The short handles for pulling the carts were replaced with longer ones and reinforced, the crossbeams planed and sanded until smooth and splinter free. Finally, even Alfred was halfway satisfied.

"You can't do more with a sow's ear," he muttered, giving the carts one last critical inspection. "At least the axles won't wear through."

Needless to say, the twenty in Alfred's group were delighted with the improvements. While the men were gone making the carts, the women sorted, sifted, and sold or reluctantly discarded personal belongings that put them over the weight limit. Tregale warned them that there would be no exceptions, so teapots and china and clocks and nicknacks were sadly put aside. Some were sold for next to nothing in Iowa City, some merely given away.

"You've done well," Tregale told them, upon completing inspection and weigh-in Thursday afternoon. "You've all made the limits and packed tight."

"When will we be leaving for Florence?" Annie Kimberley asked.

"Saturday morning, with any luck," Tregale answered.

"How far is it?" George Kimberley inquired anxiously.

"A little under three hundred miles," Tregale said, trying to sound reassuring. "It's a long walk, but look at it this way—we'll have gone almost a fourth of the way to Salt Lake."

Maude Tate gasped. "Only a quarter way? I had no idea Utah was so far—"

"We'll have a thousand miles more to travel after Florence," Tregale told them, "but we should go faster with these carts than with a wagon. That's why the wagons are in the rear—they'll be hard pressed to keep up with us."

"How long will it take us to get to Florence?" Annie asked, still concerned despite Tregale's attempt to make light of the journey.

"We should make fifteen or twenty miles a day and that will put us in Florence in about three weeks. However, since this will be our first stretch on the trail, we might take a little longer. Depends on how the handcarts hold up and how quickly we all get used to pulling and walking."

"We've each got our cooking pots on the carts, but what about the food?" Agatha Harbon asked. "Who carries that?"

"Each group of a hundred has a wagon assigned. The tents and food and other supplies will be carried on that."

"What about the tent?" Agatha queried further. "Who's responsible for putting it up each night?"

"I'm asking Sam Williams to be in charge of that—to be tent captain. It will take all of you working together, of course, to put up the tent—and take it down and stow it on the wagon every morning. Will you accept that assignment, Brother Williams?"

Sam nodded eagerly. "Happy to serve, Brother Tregale."

"Sam will be the man you go to with questions and problems," Carn added. "I'll not have much time once we start on the trail, not with four hundred to be checking on—six hundred after we leave Florence."

"Will you still be sleeping in our tent with us, Brother Tregale?" Sam asked.

"I will, though I'm not sure I'll be there when the bugle sounds."

"Then we'll see to it that a space near the entrance is kept for you."

Tregale glanced around the group of faces, pausing for a moment as his glance locked with the eyes of Heather Lee. She looked tanned and healthy. Her hair was pulled back into a bun and she was dressed in a simple, long frock of flowered material. He noticed how small her waist looked in it. Then he continued searching the faces in front of him. There were no more questions.

Tregale smiled. "Very well. Let me congratulate all of you again on such fine preparations. We'll be in the lead on the trail—and I for one can't wait for Saturday."

Saturday came quickly, another hot morning that promised to turn into another blazing afternoon, but the heat wasn't bothersome today. This was the start of a whole new experience.

The four captains of the groups of one hundred met at sunup

with Tregale to report that their companies were ready for the trail. Tregale's twenty moved out with their handcarts at nine o'clock, leading off the long line of emigrants. Harriet and Lydia Hilliger were pulling side by side in the yoke, with Heather Lee and Derek and Gwen Pitts pushing from the rear. The personal belongings and cooking utensils piled on the cart weighed almost a hundred pounds, but the load seemed easy to pull.

Next came the Tate family, with Willie and Maude at the yoke and Freddie and Teddie pushing. Beryl carried little Dolly, and Maggie skipped alongside, smiling from ear to ear, lighthearted and happy.

Alfred Cunningham and his son, Aaron, pulled the third handcart. Esther pushed at the rear, and George and Annie walked alongside. The elderly couple had protested that they could help, but Alfred had assured them they would have plenty of time to take their turn.

Sam Williams and Art Smith pulled the last cart in the twenty, with Jim Wilson and Agatha pushing from the rear. Beth, carrying little Nancy, walked beside her husband.

Carn visited briefly with each handcart group as they headed out, smiling and encouraging them. He took a few extra moments to walk beside Heather. She greeted him warmly and he was pleased to see her in such high spirits. He was struck again by how different she looked, tanned and lithe, completely at ease pushing behind the cart. There was no connection between this woman, he thought, and the genteel young lady of society he had seen on the Liverpool dock. They chatted for a moment, then Tregale turned back to supervise the rest of the handcarts slowly forming into a line.

Carn spotted Ed Martin beside the wagons, in the middle of the confusion, busily checking off lists with the wagon masters, nodding as all seemed in order. Martin saw him and waved.

"All's well, Carn?"

Tregale nodded. "How far do you want to go today?"

"Fifteen miles, if it's possible. No less than twelve."

"We'll make it. Everyone is in such high spirits you'd think the carts were empty."

And make it they did, easily. They traveled fourteen miles from Iowa Hill by early evening. When the line of handcarts topped a long incline, the emigrants found themselves on a large, grassy plateau. Word passed down to form a circle with the handcarts and wagons for the first night's encampment.

With the evening meal out of the way, tents started mushrooming inside the circle. The bugle sounded, as it had at Iowa Hill, calling people to evening prayers. After that, the chatter and exchange of tales quieted. By the time Tregale finished his final round, cautioning the captains to ensure that guard schedules were followed throughout the night, the camp was mostly asleep.

The bugle sounded again at five the next morning, bringing a noisy outbreak of sighs and moans and protests from inside the tents. Muscles that had merely ached the day before were now stiff and painful. Breakfast was a halfhearted affair, mostly bread rolls left over from dinner the night before and mugs of steaming coffee and tea.

The emigrants took down the tents and stowed them on the wagons and carefully extinguished their fires. Two hours after rising, under Carn's diligent urging, the entire company moved out. There were a lot more menfolk at the yokes this morning, for most of the women with young children had still-sleeping bundles in their arms. Carn watched his own group take the lead again. They too were more subdued than yesterday, but Heather flashed him a cheery smile as she passed by.

The Iowa countryside they passed through was pleasant and green, dotted with frequent patches of forest amid gently rolling hills and grassy valleys. Streams were abundant, seeming to run in every direction, gentle and meandering. It was settled country for the most part, with small communities and outlying farms. Tregale met several of the Iowans and found them to be friendly and helpful in giving directions, although the trail ahead was clearly marked by wagon ruts and the lighter tracks of handcarts that had passed earlier in the season.

Shortly before noon, as the lead handcarts passed near another small township to the north, a group of hard-riding men, about a dozen in all, bore down on them. They were headed south, and it appeared for a moment that they might crash right through the handcart train. At the last minute, they reined in, right next to Sam Williams's cart.

One of the bearded riders glared at the emigrants. "You people slavers or free men?" he shouted.

Sam had stopped the handcart, fearful of being trampled, which brought the train behind them to a ragged halt. He answered with a nervous quaver in his voice.

"We know nothing about slavery. We're Mormons, on our way to Utah Territory."

The man on the horse waved an arm in dismissal of his previous challenge. "We have no quarrel with Mormons. We aim to stop any more slavers settling in Kansas—that's where we're headed."

"You seem in a mighty big hurry to get there," Jim Wilson said. "Is there trouble in Kansas?"

"Trouble and a lot of bleeding," the rider responded. "Good men are dying, and we're going to see justice prevail. None of Douglas's laws will be binding in Kansas, or any other territory. We'll have no slaves in these parts—it goes against the will of God, that it does."

"Then pass on through, friend," Sam called out, not understanding what the man was talking about but sympathetic to any just cause, "and Godspeed."

Two more groups of armed, grim-faced men crossed the train that afternoon, both heading south as had the earlier group. Tregale and Martin watched them as the riders waited for the handcarts to stop and make room for them to pass. Neither of these groups said anything, nor showed any friendliness. Obviously, important things were happening in Kansas Territory, but among the emigrants, only Martin had heard of Douglas or knew anything about the contest between north and south or the rush to settle the new territories of Kansas and Nebraska with settlers favoring one side or the other of the slavery question.

"If we say we're going to Utah," Martin told Tregale, "they'll ignore us."

That night the wagons and handcarts circled again, having been on the trail four hours longer than the day before but traveling only about the same distance. Carn went to check his group. Everyone was tired and sore, limping from blisters on their feet, still not conditioned to the rigors of pulling the carts. Everywhere conditions were the same. Shortly after the bugle for evening prayers, the camp settled into weary and grateful slumber.

Before Tregale could turn in for the night, Ed Martin came to find him and talk about the day's progress. They passed outside the circle of carts and wagons, pleased to see that an alert sentry challenged them. The two men walked a ways up the trail so their voices would not disturb those in the tents.

"A fair day's march," Martin said, looking up at the stars. "Took us longer than yesterday, but good under the circumstances. Hopefully, we'll do better in the days ahead."

"I think we will," Carn replied. "But the soreness will work out in another day or two, and the blisters will toughen. People have a good attitude, and the carts seem easy to pull."

"I agree—it all seems in our favor for the moment."

"You're being mighty cautious," Tregale said. "You expecting things to turn bad?"

"We'll be having trouble with the carts, that I know. I just hope we have the parts to keep them on the trail."

Tregale glanced back at the darkened encampment. "When I think about how tough traveling less than thirty miles has been, I hate to think about thirteen hundred."

"Just take it in sections," Martin advised. "We've gone a tenth of the way to Florence in two days—does that make you feel better?"

"Not much. A family pulled out today, I hear."

Martin nodded. "The Hargreaves, out of the third hundred. Decided to pull out and settle in that township we passed early this afternoon. We'll probably lose more before we get to Florence. This is good country, and the settlers here are friendly to Mormons. The Hargreaves have two small babies—one only a month old and a toddler not yet two. The mother had a difficult birth, I'm told, and hasn't fully regained her strength. They thought it best to wait in Iowa, possibly earn enough to join a wagon train next season."

"Can't blame them," Carn said, "not with having to carry both babies as well as pulling a cart."

"How about your people?" Ed asked. "How are the Kimberleys holding up?"

"They're managing, but it's all they can do to keep up just walking. It's hard on the Cunninghams, not having the extra help on the handle. I'm thinking of moving Art Smith to their handcart—that will give the Cunninghams some relief. George and Annie can't do any pulling, and no one expects them to—we'll all be satisfied if they just stay healthy and able to walk."

"How is Heather Lee doing?"

"Haven't spoken a dozen words to her. She's pulling her share, and more. She gets along well with the Hilliger sisters and even Agatha, and I've noticed she's a big help to the Wilsons—"

"You seem to be noticing a lot about Sister Lee," Ed said, stifling a grin. "I hope you're not hiding your feelings from her—"

"I have no feelings to hide—"

"Don't try to fool me. I've seen you around her—we both know she stirs something inside you."

"It's only been eight months since I buried my wife, Ed."

"And this is a new world, Carn. England and its memories, good and bad, are behind you now. You need to think of the future."

"I am thinking of it," Carn muttered, "more than I care to admit."

The company made good time the next day, traveling over sixteen miles. It seemed people were indeed getting more used to the walking and pulling and pushing. Muscles responded with less protest; minds and bodies worked together with less fatigue. When the point of the train pulled in sight of a small farming community named Marengo, another halt for the night was called.

While the rest of the handcarts were slowly coming into the campsite and preparing to form a circle, a bunch of riders bore down on the handcarts already in place. This time, however, they were not dedicated men riding to Kansas; they were a group of rowdy youths. They immediately picked out the Hilliger sisters and Heather and started to ride in circles about their handcart, whooping and yelling.

Circling the handcart several times, they waved their hats and yelled crude invitations to the three young women. The galloping horses nearly smashed into Willie Tate's handcart. Little Dolly started to cry.

Suddenly one of the youths reached down and snatched at Heather's arm as he galloped past. Heather screamed and fought clear, huddling back against the handcart. The young man turned the horse sharply, reaching out for another try. But before he could get there, Carn Tregale grabbed his outstretched arm. Carn had come running for the head of the column when the toughs first rode into camp. The man was jerked out of the saddle and landed on his back in a cloud of dust. Tregale piled on top of him, ignoring the other circling men. He pressed the point of the metal hook into the man's throat, felt the fight give way to fright. Only then did Tregale look up at the half dozen other riders who now had stopped their mounts and were staring down in startled surprise at the plight of their companion.

"What's it to be?" Tregale grated harshly. "Do I rip out his throat, or do you men ride out of here as fast as you came in?"

Tregale saw the frightened expressions on their faces, saw they were indeed only youths, probably seventeen or eighteen for the most part.

"Let him go, mister," one of them pleaded. "We was only having some fun—"

"You nearly trampled these people. And you tried to abduct one of these young women—"

The youth on the ground raised a hand, not daring to move his head. "I was only funnin', mister. I didn't mean no harm."

"Well, you caused harm," Tregale growled. He lifted the point of the hook from the youth's throat, keeping it a threatening inch away. "Are you boys ready to ride out of here?"

The youth Carn was straddling put a hand to his throat, feeling for blood. He looked at his fingers, obviously relieved to see no blood on them. "You let me up and we're gone, mister. You'll see no more of us, I swear by my mother's grave."

Tregale stood up, extending a hand to help the youth to his feet. The young man reached for his horse and vaulted into the saddle. Moments later, the now-deflated bunch of rowdies went racing back toward Marengo.

Tregale turned, and Heather rushed into his arms. She was sobbing, still frightened by what had happened. He put his arms around her to comfort her. Harriet and Lydia crowded around, beaming proudly.

"You sure took the starch out of them," Lydia said excitedly. "No telling what they might have done."

"It's over now. We won't see those lads again," Tregale replied, embarrassed by the flood of congratulations that poured from Willie Tate and his family and the others.

But what Tregale was feeling most was a strange burning inside him from the closeness of Heather Lee. She suddenly realized she was clinging to him and stepped back, the look on her face a mixture of embarrassment, gratitude, and something else Carn couldn't quite define.

CHAPTER NINE

WINTER QUARTERS
LATE AUGUST

It took twenty-seven days for the Fifth Company to cross Iowa and reach Council Bluffs, arriving on the twenty-first of August. They wound their way up the bank of the Missouri River and camped on Pidgeon Creek, near the ferry crossing. The next day the entire company ferried across the Missouri, and the emigrants came to a weary halt beside the old Mormon sawmill at Winter Quarters, just outside Florence. The first two hundred emigrants greeted the new arrivals, and the entire company again joined together under Captain Martin.

Not that they had time for resting or reminiscing. The campsite was abustle with activity, mostly repair work on the handcarts. Ed Martin made it clear that the company had to make up lost time, so there were many groans of dismay that they would enjoy not even one day of rest after arrival at Winter Quarters.

Alfred and Aaron Cunningham set to work inspecting the handcarts in their hundred, making what repairs could be done to those that had developed problems. Alfred was squatting down to study the damage to a cart that had hit a rock the day before when leaving Pidgeon Creek. One wheel had three spokes missing, the rim of the wheel had cracked badly, and the metal was worn away. The wooden rim measured less than a quarter inch thick in several places. Cunningham had no idea how the wheel had held together long enough to reach Winter Quarters. He looked up at the anxious faces of the family who had pulled the cart.

"That wheel's gone, and the other one is close to it."

The bearded father hunkered down beside him. "Can you fix it enough to keep us going? Don't know what we'll do without the handcart. There are four young'uns, as you can see, and the wife is six months along with our fifth. We need our belongings—"

Cunningham shook his head despairingly. "Let me find out if any spares are left. Nothing will put this wheel back on the trail."

He returned in a few minutes, triumphantly holding up one new wheel. As the family crowded excitedly about him, tears ran down the face of the mother. "Bless you, Brother Cunningham," she cried.

"Well now," Alfred said awkwardly, "no thanks is due until we get two wheels under this cart."

Replacing the damaged wheel was not difficult once the family had unloaded all their belongings onto the ground. The second wheel was what caused Cunningham grave concern. All the metal had worn off and there were several badly worn spots on the wooden rim. At least all the spokes were still in place. When Alfred took the second wheel off, he immediately saw the real problem. The axletree was in almost the same shape as the rim.

"You folks got any tin cups or plates?" Cunningham asked.

"Got some cups," the father replied. "The plates is all stoneware. The teakettle is tin though—"

"Get me all the tin you got. We need to wrap this axle at both ends and put some on the wheels, if there's enough."

The mother signaled to her oldest daughter, who began digging through their belongings.

"Another thing," Alfred said. "You happen to have any bacon left—or anything you can melt down for grease?"

"Got a small end piece we were saving for the next rest day," the mother said.

"Put it in the skillet and render it down," the father told her.

"Don't know what else would go to grease," he told Alfred. "It's slim pickings these days."

Cunningham spared the family a thin smile. "You got tin, and you got grease. We'll get this broken-down piece of junk back on the trail—and who knows, with that axle getting some protection, it just might last all the way to the Great Salt Lake."

The Cunninghams and the other carpenters in the company worked through the day making repairs. Alfred and Aaron alone repaired more than a dozen handcarts. By the end of the day, there were few tin plates or cups left anywhere, and no bacon.

President Franklin Richards and the last party of returning missionaries caught up with the Fifth Company the day they arrived in Council Bluffs. They had left Liverpool on the twenty-sixth of July, crossing the Atlantic by steam packet and riding horses and light carriages after reaching the railhead—all in less time than the emigrants took to cross Iowa. President Richards had been responsible for the emigration of more than three thousand European converts in just this one season.

The day after arriving at Winter Quarters, President Richards called for a meeting of all emigrants. They gathered expectantly, wondering if some new direction was to be given. The mission leader stood on a mill platform to address them.

"This is August the twenty-third," Richards began, "and it's more than a full month—almost two months, really—later in the season than it should be. It's time for decision. You still have over a thousand miles to go to reach the Salt Lake valley. There's a chance you could run into severe weather. Winter has been known to come as early as October, although it's usually November or December before the heavy snow falls. Several of us here today have made this journey more than once, and not all of us feel comfortable about the company leaving so late. Some feel that waiting here in Winter Quarters until spring is best. You emigrants must decide—wait it out, or continue on as quickly as possible."

One of the emigrants in front called out to him. "What are you going to do, President Richards?"

"I'm going on with the missionaries," Richards answered, "but we have fast horses and are traveling light. President Young is awaiting my report before general conference, so I need to make it back to Salt Lake City as soon as possible. If I were you folks, pulling handcarts, I believe I would still push on. However, you people must decide that for yourselves."

George Grant, one of the missionaries involved in making arrangements for the P.E. companies for the past five months, clambered onto the platform. Grant, who looked older than some of the other missionaries, was clean-shaven except for long sideburns, his hair free and windblown.

"I'll give you my opinion," he told the crowd. "It's late, no doubt about it, but you people are used to the trail now, and from what I've seen yesterday and today, the handcarts look to be in fine repair. Waiting out the winter here will be no picnic, I tell you that, so I urge you to get on the trail and put your feet toward Salt Lake."

Another elder climbed up beside Grant. William Kimball, a younger man than his companion, had penetrating eyes, a wide mouth, and a thin circle of beard around his face. He also had worked for months to prepare the outfitting of the handcart companies.

"I'll add my testimony to the others," Kimball said. "There could be snow, it's true, but you'll make it to the valley in time. Push yourselves now, and spend the winter in Salt Lake beside a fireplace with friends and family. That's what I'd do if it were up to me."

Then a grizzled stranger to the emigrants jumped onto the platform. President Richards introduced him as Elder Levi Savage, returning from a mission in Siam and Ceylon. He was thin, deeply tanned, and he wore a full beard.

"I understand your eagerness to get to Salt Lake," he said in a booming voice, "but the season is far advanced, and the risks are great of running into cold weather and snow. Far better to go into winter quarters here, where it's safe. If it were me, I'd wait until spring, then continue on the trail."

When he finished, the crowd began to buzz noisily as they discussed the advice of President Richards and the three missionaries.

"Where's Captain Martin?" someone shouted. "What are his feelings in the matter?"

There was a chorus of calls for the man who had brought them this far and Ed Martin finally climbed up on the platform beside President Richards. He raised his arms for quiet.

"There's a chance we could run into bad weather, no doubt about it, leaving this late. I think it will be close, but I believe we can outrun winter. A thousand miles is a long way, and I'm concerned, but I'm not against going on, if that's what you want to hear."

That *was* what everyone wanted to hear. Soon after, a vote was taken, and the forest of upraised arms left no doubt about the decision.

President Richards stepped forward on the platform. "The Lord bless you. Rely on him, and Godspeed on your journey. I have some Church business to take care of here before I leave, but I'll meet you on the trail again." The company was dismissed to prepare for departure. Each handcart group received an additional hundred pounds of flour, which they loaded on their carts because the supply wagons were full. The combined count of the company now totaled five hundred and seventy-six men, women, and children. There were one hundred and forty-six handcarts and seven wagons.

Midmorning of the twenty-fifth, the first of the handcarts began moving out of Winter Quarters. Tregale's twenty, as they still liked to look upon themselves, again took the lead. The two hundred that had arrived earlier now was assigned to bring up the rear of the column.

There hadn't been much time for rest during the past few days, not with all the repairs and preparations. People were still weary from the haul across Iowa, but the excitement of starting out on this final leg of the journey lent fresh strength.

The emigrants soon found that the extra hundred pounds of flour on each cart was a greater burden than expected. Those pulling and pushing adjusted stances and drew deeper on muscles to move the handcarts along. They traveled only two-and-a-half miles that first day, to Cutler's Park, before word was passed to make camp. That gave people a chance to rest and allowed the handcarts to close up ranks, for many had struggled and straggled in a ragged line out of the campsite. Some handcarts, for one reason or another, failed to leave Winter Quarters at all.

The company stayed at Cutler's Park all the next day. About noon, Colonel Almon Babbitt, the secretary of Utah, entered the camp in his carriage, pausing to visit a few minutes with Ed Martin. Babbitt, dressed in corduroy pants and a woolen shirt, was jovial and in high spirits. He had conducted some business in Washington on behalf of the Territory and now was anxious to get back to Salt Lake City.

"Your company looks in fine shape," Babbitt told Ed. He looked around from his vantage point in the light, horse-drawn carriage he was traveling in, taking in the mass of handcarts and emigrants. "Seems the handcarts are doing the job for which they were intended."

"If they hold up another thousand miles, I'll agree with you, Colonel," Martin replied. He had met the secretary several times in Salt Lake City in the months after the Mormon Battalion returned to Utah. "You'll be making it to the Valley in better time in this rig."

"Hope to be there in fifteen days at the outside," Babbitt said. "I have four wagons ahead of me on the trail—did you happen to see them at Winter Quarters?"

Martin shook his head. "Must have left before we got there. They'll be at least four days ahead of you."

"Glad to hear that," Babbitt said, nodding in satisfaction. "There are some important papers and a considerable amount of Church items that need to reach the valley with all haste."

"You'll probably catch up to them tomorrow or the next day," Martin assured him.

"Well, best be getting on. Godspeed on the trail, Captain Martin." Babbitt picked up the reins, clucked at the horses, and went cantering out of camp.

CHAPTER TEN

NEBRASKA FRONTIER

EARLY SEPTEMBER

It took two days for the handcarts to reach the Elk Horn River crossing. The emigrants camped on the eastern bank, waiting until morning to cross. At this spot the river was shallow and placid, the bottom hard shale, so no one had any difficulties in pulling the handcarts across.

Everyone settled into the routine of travel. Despite the added weight of the flour, which diminished every day by several pounds, the miles slipped by with surprising ease. People became hardened to the rigors, accustomed to long hours of pulling and pushing. Each evening found the emigrants tired but in good spirits, light-hearted for the most part, ready with a laugh and a joke about some occurrence on the trail. They sang around the campfires, a song often starting with one group then spreading into a loud chorus as adjacent groups picked up the words. Sometimes a song carried through the entire camp. The evenings always ended with bugle call and prayers.

On Saturday, the sixth of September, there was a sudden sweep of apprehension as a group of several hundred Indians passed less than a half mile from the handcarts.

"How many do you think there are?" Beth Wilson asked her husband nervously.

"Difficult to guess," Jim replied, awed by the sight. "At least four or five hundred, possibly a lot more."

The emigrants crowded closer together as they watched the Indians, seeing no signs of hostility, yet all the terrible stories they had heard about attacks and massacres flooding fearfully into thoughts.

Tregale, who had been up ahead on the trail with Ed Martin, came striding back toward the first handcarts.

"Can we expect trouble, Brother Tregale?" George Kimberley asked.

Tregale shook his head. "That's what I came to tell you. Captain Martin tells me these are Pawnees—they're peaceful enough. Just moving out of the high country for the winter, Captain Martin thinks. Pass the word back, will you, Aaron—"

The scare caused by the sight of so many Indians quieted when they passed without incident, disappearing into the east. The fears all came rushing back later that afternoon when the company met a small wagon train headed east.

A bearded man in the lead wagon called a rough command to the team of oxen, and the wagon halted. The others behind also stopped, as did the train of handcarts. Ed Martin and Carn Tregale crossed toward the bearded man and exchanged greetings. They learned that the train was comprised of several California families who were disillusioned about opportunities in the West and had decided to return east to farm in more settled country.

"You'd best be on alert," the wagon master warned the two men. "There was a wagon train massacred not too far back a few days ago. The Babbitt train, we were told. Four wagons burned and looted. Two teamsters killed, and a baby. Its mother was dragged off by the savages."

"Do they know what tribe?" Martin asked. "Were they Pawnees?"

The bearded man shook his head. "Cheyennes. The soldiers at Fort Kearney raided one of their camps a while back, killing some, and the Cheyennes are looking for revenge. There are several war parties about, so I hear."

"Appreciate the warning," Martin said, the expression on his face grave. "We'll take extra precautions."

"Probably won't attack you." The Californian spat a stream of tobacco juice onto the ground. "Too big a train, I suspect. But I'd be careful about stragglers."

"By the way," Martin added, "there's a large party of Pawnees a few miles east. Seemed peaceful enough when we passed them, but you might want to steer clear."

"Seen their tracks," the wagon master said, "and wondered who they might be. Peaceful, you say—"

"Looking for nothing more than a place for wintering, in my opinion."

"Thanks for telling us. Those Cheyennes ahead of you ain't peaceable, that's for sure."

The news about the Babbitt train massacre had a chilling effect on the whole train. This was real, not stories told of faraway events in other times. These were real people like themselves killed on the trail by Indians, just a few miles from where they were. Real Cheyenne war parties searching for vengeance—and the train of handcarts was heading directly into the country being ravaged. Everyone was shaken and alarmed.

Needless to say, those in the rear crowded closer to the main body as the train resumed its journey westward.

On Sunday, probably spurred by the haunting pictures in everyone's mind, the company made sixteen miles before camping. They pulled into a tight circle, and the guards quickly took positions. As they were doing this, President Franklin Richards and the small company of returning missionaries rode into camp. The emigrants hailed them warmly as the party brought their carriages and horses to a stop beside Martin and Tregale.

"You've made good time," Franklin Richards commented as he shook hands with them.

"We're averaging about a hundred miles a week," Ed told him. "That's pretty good for all the young and feeble we have."

Richards nodded agreement. "Passed the wagon trains a ways back. Hodgett is about ten miles behind you, and Captain Hunt planned to spend the night at Loup Fork, about forty miles to the rear."

"Did you hear about the Babbitt train?" Martin asked.

They hadn't, so Ed related the news. It sobered the previously jovial group.

"We'll have to move fast and keep our eyes open," Richards said. "We'll visit with the authorities in Fort Kearney and get a reading on how serious this business with the Cheyenne really is. If it's just a few disgruntled Indians skulking around, probably won't be any danger to a party your size."

"That's what we're hoping," Martin said.

The party of missionaries remained only a brief while, then continued up the trail. They intended making several more miles that evening before halting for the night.

The next day the handcart train climbed into the hills that separated the Loup Fork valley from the Platte valley. The climb was not difficult, but the country was dry, with no more of the frequent freshwater streams that fed the Loup Fork river. The barrenness continued on Tuesday into the afternoon. None of the travelers had prepared for such a long stretch between drinks and many suffered from the heat and dryness. That afternoon the company came upon a round, shallow pond of water. No stream fed into it, so an underground spring must have been the source. Seeing the water glinting in the sunlight, the Pitts and the Hilliger sisters, who were in the lead, sped up, eagerly anticipating the taste of fresh water again. Word rapidly passed behind that they had sighted water.

However, the cattle had suffered the same privations the past two days, and when they smelled water, the entire herd broke. They stampeded into the pond and when the first handcarts arrived a few moments later, the fresh water had been churned into mud. Even after the cattle had been driven out of the pond—not an easy task to accomplish—the water remained thick and black.

The emigrants gathered the liquid in pots and pans, facing the fact that it would not clear for several days. They prepared the afternoon meal with what they had, but the hastily cooked breads, puddings, and dumplings cooked up as black as the water. Still, it was food, and the muddy water just made the tea and coffee that much stronger.

Tregale took one of the horses and rode ahead to locate the campsite Ed Martin was determined to make that day. It was some nine miles farther west, a place called Prairie Creek. He returned with the good news that a clear stream awaited them at the campsite.

The company did not start back on the trail until seven that evening. As a result, they arrived at Prairie Creek just before midnight. People drank draughts of the fresh water but were too tired to prepare an evening meal. They put up their tents, posted guards, and fell exhausted into sleep.

Tregale rose early the next morning, before the bugle awakened the company for morning prayers, and stepped outside. He found Agatha Harbon sitting beside the fire she had started, sipping a cup of tea. She offered him one and he gratefully accepted, sitting down beside her.

"Nothing to eat yet, I'm afraid," Agatha said. "Waiting until the others get up before starting any cooking."

"This is all I need," Tregale murmured, sipping at the tea.

"Of course, it's none of my business," Agatha said, giving him a sidelong glance, "but I can't help wondering about you and Heather. You intend to do anything about that?"

"About what?" Tregale said, flustered.

"You know what I mean," Agatha snorted. "You and Heather."

"There's nothing but friendship between us—"

"There's more than that on Heather's part, and you know it. What I want to know is how you feel about her."

Carn took a few sips of the drink in his hand. Agatha's pointed questions had caught him completely off guard. "I think you're mistaken, Agatha," he said finally. "Heather is a good person who reaches out to everyone. If you've seen anything, it's her natural kindness—"

"That's tripe," Agatha interrupted. "She's interested in you, and it's preying on her that you don't seem to return that interest."

Tregale looked squarely at the older woman. "Agatha, if I do have feelings for her, I should discuss them with her, not you, don't you think?"

"That's exactly my point," Agatha snapped. "It's eating at her, you being so standoffish." She raised a hand to cut off his protest. "I know your time is taken up most of the day. But for heaven's sake, you can give her a smile and a friendly word now and then, can't you—I know very well you have feelings for her."

Tregale stared into the fire, took another slow sip of his drink. Finally he nodded, looked over at Agatha, and grinned sheepishly. "You don't miss much, do you."

"Not when it's obvious," Agatha retorted. "I understand what might be holding you back—she's a woman of fine upbringing. She probably makes you feel a little inadequate in the social graces."

"A widower with one hand and a hook can't presume much, can he."

"Nonsense. That hook is new to you, Carn Tregale, but the rest of us have never seen you without it. It's part of you, and no matter if a person likes or dislikes you, the hook goes along with it."

"It's still not something that's suited to courting a young woman of breeding—"

"More nonsense. You do Heather wrong by even thinking such things. There's strong character in both of you, and both have something that reaches out to the other. That's the important thing. Anyway, you're both starting from the same patch of ground now, aren't you? You'd better give heed, Carn Tregale, and do something about it. I like that young woman."

Tregale stared into his now-empty cup. He suddenly held it

over for Agatha to refill. "I like her too, Agatha. I'll take your advice and make sure she knows it."

Tired by the late-evening march the day before, the company made only twelve miles that day, camping early in the evening in a wide valley on the western side of the dividing hills, overlooking the broad expanse of the Platte basin. After dinner, Carn approached Heather as she and the other women were cleaning up.

"It looks as though it might be a beautiful sunset," Carn said to her. "I wonder if you'd care to watch it with me?"

Taken aback, Heather stood silently without answering. Agatha reached over and started untying Heather's apron. "We'll take care of this mess," Agatha said. "Can't remember when a man last asked *me* to watch the sunset." Carn thought he detected the merest flicker of a smile on Agatha's face.

Carn and Heather walked out of camp, strolling along the clearing, not saying much. Crossing a small ridge, they suddenly passed out of sight of the cluster of tents and handcarts. Carn pointed to a fallen tree a few yards farther on. "Looks like a good place to sit."

They settled on the log and stared out over the panorama of rolling hills, vast grassy plains, and huge patches of forest below them. They could see the Platte and a number of smaller rivers and tributaries feeding into it.

"Once we make the last crossing of the Platte," Carn said, "we'll be in high country and on the last leg of the journey, Ed tells me. Looks easy enough from here."

Heather shivered and pulled her shawl tighter about her shoulders. "Have you felt the chill in the air? The weather is beginning to change. You can see autumn in the trees."

"It'll be a little more pleasant pulling the handcarts without so much heat."

Heather abruptly changed the subject. "We don't see much of you these days, Carn."

"Keeping everyone on the move takes more time than I expected. Ed warned me that's how it would be."

"Have you got used to being around so many Mormons?"

"There are some I'd like to shake now and then, but that's the same in any group. On the whole, I admire and respect them."

"Any interest in our faith yourself?"

Carn shook his head. "Truthfully, no. I haven't had time to give it much thought. Ed and I talk about religion now and then, but neither of us has much opportunity. I know Ed would like to see me struck by lightning, or whatever it is that happens, but I don't think it will."

"Why is that?"

Carn shrugged. "I don't rightly know. Nothing inside me gets excited about religion, not like the rest of you."

"Well, if you haven't been told much about it, you can hardly be expected to get excited about it. Would you like to know more about the Mormon faith?"

"I can't honestly say I do."

"Why not?"

Carn smiled. "I knew you were going to ask me that. I don't have an answer."

"There must be something that troubles you about our faith," Heather pressed. "Do you know what it is?"

He thought for a moment. "I wouldn't exactly call it troubling, but there is one thing I don't understand."

"I'd like to know what it is—"

"I'm not sure I can explain it. It's the way you all seem to be not very concerned about now—today, or even tomorrow. You seem to live for the future—a life in another world that none of you can be sure exists. It doesn't seem natural not to worry about what's going to happen in my life next week, or the next few months. I suppose the truth of the matter is, I simply can't bring myself to believe in this life after death that means so much to you Mormons."

"I'm surprised to hear you say that," Heather murmured. "I

would think a man who has so recently experienced the death of a loved one would feel a closeness to the idea."

"It's going on without her that's more of a challenge. The whole purpose of life changes so you try to find new meaning, a new direction."

"That's where we differ, I suppose. I know what you're saying, and it's true, but the real purpose hasn't changed—not the eternal purpose."

Tregale shrugged again. "I know nothing of eternity. I can deal only with the here and now."

"But life is more than that," Heather said, her voice insistent. "We lived with our Father in Heaven before we came to this earth. When our stay in mortality is finished, we return to his loving arms, hopefully a better and stronger person for the experience."

"Is that why you gave up your cabin aboard ship—why you chose to travel with the handcart company instead of riding with the wagons? You thought it would make you a better and stronger person?"

Now it was Heather searching for the right words. "Well, I certainly didn't do it with that in mind—"

"But you were determined," Carn insisted. "It was written plain enough on your face—no one was going to talk you out of it. I'm curious what prompted you to do that."

Heather gave a little shrug of her shoulders. "I really don't know. I think I felt some guilt, perhaps, about having my own cabin when so many others were less fortunate. You even accused me of being spoiled, as I remember—"

"I didn't mean it that way. But you were being so—direct."

She smiled. "I did act rather strangely that night, as I recall. Perhaps by giving up the cabin, I was hoping people would treat me like I was one of them—that I wasn't someone who didn't know how to join in. It isn't my fault that my parents are well-to-do or that I was brought up in a sheltered atmosphere. I was trying

FIRE IN THE SNOW

to prove something, I suppose—probably more to myself than anyone else. Does that satisfy your curiosity?"

Carn half-turned, facing her squarely. He reached out and took
hold of her hand. "It's just that I want to understand how you think
and feel. I know you feel deeply about your faith, and I envy you
the inner peace you enjoy. I'm not much for dealing with things
that in my opinion have little to do with the business of life. To be
truthful, that has been my main obstacle in letting myself have feelings for you."

"Because you feel there is little chance for us?"

"As I told you once before, your station is—"

"—sitting here on the same log with you, looking at the same
horizon. You say you prefer to deal with the here and now. Well,
this is it. The past, for both of us, has no bearing on today or tomorrow. I have feelings for you, Carn, and I feel bold enough to
admit it. I couldn't bring myself to say that to a man a few weeks
ago, no matter how much I cared for him, so I know I've changed
in that, along with about everything else in my life."

"It doesn't matter to you that I'm not a Mormon?"

"It matters, yes, but I'm content with the man you are. You're
kind and sensitive and thoughtful of others—I've seen that in you,
and others can see it too. Perhaps one day the Spirit will touch your
heart, and I'll pray it does, but it's who you are now that I've been
drawn to."

Tregale drew in a deep breath, feeling sudden elation. So
Agatha was right; this young woman whom he admired but from
whom he kept distant did have an interest in him. He released his
breath slowly. "Perhaps we could walk together on the trail when
I have the chance. And watch another sunset—"

"I'd be pleased and flattered."

He squeezed her hand. Heather returned the pressure and
smiled at him, seeing for the first time the glistening of moisture in
the corners of Carn's eyes. She instinctively touched his cheek with

105

a fingertip. "Why, Carn Tregale, is that a hint of tears? I hope it's not sadness."

He shook his head. "You make me feel alive, Heather, just with a few words—almost like a young lad again. I've felt dead these past months since I lost Elsie. Suddenly I have feelings inside, and I have you to thank for it."

Nothing more needed saying. They sat together until the sun sank low in the horizon, holding hands, content with the warm pleasure of each other's company.

CHAPTER ELEVEN

INDIAN COUNTRY
LATE SEPTEMBER

T he lead handcarts came upon the sign early the next afternoon. A board was propped up between a pile of rocks at the side of the trail, a piece of paper with crude lettering fastened to it.

> Omahas not kill
> men and baby
> Omahas
> at peace

There was a signature, although no one could make it out. The note obviously referred to the recent attack on the Babbitt train that had killed two teamsters and a baby.

Ed Martin joined the group gathered beside the sign. "It's the work of the chief of the Omahas," Ed told them. "That's his sign at the end. He wants everyone to know that his tribe is not responsible for the Babbitt massacre."

"How many tribes are there in this country?" asked a nervous Gwen Pitts.

"Quite a few. Some live in these parts, and others are just passing through to get out of the high country for winter."

"How do you know which Indians are friendly and which aren't?" Beth Wilson asked.

Her husband gave a short laugh. "If they try to kill you, they ain't friendly."

"Most of the Indians are friendly these days," Martin said, trying to reassure those around him. "According to the Californians we met, the Cheyennes went on the warpath only to avenge an attack by soldiers out of Fort Kearney."

The lead handcarts continued on, and as the other handcarts trailed past the sign, all heads swiveled to read it. The word was passed that it had been put there by friendly Omahas, but that brought little consolation. The sign served as a grim reminder that violence and death had erupted along this trail just a few days ago.

Two miles farther on, the company passed the graves of the three people killed by the marauding Cheyennes. They were in a row at the side of the trail, rocks piled on each grave, one pitifully small. The Californians had said they'd heard the baby was only two months old. The burnt wagons and a few personal belongings were scattered along the trail. It was still possible to see the marks of blood on nearby rocks apparently left by the unfortunate mother who had been dragged off by the Indians. The scene was sad and frightening.

Four days later the handcarts approached Fort Kearney, a small fort set on a plain beside the Platte River. The emigrants were not scheduled to camp at the fort, and the long train of carts kept moving past the military outpost. Ed Martin and Carn Tregale mounted two of the horses assigned to the stock herders and galloped into the stockade, anxious to talk to the post commander.

A soldier showed them into the office of Captain Wharton, a swarthy-faced, short man with a moustache drooping down at the corners. He was in his shirt sleeves, and his pants were dusty and wrinkled. He looked tired. The three exchanged greetings and Captain Wharton motioned for the two trail captains to sit in the hard-backed chairs in front of his desk.

"Talked to a Franklin Richards about six days ago," Captain Wharton began. "He told me about your company, Mr. Martin. Don't envy you your task, not with all those people having to pull handcarts through the high country. Understand you have a lot of young'uns and old folks in your party."

Ed nodded. "Got our share. But it's working out better than I hoped. We passed the Babbitt train, or what's left of it, a few days back. How bad is the Indian situation, Captain Wharton?"

"Those crazy Cheyennes are the ones causing all the trouble. They've been raiding and causing trouble for months. Sent a company to one of their villages a while back to let them know there's some authority in the territory. We killed ten braves in the skirmish and that sent them on the warpath."

"Is it a general uprising?" Martin asked.

The commander shook his head. "Just a few parties of maverick braves and discontents. None big enough to attack anything but small wagon trains. But we're standing double guards at night."

"You think they might attack the fort?" Tregale asked, surprised.

"They're mad enough to do it," Wharton replied, "but I don't think the chiefs will stand for another full uprising. Leastways, I hope not. We don't have the manpower to hold the fort if all the Cheyennes decided to band together."

"So you think we might be in danger from the Cheyennes?" Tregale thought of the handcart company's store of rifles, which seemed now to be pitifully small.

"Not unless the situation gets worse," Wharton said. "Like I said, the Cheyennes are attacking only small parties. There was a California family traveling alone a few days back, and the Cheyennes attacked them. The husband escaped, his wife was killed, and his boy, about four years old, was taken prisoner. The man made it here the same day as your Franklin Richards. Then there were the Margetts and Cowdy families, massacred about a hundred and twenty-five miles west of here. Traveling out of Laramie. Got news of that attack the same day. But the pattern's the same—the Cheyennes are attacking only the small, weak outfits. It's fair to assume they'll steer a wide path around any group numbering in the hundreds, like yours."

"Then you think it's safe for us to continue west?" Ed asked.

Captain Wharton nodded firmly. "I'll be sending a company west to Fort Laramie in about a week. Seeing that many bluecoats should keep the Cheyennes up in the hills. Do you have sufficient firepower if you do come under attack?"

"Not as much as I'd like to have," Martin replied.

"Keep the guns handy and have the guards armed at night," Wharton advised. "I'm sure you've already warned your people about keeping together. I wouldn't put it past the Cheyennes to try to pick off a small group of stragglers."

The handcarts and wagons circled for the night beside the Platte about six miles northwest of the fort. The word was passed that Captain Martin wanted to address the entire company after the evening meal.

Sam Williams and the other men of Tregale's unit saw to putting up the tent and starting a fire, while the womenfolk prepared dinner. Fred and Ted Tate left camp on their usual chore of scouting for hardened buffalo chips and other firewood. The company had spotted buffalo regularly these past weeks, although the animals were usually far off in the distance. Droppings were plentiful, the dried and hardened dung making good fuel for the fire. The twins soon found some buffalo droppings fresh enough to not be fully hardened and immediately started a dung fight. When they returned to camp, Willie took the boys by the neck, hauled them to the nearby creek and dropped them in, clothes and all.

The meals finished, people began gathering inside the circle near the river. Fred and Ted, now changed into dry clothes, slipped away from their group and headed to the far side of the encampment. They were not specifically bent on mischief but were ready for any opportunity. It came several minutes later when they found a group fire left completely unattended, the people now gathered among the hundreds awaiting Captain Martin's remarks.

The fire wasn't what caught the boys' attention; it was the tantalizing smell of fresh-baked bread. It smelled unbelievably good, though they could see no bread anywhere. They had almost decided the group had eaten all the bread before departing when Ted spotted something under the bed of a nearby wagon. They quickly crawled under the wagon and to their delight found two loaves of fresh bread cooling in pans under a cloth.

The aroma was more than the boys could resist. Fred spotted a knife beside the fire and scooted out to grab it. Once again under the wagon, he neatly cut off the end crust of one of the loaves. He handed the knife to Ted, who did the same to the other loaf. Then the boys reached in and began scooping out the warm bread. In only a few minutes, they had completely hollowed out the loaves, stuffing themselves with the delicious, fresh-baked bread inside. Then giggling, they pressed the end crusts back onto the shells, put the hollow loaves back into the pans, and again covered them with the cloth.

It would have ended there as a boyish prank, but as they crawled out from under the wagon, Ted kicked something. There was a strange rattling noise, then Fred cried out as he felt a sharp pain in his leg. He looked down and was horrified to see a coiled snake drawing its head back, preparing for another strike. A screech of fright broke from both boys and they shot out from under the wagon.

"It bit me," Fred gasped, reaching down to grasp his leg.

"Can you run?" his brother asked, looking back to see if the snake had followed them. It wasn't anywhere in sight. He glanced nervously to see if anyone had heard their yelps of fright but apparently no one had. Everyone was still over by the river, listening to Captain Martin.

"Can you run?" he asked again, peering down at his brother's leg. They could see two puncture marks where the snake had bitten Fred just above the ankle.

Both boys began running and they didn't stop until they were safely inside their own tent. There, Fred fell to the ground and clutched his leg.

"It's really hurting," he said, grimacing.

Ted's eyes widened as he looked down at his brother's leg. It had begun to swell. "I'd better get dad," he muttered. "It must have been a rattlesnake—those are poisonous. I heard it rattling just before it bit you."

"Just after you kicked it, you mean," Fred growled.

"I didn't see—" Ted protested.

"Well, you kicked it. It should have bitten *you.*"

"Do you want me to get dad or not?"

Fred's leg was swelling at an alarming rate. It throbbed with pain and he was beginning to feel a little sick to his stomach.

"Okay, but let's tell him we were just walking around the camp and the snake crawled out from under one of the wagons—"

"I'm not going to tell him what really happened, you idiot."

Ted rushed from the tent in search of his father, leaving his brother clutching his leg and watching in horror as it continued to swell. The lower part was now twice its normal size.

Captain Martin lifted his voice out over the sea of heads gathered beside the river. The emigrants were seated on the ground so his words would carry better. He repeated much of what Captain Wharton had said earlier. Gasps of dismay followed his news of the other recent Indian attacks.

"So it's important to stay close together," Ed repeated. "Those in the rear should try to double up—go two abreast where possible, and stay up with the rest of the company.

"Those of you on guard duty, draw rifles from the wagon master and stay alert. No sleeping on guard duty—everyone's safety could depend on it.

"From now on, the oxen and cattle stay inside the circle at night. We've been lax before, but there's a real danger now in leaving the stock outside. Make a bigger circle to allow for them. The Indians have a fancy for running off livestock at night. There are enough mothers with small children to know the importance of not losing the cows and the milk they provide."

George and Annie Kimberley were seated near Martin. Annie raised her hand and Martin acknowledged her. There was an anxious tremor in Annie's voice. "How much farther do we have to go, Captain Martin? The nights are turning colder. Will we make it to the Salt Lake valley before winter hits us?"

Martin paused before answering. He had struggled with this question himself these past few weeks. The company was making good progress, but no one could deny the weather was turning cold. And they were not yet in the high country.

"I wish I could give you a proper answer, Sister Kimberley. We're right on schedule—maybe a little ahead. If all goes well, we'll reach Fort Laramie in about three weeks. From there, it's only a few hundred miles to Salt Lake City. I don't know about the weather. It's turning cold, that's true, but I still believe we'll make it to the valley before winter sets in."

The meeting broke up after a few more questions, mostly about equipment and repairs. So far the handcarts had held up remarkably well—miraculously well, in Alfred Cunningham's opinion. As Tregale's group was returning to its campsite, Ted Tate found his father.

"You best come quick, dad," the boy cried. "Freddie's been bit by a snake."

It brought a cry of alarm from Maude. "Where is he?"

"In the tent. His leg's swelling up real bad."

When the family rushed into the tent and saw the condition of Fred's leg, Maude burst into tears. The leg had swollen to at least three times its size and looked as though it would burst. Maude dropped beside her son and clasped Fred's head in her arms. The boy was sweating profusely and breathing heavily.

"Do something, Willie—" Maude pleaded.

"I don't know anything about poisonous snakes," Willie muttered. He stooped and gently probed the puffy flesh of his son's leg. "Does that hurt, son—?"

Fred nodded, feeling too nauseous to talk. His head was swimming, and he felt like he was going to faint. He couldn't look at his leg—it was too frightening.

"Ted, run and get Captain Martin. Tell him what's happened," Willie said, trying not to show his deep concern as he looked at the swollen leg. "Captain Martin will know what to do—"

Several minutes later, Ed Martin, accompanied by a worried Tregale, arrived at the tent. Ed knelt beside the boy and examined the leg, seeing the two punctures. "How long ago did this happen?" he asked Ted.

"About half an hour ago. I couldn't find my dad in the crowd at first."

Ed pulled out a hunting knife. Fred's eyes widened in fear. "You're not going to cut off my leg, are you, Captain Martin?"

Martin smiled and shook his head. "Just going to make a little cut so the poison can come out. You won't even feel it."

With two quick strokes, he cut an X between the puncture wounds. He didn't need to squeeze. A watery fluid spurted from the cuts, splashing onto Fred's sister Dolly, who was kneeling close to watch the proceedings. Dolly screamed and jumped back, clinging to Beryl as she brushed at the brownish fluid on her dress.

Maude reached out and gathered her into her arms. "That's all right, Dolly. It won't hurt you."

Fred saw the cut, saw the fluid spurt out, and fainted dead away. That was probably for the best, because Martin started to squeeze the leg to keep the liquid flowing from the cut. It was unbelievable how much came out. Finally mostly blood began to flow from the wound. Tears streamed down Maude's cheeks as she held her son's head in her lap.

"Will he be all right?" Willie asked. His face had drained of all its color. "The poison won't do any permanent harm, will it?"

"From what Ted said, a rattler bit him. The swelling should start to go down now. The boy will feel sick for a day or so, probably have a fever while the poison works out of his system. He'll be his normal self after that."

"Don't know if that's good news or bad," Maude muttered, but she was smiling through her tears.

"Get a hot bread poultice on that cut," Ed advised. "It will help pull out the rest of the poison."

The attention of everyone in the tent had been so focused on Fred that no one heard the outburst of angry cries that sounded from across the encampment. No one except Ted, that is. Even with the seriousness of his brother's injury, he had difficulty keeping a smirk off his face. The identity of the culprit who had left the hollow loaves was a topic of conversation for many days after, but it was a mystery never to be solved.

Fred still felt miserable the next morning, but he was cheered when Ed Martin ordered him to ride on one of the wagons. His mother put another poultice on his leg and was reassured by the signs of her son's recovery. Fred felt well enough to pull faces at his brother as he was lifted up onto the wagon.

Another three days passed, each one marking a good march of fourteen or fifteen miles. The train of handcarts moved more tightly as people kept a wary lookout for signs of Indians. After two days, Fred's leg had healed sufficiently for him to take his place again pushing the family handcart. The days of riding in the wagon had thoroughly spoiled him, and the youngster protested loudly that he wasn't in any condition to walk. But after an hour or so, he and his brother were arguing as usual about nothing and everything.

The feelings of nervousness among the emigrants began to ease but on the fourth day they met an eastbound train of three wagons. The small group was from a tiny settlement called Green River, the teamsters told Martin and Tregale, located in a western basin of the Rockies about a hundred and fifty miles east of Salt Lake. They were on their way to Florence for supplies, planning to return early in the spring. The news they brought cast another pall over the entire company.

Almon Babbitt, traveling with a man named Thomas Sutherland and a driver, had been attacked and killed by Cheyennes not more than fifty miles west of where they now were. Many remembered seeing the secretary of Utah when he had visited briefly at Cutler's Park, just west of Florence. That made his death more personal, brought it closer to themselves. A sense of danger again pressed in upon the people pulling handcarts.

Four days after the meeting with the Green River wagons, the Pittses and Hilligers called out the scene where Babbitt and his companions had been murdered. About fifty or sixty yards off to the left, they could see the remnants of the outfit: the wheels, the springs of the burnt carriage, some of the harness, a few scattered personal items. Apparently the bodies of the three men had been taken somewhere for a proper burial.

A silence fell over the entire train as it moved past the site, a lot of fervent prayers rising that this would be as close to the horrible vengeance of the Cheyennes as they would come.

Fortunately, only two miles farther up the trail, the lead hand-carts came upon another sight that helped push away the feelings of despondency. Captain Hodgett from the wagon train following them, along with two other men from the wagons, were not far from the trail, busily skinning a massive buffalo they had chased and separated from the herd, then killed. Tregale was among the first to reach the men from the wagons.

"Captain Hodgett," Tregale called in greeting. "Looks like you had a successful hunt." He stared at the carcass. Till now, he had seen the animals only from a distance. He had never encountered an animal so huge.

"That we did, Captain Tregale," Hodgett replied. He motioned to the two men with him. "Don't know if you've met Moses Cluff here and Nathan Porter. We've had a busy afternoon. Already skinned out one for our wagons. Got this one for your people—thought they could use some fresh meat."

"That's very thoughtful of you, Captain Hodgett. It will indeed be welcome."

The crowd watched the men cut up the buffalo, overwhelmed at its size. They had seen nothing like it in England or in any of the other countries of Europe. Tregale detailed four handcarts to distribute their loads among their neighbors and stay behind to bring the meat into camp. When Hodgett and his companions were finished, all four carts were loaded to capacity with the dressed-out cuts of meat.

Every adult received about one pound of fresh meat that night, and the smell of sizzling buffalo meat filled the camp. Most enjoyed the taste, though it was wilder in flavor and a little coarser than beef. It was good to see people laugh and enjoy themselves again, Tregale commented to Martin, for these past days in Indian country had seen a weary soberness settle over the company. The excitement of a close-up contact with the huge buffalo gave people something new to talk about and lifted everyone's spirits.

After the meal had been cleared and all chores taken care of, Lydia Hilliger saw Aaron Cunningham approach her. The two had spent considerable time together on the trail, Aaron frequently trading with Harriet to spend a turn pulling beside her sister. The young couple now wandered off by themselves, walking around the perimeter of the circle. A clear space was always left these nights between the tents and the protective circle of carts and wagons. This provided greater security and gave the livestock an area to wander in if they chose. Most of the animals, though, settled down to rest in the evenings as soon as they were fed.

Aaron seemed particularly preoccupied with something this evening, Lydia thought, casting a sideways glance at him. He had not spoken since they started walking. She quickly thought back to see if she had said or done something that might have offended him.

Finally Aaron cleared his throat several times and said, "I've grown very fond of you these past months, Lydia."

"I feel flattered about that, Aaron."

"I wonder how you feel about me?"

A slight hesitation, then a visible indrawn breath. "I like you, Aaron. I feel very comfortable and protected when I'm with you."

Aaron reached over and took her hand. Lydia flushed with warm excitement. In all their walks, he had never taken her hand before.

"I want to marry you, Lydia," he blurted.

She stopped, turning to face him. Her cheeks flamed with the unexpected surprise of his declaration. She knew Aaron liked her, liked her a lot, but she had not expected a proposal of marriage.

"Well, what do you think—will you marry me?" he asked again.

"It's such a surprise," she said finally, finding her tongue. "My mind can hardly cope with it—"

"I love you, Lydia. I've loved you since the first day I saw you on the boat. I knew then I wanted to marry you."

"I never thought you felt that strongly—"

Aaron smiled. "I'm not much with words, as you've noticed. But all this worry about Indians has made me bold. I want to be your husband, Lydia, and protect you against every bad thing that might come."

"I feel you do that already."

"But I want you as my wife, Lydia. What do you say—do you love me as much as I love you?"

For answer, Lydia reached up and put her arms around his neck, pulling his face down to hers. They kissed, long and tenderly. His arms tightened about her waist, pressing her against him. When they broke the kiss at last, Lydia was breathless. "You're a good kisser, Aaron. And you'll make a wonderful husband. Yes, I'll marry you."

They kissed again, more fervently, more passionately. The

embrace ended, and Aaron broke into a broad smile. "You've made me so happy, I want to shout—"

"You'd better not," Lydia said, returning his smile, "or people will think the Indians are attacking."

"When shall we do it?"

"Get married? I'll need time to think about that."

"Let's do it now—tonight. Captain Martin can marry us."

"We can't," Lydia said, laughing. "It's too sudden."

"Well, tomorrow then—"

She put a finger against his lips. "I'll be your wife, Aaron, but we must find the proper time. That's not here on the trail."

"Why not—?"

"Well, for one thing, I don't want to spend our honeymoon in a tent with twenty other people."

Aaron grinned self-consciously. "Well, I hope you're not suggesting we wait until we reach the valley—"

"Perhaps that will be best. It's only a few more weeks."

"I can't wait that long. I want you to be my wife, Lydia."

She reached up and kissed him again. "You'll be my betrothed. We'll be together almost all the time—side by side, pulling together." A thought struck her. "Do your parents know about this, about asking me to marry you?"

Aaron shook his head. "We'll tell them together. They already know I'm crazy about you, of course. I doubt if they'll even be surprised."

"You don't think they'll mind—"

"They like you, especially mother. Father doesn't think much about anything but the handcarts and getting to Salt Lake."

Lydia squeezed herself against him, pressing her cheek against his chest. "I'm so happy, Aaron. I truly am. Waiting till we reach the valley will be hard for me too."

Aaron held her close, closing his eyes. His heart had hammered in his chest all day long, awaiting the moment. He felt a deep contentment now that it was settled.

The sense of well-being that pervaded the camp seemed to bring renewed energy to the company. All the next morning songs drifted along the trail, and people called out to each other again, not so absorbed in themselves. There were jokes about harnessing huge buffalo to each of the handcarts. The tension that had been building inside people as they passed the signs of Indian savagery seemed greatly eased.

It was all shattered shortly before noon when the company came upon the Margetts and Cowdy family massacre. The train halted, and people walked over to inspect the remnants of the tragedy. Evidently other settlers or soldiers had cleaned up most of the debris, but enough was still cast about to paint vivid pictures of horror in the mind.

"What are all these feathers from?" Beryl asked, pointing to several dozen scattered on the ground. "The Indians?"

"Hush," Maude Tate said. "They're probably from pillows or bedding." Her voice trembled as she talked.

Agatha stooped over and picked up what was left of a blood-stained shirt. The air still seemed to quiver with unheard sounds of attacking Indians and cries of wounded, dying settlers. Heather Lee saw Tregale and walked over to him, putting her arm in his as she shuddered.

"It's all so sad," she murmured, looking around at the signs of violence. "Two whole families murdered. It must have been horrible for them."

Close beside her, Harriet Hilliger suddenly shrieked and covered her face with her hands. Tregale and Heather saw instantly what had caused the scream of anguish. Other people rushed over, and then they too backed away, horrified.

It was a child's skull, almost hidden between two rocks. The skull had already lost all flesh and hair, and black streams of ants crawled over it. There was no way of telling how the child's head had become separated from the body, but it spoke with terrible eloquence of the nightmare that had engulfed these two families.

The finding of the child's skull filled everyone with revulsion, and there was no longer any curiosity about probing the site. People returned to their handcarts, and the train was soon on its way again. There were no more songs or laughter that day, for the fears that had gripped them earlier had now returned in greater intensity.

The next afternoon, the lead handcarts stopped abruptly. "Indians!" Derek Pitts yelled, pointing to a patch of forest. Five braves on horseback, with squaws and children trailing behind them on foot, could be seen breaking into view. The Indians swerved toward the train of handcarts.

"Cheyennes!" Martin said, the word quickly rippling through the company. Martin and Tregale each grabbed a horse and galloped the length of the train, making a show of brandishing rifles.

"Show your weapons," Tregale shouted to the men as they rode past the handcarts. "Let them see we're armed and ready."

"If you don't have a weapon," Martin added, "show yourselves, and look like you're ready for a fight."

Men ran to put themselves between the Indians and the handcarts. It served the purpose; the braves passed within a few hundred yards, close enough for the emigrants to see the streaks of war paint smeared on their bodies and faces. The Indians saw the array of rifles pointed toward them, and at least a couple hundred belligerent men. They swerved back toward their squaws and continued eastward. There were audible sighs of relief as the Indians passed from sight.

Martin called the company together again that night. "We have a little more than a hundred and fifty miles to Fort Laramie," he told the gathering. "If we keep up our pace, we should be at the fort in less than two weeks. We pick up supplies there—President Richards will have arranged for food and blankets. After Laramie, we'll probably see no more Indians. Weather and the high country will be our challenge the rest of the way."

A week later, the company passed near Chimney Rock, a pin-

121

nacle of stone that had marked the trail since the earliest wagons had headed west. The emigrants marched another five days before they saw the walls of Fort Laramie rising ahead of them. They camped that night about a mile east of the fort, tired but happy to be within touch of civilization.

Something, however, drew their attention beyond the fort, something awesome in size and grandeur. Rising on the horizon, dwarfing the fort, were the rugged heights of Laramie Peak. The mountain reached up into the clouds and already wore a mantle of snow. It was the emigrant's first sight of the Rockies, stretching with jagged teeth as far north and south as the eye could see.

With the sighting of the mountain came the first realization of what lay ahead in the high country they had heard so much about. The view was overpowering, striking a chill into every heart.

CHAPTER TWELVE

FORT LARAMIE
EARLY OCTOBER

Ed Martin found Carn early the next morning eating a leisurely breakfast with his group. No bugle had roused the company this morning since the leaders had declared a day for resting and repairs, the first since leaving Cutler's Park nearly seven weeks ago.

Agatha looked up at Martin. "There's enough food if you care to join us, Captain Martin."

"Already had breakfast, Agatha, thank you." He glanced over at Carn, sitting beside Heather Lee, a nearly empty plate on his crossed legs. "Thought you and I might ride into the fort, Carn, and see what supplies President Richards set aside for the company."

Martin's glance took in the gathering about the small fire. "Everyone here fit and well?"

A chorus of cheery replies answered him. The two men strode off to where two saddled horses waited beside one of the wagons.

"I wish everyone felt as good as they pretended," Carn said. "Some are just about played out, I'm afraid."

"It's the same throughout the company," Ed responded. "I don't know how some of the older ones are managing to hold up."

"How much farther beyond Laramie?" Carn asked.

"About three hundred and fifty miles—and it's the toughest stretch of the journey."

The post commander was pointed out to them as he walked

across the parade ground toward his office. They caught up to him and he swung about, scrutinizing them. The commander was tall and thin, with a stiff military bearing and piercing blue eyes over a bushy moustache. His uniform was brushed and clean, his boots shined. "I'm commanding officer Colonel Hoffman. You men from that handcart company out there?"

"Captain Ed Martin, and this is my assistant, Carn Tregale. We'd like a few minutes of your time, Colonel."

"Understood," the commander said brusquely, nodding. "Might as well cut right to it. Wish I had good news to tell you, but I don't."

Martin frowned. "Would that have anything to do with the provisions set aside for us?"

"I know what you're expecting, gentlemen," the colonel said, "but there are no provisions, I'm afraid."

Both Martin and Tregale were stunned. "We're desperately in need of food and supplies, Colonel," Martin said. "We've counted on getting fresh provisions—"

"I know, I know," the colonel interrupted. "A man by the name of Richards was here a few weeks ago, trying to make the arrangements. I'm sorry—I truly am. But supply has been fouled up all summer. Three supply trains were scheduled to arrive from the east in the past six months. None of them did."

"Was that due to Indians?" Tregale asked.

The colonel made an impatient gesture with his hand. "Indians these days know enough not to attack a military train. It's what's happening back east that's upsetting the supply system. All priorities are going to commands that might face immediate action if war should break out with the Southern States. Not likely, I say, at least not this year, not until the elections are settled. I'll be glad when the next few weeks are over—perhaps then we'll have some idea of what the politicians are up to. But there is a possibility of war in the near future, and that's what's on the minds of the generals and quartermasters these days—that and all the trouble in the

Kansas and Nebraska Territories. Seems anyone stationed out here has been forgotten. I've received notice that no supply trains will come in until spring."

"So nothing's set aside for us?" Martin asked again.

"Check at the sutler's. I believe Richards purchased some buffalo robes and earmarked them for your company. But food—not a sack of flour or a barrel of jerky to spare. I'm sorry, for I know your people must be in need."

"We can't go much farther without food," Carn said, looking at Martin. "As it is, we're losing miles every day because of the condition people are in."

The commander stroked a finger at the bushy moustache, uncomfortable before the troubled expressions of the two men.

"I know it seems a military post this size should have plenty to spare, but believe me, Captain Martin, our position is almost as precarious as yours. I've had the men on reduced rations for a month now, and those are due to be cut again. Fort Kearney is as bad, if not worse, than we are. We'll be facing starvation if it's a long winter. I've written several dispatches, even sent an officer back east to see if he could get the generals to realize our urgent situation. All he brought back was a reprimand for myself."

Martin and Tregale looked at each other in despair.

"Is there any other outpost where we can get supplies?" Carn asked.

Martin shook his head. "This is our last hope."

The colonel nodded. "He's right about that."

"Then we need to think seriously about how far we can go before running out of food," Carn said grimly.

Martin glanced across the parade grounds in the direction of the handcarts. "Not far, I know. Perhaps we'll have to winter here in Laramie."

Colonel Hoffman started stroking his moustache again, frowning at the prospect of six hundred starving civilians on his hands for the next five or six months. He came to a decision. "If your situa-

tion is that desperate, Captain Martin, we will have to do something to help, no matter what our own straits may be. Your company is the last westbound this season, I'm told, along with the two
wagon trains accompanying you. Tell your people I'll open the
post store to them this afternoon. They can buy whatever is available. I'll have the quartermaster fill the shelves and mark prices
plainly."

The colonel's gaze slid down to take in the dilapidated condition of the two men's boots. They looked as if they were barely
holding together. "I'd be pleased to have the quartermaster issue
new boots to the pair of you," Hoffmann said, "compliments of the
United States Army. They're a poor substitute for the provisions you
need, but the fact is, feet are almost as important as the stomach on
a march like you people have ahead of you."

Both Ed and Carn thanked him, accepting the offer gratefully.
Practically everyone needed new footwear, even those who had
included extra pairs of shoes in their seventeen-pound limits.
People had walked over eight hundred miles from Iowa Hill, and
the cutting and tacking of leather hides onto worn-out soles had
become a regular activity. Carn had already gone through three
soles on his boots, which had been sadly worn to begin with. Much
of the footwear had gone beyond repair, and scores of people,
both children and adults, had taken to walking barefoot. Despite
the initial discomfort, feet soon hardened, and the trail in most parts
was smooth and grassy.

The colonel had one other suggestion. "The sutler, J. W. Tutt,
has some provisions not under military control. I suggest your people also buy what can be had at his store. You'll have to pay his
prices, of course, but it's better than going without. To be frank, as
soon as your company leaves, I'll be commandeering whatever
supplies the sutler has left. In deference to your needs, Captain
Martin, I'll not issue that order until your people have a chance to
stock up whatever they can. That's all I can do for you, I'm afraid."

The two men obtained new boots at the quartermaster's store, stopped in at the colonel's office to thank him again, then headed back to the handcarts. Ed Martin called a general meeting that morning to make the report. Everyone had noticed the supplies dwindling each day, but none had been concerned till now because everyone expected ample provisions to be picked up at Fort Laramie.

"I know few of you have money to spare," Ed told the gathering, "but I urge you to take what you have and buy food at the fort. Pool resources if you have to because you'll have no opportunity to buy anything after we leave Laramie. For most of you, it will mean using money put aside for clothes and shelter in Salt Lake. Have no doubt that using it to buy food now is by far the more urgent need. We'll be climbing into high country after we leave Laramie, and the going will be a lot harder than it's been so far. You'll need all the strength you can muster to pull these handcarts over the mountains."

Martin pointed down to the new boots he was wearing. "The commander was kind enough to take pity on Brother Tregale and myself and provide us a gift of new boots. If you can spare any money from buying food for your families, purchase new shoes. Remember, we still have another five hundred miles to walk."

It was a busy, frantic afternoon as members of the handcart company crowded into the fort's supply store and bought practically everything in sight. The prices were plainly marked, as Colonel Hoffman had promised, and fair enough. Bacon was fifteen cents a pound, and the women from Tregale's group, shopping together, bought a whole slab. In addition to tasty breakfasts, it would replenish the supply of much-needed grease for the axles of the group's handcarts. The women bought tins of hard biscuits, one of the higher-priced items at fifteen-and-a-half cents a pound. They added three sacks of flour, a bargain at twelve cents a pound, and a sack of rice, expensive at seventeen cents a pound, but a welcome addition. They bought some sugar and butter and even found some tins of tea, which they quickly snapped up. Maude found a desperately needed treasure at the sutler's store: children's shoes in sizes to fit both Maggie and Dolly. There had been a dozen or so pairs of women's shoes on the shelf at the sutler's, but the first customers had immediately bought them.

The women piled their purchases onto the handcart they had brought with them and they headed back to the camp, excited and pleased with themselves. There was enough extra food on the cart to supplement their daily rations sufficiently to last the journey, even if rations were reduced, as Captain Martin had hinted this morning might be necessary.

Many of the emigrants who had almost no money faced much harder choices. For these, the priority was staples, flour and a little rice. The two young married couples, the Pittses and the Wilsons, quickly ran out of money at the military store where purchases were on a strict cash-and-carry basis. The couples managed to buy some more at the sutlers, for Tutt was willing to barter. Derek Pitts was able to sell his watch, and Beth Wilson got a fair price for a gold necklace that had been a wedding gift from her mother. She felt a twinge of regret as she handed it over to the sutler, but that quickly faded as Jim picked up an entire sack of flour in exchange. There was little sense in being buried along the trail with a gold chain about her neck, Beth admitted to herself.

Carn and the section leaders distributed the hundred buffalo skins Franklin Richards had purchased weeks before. There were enough hides to provide three each for the larger tents and at least one for the smaller ones. The skins were large and heavy, good protection from the cold ground.

The handcarts and tents needed more repairs than expected, and both men and women worked all the next day to complete them. Not until the evening was the company ready to leave. Despite the lateness of the hour, Ed Martin decided to move on, if only for a few miles. The tents and handcarts were all packed and ready for the trail, and Ed and Carn agreed this last leg of the journey should get under way without further delay. A rider from

Hodgett's wagon train had ridden into Fort Laramie late that afternoon, informing Martin that the wagons were only about a half-day's journey behind them, some seven miles.

After the company left Laramie, the weather turned cold. A strong wind blew in their faces during the day, continuing through the night as temperatures dropped to near freezing. Each morning heavy frost lay on the ground. The company had begun to climb now, and the handcarts bumped and jarred along a trail strewn with large rocks and stones.

Progress slowed down some, but people worked harder at pushing and pulling and the company managed to average twelve to thirteen miles a day. At night, men scurried to repair handcarts, which were taking a beating on the rocky trail. The livestock became more difficult to handle, for they could find little feed in the changing, increasingly hostile terrain.

Two days out of Laramie, Martin ordered daily rations of flour cut from one pound to three quarters, even though people were working harder now and feeling a greater need for food. There were complaints, but in general the order was accepted as necessary. People furtively began to use the supplies they had purchased in Laramie, despite a strong warning from Martin and the other captains that they should get along with the reduced rations to stretch supplies as far as possible.

On the fifth day into the high country, the emigrants encountered an eastbound train of wagons. The train appeared to have about a hundred or so people, and the two companies halted to exchange greetings.

The leader of the wagon train was a bearded man who introduced himself as Jonathan Grimshaw. Martin and Tregale and a small group of the emigrants gathered around the lead wagon as Grimshaw frowned at the sight of the handcarts stretching at least a mile along the trail.

"You must be the company we've heard about," Grimshaw

said. The others placed the man's heavy English accent as the Midlands. "Last train west this season, I'm told."

Martin nodded and looked back at the line of wagons. "You people out of Salt Lake?"

"That we are," Grimshaw said heavily, "and glad to be rid of it, I might add."

The group of emigrants were surprised at the anger in his voice. "Things not go well for you in Utah?" Martin asked.

"Things ain't going well for anyone in Utah these days," the wagon master growled. "You folks will find it's not the paradise you expect. Hasn't been for us, anyway."

"You're from England?" Alfred Cunningham asked.

Grimshaw nodded, a dour expression on his face. "Going back as soon as we have the passage. Plan on getting jobs back east. I'll give you fair warning, there are no jobs to be had in the valley."

"Sounds as though you people have had a rough time," Martin said, concerned about the looks he saw on the faces of those around him. This was no time to weaken resolve. "Is it your faith that's in question?"

"It's the times," Grimshaw replied. "There's been famine for the past two years. Little food and less work. The brethren do their best, I suppose, but emigrants like yourselves keep flooding in and that makes things all the harder. We just decided to pack it in and head back."

"These are tough times in England too," Art Smith told him. Tregale was surprised, for this was the first time he had seen Art voluntarily join in a conversation. "I don't know how long it's been since you left, but you'll not find much in England to your liking when you get back."

"Can't be worse than what you'll be finding in the valley," Grimshaw retorted.

"Is the Lord telling you people to do this?" Art asked, his voice insistent.

The wagon master was openly antagonistic now. "That's our

business, isn't it. You people listen to your voices, and we'll listen to ours. We've had enough of promises and all the talk about how wonderful the next life will be. It's this life that needs getting through. And I tell you people straight, it's hard times you'll be finding in the valley."

"Well, we wish you well," Martin said, anxious to end the meeting. "May you find all you hope for in England. How about the trail up ahead—anything we should watch for?"

The wagon master picked up the reins, shaking his head. "Just the weather. We hit a little snow about a week back. Probably just a passing storm, though. You should have no trouble." He put a hand to the straight brim of his hat. "Didn't mean to sound too sour. There are those in Zion doing fine, I suppose. Wish you people the best—but we're glad to be heading home."

The cold increased as the handcart company climbed higher into the mountains, the emigrants casting anxious eyes toward the towering, cloud-shrouded heights of Laramie Peak. The snowy slopes were an ominous foreboding of the winter weather they desperately hoped to avoid. The cold during the day was bearable because of the body heat generated by the exertion of pulling carts over the rocky trail, but at night the temperature in the tents fell to chilling levels, and the ground felt cold even through the buffalo hides. In the days after leaving Laramie, the company experienced at least one death each night as the grueling physical hardship and reduced food rations began to take a toll among the elderly.

Tregale had the captains take an inventory of the food in the wagons and it became painfully clear that, at the present rate of consumption, provisions would not last through the weeks it would take the company to reach the Salt Lake. Two days after meeting the wagon train, Ed Martin ordered the daily ration of flour reduced even further to half a pound for each adult. That meant hunger was now to be a constant companion for those who tried to survive on the approved rations. More of the company began supplementing their meals with food from their private stocks purchased in Laramie.

On the evening of the ninth day out of Laramie, on Saturday, the eighteenth of October, the handcarts made camp at Deer Creek, a spot some five miles from the North Platte River. The campsite was a beautiful sweep of high meadowland, a favorite spot for Indian tribes during the summer, Martin explained. The company had traveled one hundred and twenty-five miles since leaving Laramie. They faced one more large river, and then only four hundred more miles. That news made for a cheerful camp despite the bone-weary fatigue and chilling cold.

CHAPTER THIRTEEN

NORTH PLATTE RIVER
MID-OCTOBER

Martin and Tregale rode out of camp even as the handcarts were circling at Deer Creek, galloping ahead until they reached the bend in the North Platte where a pontoon ferryboat normally bridged the river. This was to be the spot where the handcarts crossed and Martin wanted to be sure all was well. Mormon pioneers had built the ferryboat nine years ago during their western trek from Missouri to the Great Salt Lake Basin. The bridge had been maintained since its construction and was now an important station along the trail for all travelers, for the North Platte could be a formidable river to cross.

Looks of dismay crossed the two men's faces as they saw the ferryboat pulled up onto the mud and rocks at the side of the river. They could see a couple of tents pitched near the beached bridge and several soldiers grouped beside a campfire, evidently part of the detachment of soldiers from Fort Laramie stationed at the bridge during the months when wagon trains used the crossing.

The two men dismounted and a young-looking soldier in a lieutenant's uniform rose and came forward, hand outstretched in greeting

"Lieutenant Brandon at your service," the officer said, shaking hands with them. "I hope you men are from the handcart company we've been waiting for."

"That we are, Lieutenant," Martin replied. "We're camped about five miles back, at Deer Creek."

"Good spot," the lieutenant replied, nodding. "We've been expecting you for the past two weeks."

"And we were expecting to cross over that bridge," Martin said, glancing at the ferryboat resting in the mud. "What happened, Lieutenant?"

The young officer shrugged. "We had to take it out, sir. The river has been rising rapidly—a lot of rain up in the mountains, I suspect. The current grew dangerously strong, and a week ago heavy chunks of ice began piling up against the bridge. We figure some of the higher tributaries froze up, then broke loose, putting a lot of ice in the river. Between the current and the ice, we almost lost the bridge. We had to take it out."

"Can you put it back in so we can get the handcarts across?" Martin asked.

"The current's too strong. We couldn't hold it. Especially if you put more weight on it. Even doubling up on the ropes wouldn't work. We knew it would be a problem, sir, but we had no choice."

"Can we cross here without the bridge?" Tregale asked, knowing the answer. He could see the water churning and swirling, dark and threatening in the failing light.

The lieutenant shook his head. "The water's too deep. Not even wagons could make it across."

"What do you suggest, Lieutenant?" Martin asked.

"We've scouted the river, sir, and found a suitable spot about five miles upstream. The Platte there is about a hundred and fifty yards across and not more than a foot and a half deep, maybe a little deeper in spots. But it has a good rocky bottom, and being so wide, the current's not so strong. You should be able to ford without much difficulty, I believe."

"Thank you, Lieutenant. Deer Creek is a pleasant spot, but it's no place to spend the winter."

"You're right, sir. We'll be heading back to the fort ourselves now that we've made contact. When do you plan on making the crossing?"

"We'll head out early in the morning. How do we find this crossing upriver?"

"We've marked it clearly, sir. You'll have no trouble recognizing it."

Back in camp, Tregale summoned the captains and told them about the change in plans. Then he told them of the decision he and Ed Martin had made on the way back from the river.

"The North Platte is the last major river crossing facing us, but it's also the most difficult. With the river up, we'll have our hands full getting the handcarts across. We'll need to lighten loads." There was mumbled concerns from captains, but Carn held up a hand to silence them. "The people are wearing down, and the carts are wearing out. Both are in danger of not being up to the task of making the crossing. We have to lessen the weight on the carts. Every adult must bring what they carry down to no more than ten pounds. For children under eight, the limit is five pounds."

"That's almost cutting the limit in half again," one of the captains muttered. "We have so little now as it is."

"I know it will be difficult," Tregale said, "but we must do it, no matter what."

"What do you suggest they leave?" another captain asked.

"Get rid of everything that can't be worn or eaten, for starters," Tregale answered. "Keep just the bare essentials in cookware. Leave behind all clothing not suitable for the trail. A lot of people still are carrying gifts for friends and relatives in Utah—they have to get rid of them if that's what it takes to get their load down to ten pounds."

One of the captains raised a hand. "Can't the wagons following us pick up some of the belongings left behind?"

"I discussed that with Captain Martin," Tregale answered, "but it's not possible. The wagons are overloaded as it is. They'll have to reduce loads for this last stretch too. We've sent a message to both

Captains Hodgett and Hunt, however, asking them to close up and render whatever assistance they can in crossing the river."

He looked around at the grim faces, knew what they were thinking. This was not a time to be adding to the stress of their people, physical or mental. But there was no alternative if the river was to be crossed.

"We have no choice," he told the captains quietly. "It's best your people make their decisions tonight because we'll be starting early in the morning. It's ten miles to the crossing and we need to have the river behind us before we make camp tomorrow."

The handcarts moved out at six the next morning, the meadow dotted with piles of belongings. People did not understand the need to lighten loads.

"If the river can be crossed with a ten-pound limit, it can be crossed with seventeen," Esther Cunningham had complained, voicing a sentiment common throughout the company. The captains were sympathetic but adamant.

The early departure left little time for anything other than brewing hot drinks and munching leftovers from supper. The forced abandonment of prized clothing and possessions left most of the emigrants in a sour mood as they left the meadow and headed for the river.

Ed and Carn again rode ahead to scout the crossing. At the site of the dismantled bridge, the soldiers had already broken camp. The lieutenant once more assured the two men that they would have no difficulty in locating the marked crossing. They rode on and found the markers five miles upriver, two piles of stones with boards pointing toward the river.

At first sight, it looked as promising as the young lieutenant had said. There were no banks, just a wide, gentle approach to the water and what appeared to be an equally flat area on the far side. The river was wider than a hundred and fifty yards, but that was probably because it was continuing to rise. It was now closer to two hundred yards across, they guessed. A few large boulders protruded out of the fast-moving water, but it was easy too see how a path could be threaded between them. Not until Carn edged his reluctant mount into the water did they realize fording the river would not be as simple as it looked.

The horse snorted and shied away, feet slipping on the smooth stones lining the riverbed. Carn held the animal's head tight with the reins and kicked its flanks, forcing it farther out into the water. In just a few steps, the water was almost up to the horse's belly. The stirrups went into the water, and in seconds Carn could feel a numbing cold through the leather of his new boots. He leaned over, put a hand in the river, and jerked it back. The water was bitterly cold. He backed the horse out and dismounted.

"If we cross in that," Carn said, wincing and stamping his feet, "a lot of people will freeze to death."

"If we don't cross," Ed replied, "a lot of people will starve to death. Let's find a place to ford—"

The handcarts began arriving at the river about two o'clock that afternoon. In the lead was the cart drawn by Derek and Gwen Pitts, with Heather and the two Hilliger sisters pushing at the rear. The company was spread out more than usual behind them, showing the mood of those who had not been able to summon the usual energy and enthusiasm for the march.

Carn and Ed had each located a good crossing route at both ends of the site, and the handcarts began splitting into two groups at the direction of the captains. Tregale's twenty gathered around him, looking at the broad stretch of the river with apprehension showing plainly on their faces.

"It's so wide," Esther Cunningham said. "Is it deep?"

"Not too deep to cross," Carn assured her. "I'll go ahead with the first handcart to show the way across. It's simple enough—go straight out to those boulders near the middle, then angle across toward that first clump of trees on the far side. The water won't be above your knees most of the way, although it will be waist high for some of you women about midstream. The bottom is fairly smooth and mostly small stones, so it shouldn't be too difficult a pull. There are some larger rocks, however. If a wheel gets stuck, push a little harder, and it will roll free. If you can't move, just be patient. Someone will come out to help you get started again.

"The biggest problems for everyone will be the cold and the current. The water is like ice—in fact, there are slush and chunks of ice in it—and the current is strong enough in places to push you off balance. Take your time, and hold tight to the cart if you should lose your footing."

Tregale's glance took in all of them, from poor George and Annie Kimberley, sitting weary and worn on the ground, to Maude Tate, a worried expression on her face as she held little Dolly, to Beth Wilson clutching the tiny bundle of her baby, to Agatha Harbon, standing stiff with arms folded and wearing her usual grim expression, to Heather, close beside him and trying not to show any concerns. The crossing would be difficult for all of them, he knew.

"Beth, you and little Nancy wait for the wagons. They should catch up to us within the hour. You ride across with them—we can't put the baby at risk in water that cold." He looked at Maude. "How about you, Maude—do you want to put Dolly on the wagons with Beth and Nancy?"

Maude shook her head. "I'll carry her so she can stay with the family."

"Put her on the cart then," Carn said. "No sense taking a chance on losing your footing and both of you getting dunked."

He looked directly at George and Annie Kimberley. "How about you two—I think you should wait for the wagons with Beth."

George stood up and shook his head. "Annie is not feeling well, and I would appreciate it if she could ride on the wagons. But there are more than enough sick, and babies like little Nancy, to fill whatever space there is. I can make it across by myself." Annie started to protest, but George hushed her with a gentle hand on her shoulder. "You know I'm right, Annie. I'll be fine, and the better for not worrying about you. Brother Tregale said the current is strong, and I probably couldn't hold you if you fell."

"He's right, Annie," Carn told her, forcing a smile onto his face. He knew her husband should go on the wagons too, but what George had said was true. It would be hard finding space for those who had to be put on the wagons. "We'll all be together, and we'll all be helping each other."

"Where are we going to camp, Brother Tregale?" Alfred Cunningham asked.

"Almost forgot that," Carn said. "There's a spot a couple of miles beyond the river with plenty of firewood. We'll all want a good fire tonight so just keep going after you cross the river. Captain Martin and I have already marked the spot with a pile of wood. I'll be staying behind to help the rest of the company across. Get fires going right away. Everyone will need to dry out clothing, and I promise you, a hot drink will never feel so good as it will after wading across that river."

Tregale moved to the front of the first handcart, smiling encouragement at Derek and Gwen as they took their places behind the handle. Heather and the Hilliger sisters lined up at the rear, ready to push.

"All right," Carn called, taking hold of the pulling bar along with the Pitts, "let's get this handcart across."

Gwen gasped as ice-cold water rose above her knees. She took a few more steps then gripped her husband's arm fiercely. "I—I can't breathe," she shrieked. "It's too cold—"

"Keep pulling, Gwen," Derek cried, forcing his voice past the shocking cold that was squeezing the breath from his chest. "Keep pulling—"

Carn kept a firm grip on the handle and put his strength into keeping the handcart moving over the stones of the riverbed. He heard painful gasps escape Heather and the Hilliger sisters and knew the three young women had stepped into the river and were suffering the same freezing shock as the others. At least he had known what to expect, and on top of that, his body temperature was still lowered by his earlier wading and crisscrossing of the river.

The cart rolled through the rushing water for a dozen or so yards but abruptly lurched and jerked to a stop as a wheel struck a large rock. Carn arched his body backward, pulling harder on the handle. The others responded, pulling and shoving in unison. The cart lurched again, cleared the obstacle, and once again started rolling forward.

The water rose higher as they moved farther from shore. Carn could feel the energy of the group fading as cold and shock numbed them. They were barely a third of the way across, and the wheels were now bouncing against larger rocks with greater frequency, placing terrible strain on protesting muscles.

Gwen suddenly began to sob hysterically. "I can't do it, Derek," she cried, her chin chattering spasmodically from the cold. "I can't feel my legs—"

"You have to keep going, Gwen," her husband shouted at her. "There's no going back now. Just keep pulling—we'll soon be across."

Behind the handcart, the three women were pushing as hard as they could. Keeping their footing against the rush of the current was tricky, and the water dragged with foaming force at the bulky mass of their wet, ankle-length skirts. Suddenly Harriet twisted her foot on a loose stone and staggered to one knee. The water engulfed her, and the next second she was being swept away, tumbling helplessly in the current.

Both Lydia and Heather screamed and Carn looked back to see a dark form rolling and tossing in the water. He lunged after it, forcing his legs to leap through the stream with great, stretching strides. Carn reached out and his fingers grabbed a handful of cloth. He stuck the curving hook through the cloth and plunged his other hand into the water, seeking to lift up the face of the woman. He had a desperate fear it was Heather the current was threatening to sweep from his grasp. His fingers found hair and he pulled the head above water. Harriet spluttered and coughed, still struggling, though she was aware of hands pulling her upright. Carn had time only for one quick look into that terrified face, relief sweeping through him both that the woman was alive and that it wasn't Heather.

He stiffened his body against the current, gaining balance and drawing breath into lungs that felt crushed. Harriet suddenly slumped in his arms, becoming a dead weight. He knew without looking that she had fainted. Reaching down, he lifted her in his arms and started staggering toward the north side of the river. Fortunately, the current had swept them on an angle closer to the far bank, now only fifty or sixty yards away. Carn felt grateful for that, for he knew he could not carry the dead weight of Harriet and her heavy, soaked clothing very far. He could already feel the muscles in his legs and arms quivering from the strain.

The people waiting to cross had watched in horror as one of the women behind the handcart was swept away. They saw Carn leap after her and catch the tumbling body. Cheers broke out as he lifted the woman in his arms. At the same time, Aaron and Alfred Cunningham were already splashing through the river toward the handcart. Aaron had kept his eye on Lydia since she first stepped into the water, so he knew she was not the one pulled into the current. But fear for her safety hammered inside him as he raced past his father, the shock of the bitterly cold water not slowing him down at all.

Aaron reached the handcart and threw his weight into pushing beside Lydia. She and Heather were struggling to keep the cart from being swept sideways. Moments later, Alfred splashed his way to the front and squeezed behind the handle beside Derek. With the added strength of the two men, the cart once again began to roll toward the far side of the river.

But the river was not yet ready to be beaten. Lydia abruptly cried out in pain as a large chunk of ice crashed into her thigh. The force of the blow knocked her feet from under her and she slipped completely under water. Aaron grabbed her before she could be swept away as her sister had, putting his hands under her arms and tugging her back onto her feet. Lydia seemed able to stand, but her eyes were wide in fear and shock as the freezing water cascaded from her. She clung fiercely to Aaron, almost pulling both of them back down into the water. With an arm about her waist, Aaron looked over at Heather and shouted a warning.

"I can't help you," he cried. "She'll fall if I let go."

Heather was too busy even to hear Aaron. The cart was sliding and she was fighting with all her strength to keep it from swinging sideways. Fear beat in her breast, and her body felt completely frozen. She had no idea what was happening up front, could not see Derek or Gwen, did not even know what had happened to Harriet. She had seen Carn leap after her, but beyond that, the cart had demanded every ounce of her strength and concentration. She was aware the cart had stopped again after Lydia fell, except for the grim pressure of sideways motion. Suddenly a man appeared beside her, pushing against the rear of the cart. Her mind was so numbed that she could not have recognized Art Smith even if she had been able to look up. But now the cart was moving again, as more people came from shore to help.

Heather was not even aware they had stepped on dry ground until she felt strong hands about her and looked up into Carn's face. She fell against him, sobbing, feeling her knees sag. He picked her up and carried her away from the water, away from the terrible dragging and pulling, her body exhausted and so cold she could feel nothing, not even the cold. She was aware of Carn putting her down gently, and then, mercifully, she blacked out. She had not even seen the silent, quivering form of Harriet just a few feet away.

Harriet was sitting on the ground, body hunched over, arms folded tightly about her knees. Except for the violent shaking from the cold, she was not moving. She simply stared straight ahead with unseeing eyes.

Aaron hobbled toward them, supporting a sobbing, shivering Lydia. She saw her sister and ran the last few steps, falling down on her knees in front of Harriet. She called her sister's name but got no response, not even in those blank eyes. Lydia looked up in alarm at Tregale.

"Your sister is in shock, Lydia. There's not much we can do until we make camp. Some dry clothes and hot food will help."

Lydia stared at her sister with deep concern. "Will she be all right then?"

"Eventually," Carn told her, avoiding a direct answer. "She's had a bad experience. We'll have to be patient and wait until she comes out of it."

Aaron knelt on the ground beside Lydia, putting an arm about her shoulders. "I'll have to get back to help bring our cart over. Will you be all right?"

Lydia turned her head and reached up to kiss him. "Thank you, Aaron. You saved my life."

"Well, I don't know about that," Aaron said, casting an embarrassed glance toward Tregale. "But I'm glad there's no harm done. And don't worry about Harriet—she'll be all right. I'm sure of it."

Willie Tate was second in line, and with all the difficulties plaguing the first handcart, he had waited until it had safely left the river on the far side. Agatha Harbon volunteered to help pull the Tate handcart across since Maude had her hands full with the children. Agatha took her place at the front with Willie. Maude was at the back holding onto Maggie's hand. Dolly was already seated on top of the goods in the cart, looking frightened.

"Now you stay down and hold tight," Maude told her youngest daughter, her voice harsh with concern. "I don't want you falling off."

"I'm afraid, mother," Maggie said, tugging at her mother's arm.

She stared at the swirling water with wide, fearful eyes. "Won't it go over my head?"

Willie glanced across the river, scratching his cheek. "The child's right, mother. Better put her up with Dolly. Her weight won't make that much difference, and then you can help push."

Maude hoisted Maggie onto the cart, and the two sisters immediately clasped their arms around each other.

"Lie flat, the both of you," their father ordered, "and don't sit up again until we're on the other side."

Agatha reached down and grabbed at her skirt. She pulled it up to about her knees, then knotted the material in place. "You'd best do the same, Maude," she called. "I'm sure the water pulling against their skirts was what made walking so treacherous for the girls. You too, Beryl. No time for modesty—these men have seen a pair of knees before."

They hoisted and tied their skirts. Beryl squeezed in at the front bar between her father and Agatha, while Fred and Ted leaned against the back of the handcart on each side of their mother. Willie gave a shout and pulled the handcart into the river, his shout turning to a painful howl as the frigid water closed about him. His cry was swallowed up, however, in the piercing scream that broke from Beryl as she entered the water.

The first shock of that icy water brought wild screeches from the twins. Maude would have screamed with them, but all sound froze inside her, breath snatched away by the chilling cold.

"Hang on, boys," she managed to gasp. Her eyes slid upward, making sure the girls were obeying their father. They were, lying flat on their stomachs and clinging tightly to the ropes around the belongings. Maude threw her weight into pushing. The twins got over the first shock and put their shoulders back against the cart.

The group pulled and heaved and kept the handcart moving until they neared the boulders in the middle of the river. The water was much deeper here, the rocks larger, and it was more difficult to pull the wheels of the handcart over them. Suddenly the cart slid sideways into a hole and tipped precariously. Maggie and Dolly started to scream, clinging desperately to the ropes to keep from sliding off. Willie shouted to everyone as he tried to position his feet to get a better pull.

"Push hard—give it all you've got!"

They fought to get the wheel out of the hole but the cart wouldn't budge. Water was splashing over the top of the handcart, soaking the little girls and causing them to scream even louder. Maude was desperate, but she could not even spare a glance at her girls, for the handcart was threatening to tip over completely.

Then strong hands were placed on the cart as Tregale and Martin and others from the company arrived to help. A couple of heaves and grunts, and the cart lifted out of the hole and began rolling across the bottom again. Carn lifted Beryl out from the front bar and started to carry her across. Ed Martin ducked under and took her place, putting his strength with that of Willie and Agatha. The cart made the rest of the crossing without stopping.

The Wilson cart moved out ahead of the Cunninghams—Sam Williams had helped wrestle the cart into position while Alfred and Aaron were still across the river. He and Jim Wilson were joined by a man from the first hundred, a volunteer to fill in for Agatha at the front. Art Smith, still soaked and shivering from helping the first handcart across, took a place beside Sam Williams at the rear. Art shook his head at suggestions he wait and rest.

"I'm too cold to sit around," Art told them. "I'd rather cross and get to the camp."

The group made it to the middle of the river without incident, but just when they thought all would be well, Sam Williams's knees buckled. He cried out and gripped the back of the cart. Art called out for the men at the front to stop.

Sam was deathly pale, beyond the color drained from all of them by the frigid water. He looked over at Art and gave a wan smile.

"My legs have give out, Art, and there's a terrible pain in my chest—"

Art let go of the handcart, watching nervously to see if it would slip sideways under the pressure of the current as the other carts had done. The wheels must have been lodged firmly between the rocks for it stood steady. He reached over to grab Sam by the arm.

"Can you hang on until we get across?" Art shouted.

Sam shook his head. "I don't think I can walk at all," he gasped. Water was cascading over his shoulders. "I can't even stand up."

"Let's get you up on that rock, then," Art told him. "I'll have to stay with the handcart, but you'll be safe there. Someone will come to help you across."

Sam was immensely heavy as the current pulled ferociously on him, but Art managed to push him up onto one of the larger boulders. Neither man at the front dared to let go and come back to help him. Sam inched up onto a flat spot and sat there, both legs still dangling in the water.

"You going to be all right, Sam?" Jim Wilson shouted.

Sam waved a hand. "I'll be fine."

Art took his station at the rear again as Jim threw him an anxious look.

"Can you handle it?" Jim asked.

Art nodded, hoping he did not show the utter fatigue he felt. This second crossing, along with the additional exertion of getting Sam up on the rock, had left his muscles trembling. The weariness inside him went deeper even than the cold. All he wanted to do was get across and lie down in dry clothing beside a roaring fire. The cart started inching forward again.

The Cunningham handcart was only a few yards behind them now. Two men from the company had volunteered to join the Cunninghams and Esther and George Kimberley. One of the men was up front pulling, and the other joined Esther and George at the back. The cart was having an easy crossing. George, who was too numbed and fatigued to do any meaningful pushing, was having a difficult time just holding onto the cart. He called out anxiously as they passed the boulder where Sam was perched.

"Can we help you, Sam? Do you want to get on our cart?"

Williams waved them on. "Just giving my legs a rest, George. I'll be fine."

George waved back, then clutched the end of the cart with both hands, desperately trying to stay on his feet. He thought of Annie and how grateful he was that she was being spared the agonizing cold and hammering current.

The wagons in the Hodgett and Hunt trains arrived, and soon the river was crowded with handcarts. Men from the wagons and some of the livestock drovers plunged in to help get the carts across. A man on horseback plucked Sam Williams off the rock, laying him across the neck of the horse. Waiting hands on the north side took Sam and put him with the growing number of those unable to continue under their own power. Among these, Harriet still sat hunched over and unseeing. Lydia remained beside her sister, arms locked tightly around her, lending what little body warmth was left in her. Heather had left for the campsite, shaking off the fainting spell and insisting on helping to pull their handcart to the grove.

The icy, swiftly flowing river took a harsh toll on the emigrants. None had experienced bitter cold like this before and many, like Harriet, arrived on the far side in shock. Some suffered nasty cuts and bruises from the chunks of ice churning downriver. Some of the younger women could not stop screaming and sobbing even after they were safely across. Many handcarts stalled or faced danger of being overturned, while some family members panicked during the crossing and were unable to move. Fortunately, help arrived quickly wherever it was needed, and not a single emigrant was lost in the treacherous crossing.

By four o'clock, a little less than two hours after the crossing had begun, all the handcarts had reached the north side of the river. Most of the wagons also crossed that afternoon, including those carrying the sick and the babies who could not have survived the crossing otherwise. Dusk fell early, and the remainder of the wagons and all the cattle were held on the south side, waiting for morning to complete the crossing.

CHAPTER FOURTEEN

BANKS OF THE PLATTE

MID-OCTOBER

Carn and Ed spent almost two hours in the water, rendering assistance and encouragement to frightened families. Both men had lost all feeling in their bodies, surviving the numbing cold by keeping constantly on the move. When the last handcart rolled onto the north side, they emerged from the river and collapsed wearily in the mud.

Carn's teeth were chattering as he lifted his head, blinking water out of his eyes. "You sure this is the last river we have to cross?"

"A few more," Ed grunted, "but they're small streams compared to the Platte."

A half-dozen handcarts had clustered over by the trees where people had been left who had been too weak or disabled to continue. At least a score had been injured in the crossing, including those in shock and some like Sam Williams who obviously had serious problems. After talking to Sam and examining him, both Carn and Ed were reasonably sure he had suffered a heart attack. Many more of the emigrants had been injured in one way or another, but most had been able to stay with their families, either walking or being carried on top of handcarts.

"Let's empty a couple of those carts," Ed said, "and haul the sick and injured to camp. We can send a wagon back for the rest."

Carn glanced at the sky, seeing a mass of dark, threatening

149

clouds. The light would be completely gone in an hour or less, he guessed. "Is it just because I'm frozen, or is the temperature dropping like I think it is?"

Ed's face wore a grim expression as he too looked up at the darkening sky. "I don't like it. It feels like snow."

Fires roared in camp that evening. There was plenty of firewood from the cottonwoods and willows beside the campsite, and the emigrants gathered close about the flames, shivering bodies eagerly soaking up the heat. People who could, changed into dry clothing. Most found to their dismay that the river had soaked everything lashed on the carts. The pots of tea and coffee were kept full, hot drinks warming some of the bone-deep chill that gripped everyone. Surprisingly, there was little attention paid to supper; people were too cold and worn to spend much energy on cooking.

A bitterly cold wind began howling out of the north, frustrating efforts to set up the tents and showering long trailers of sparks from the fires. It started to rain, soon turning into a downpour of freezing sleet. As soon as tents were staked and secured, people left the smoldering fires and ducked inside. Few had managed to completely dry out their clothing, and they faced the prospect of spending the night in damp misery.

Carn made his rounds of the camp, visiting with each of the captains, growing more worried with each report. The river crossing had caused widespread suffering and every captain was concerned about how his people could go on in the morning. The river had sapped the last energy from most families, and with now being forced to spend the night in wet clothing, there was a very real concern about sickness. Every captain reported that some in his hundred were in shock, hysterics, or more serious conditions. The men seemed to be in worse shape than the women, for battling the cold and current had proved to be the last straw for many already drained and exhausted. Each captain quietly confided that several of their charges were near death as a result of the crossing.

Carn could do nothing but encourage the captains to do everything possible to keep suffering to a minimum.

Tregale sought out Ed Martin and passed on the reports. They shared each other's frustrations about being unable to do anything to improve conditions. Ed stood in the rain and looked up again at the dark, stormy sky overhead.

"Let's hope it's a passing storm," he muttered. "It feels like winter, but it's only mid-October. There should be another four to six weeks before the really severe weather sets in."

"This is severe enough for me," Carn said, shivering. "What about the morning—do we stay here or move on?"

"We have no choice, Carn," Ed muttered. "We have to keep going. We have to make the valley before the food runs out—and I'm not at all sure that's possible, even now."

Tregale returned to his tent. In the flickering light of the lantern, he cast a concerned glance around. It was cold inside, and everyone was suffering from the rigors and aftermath of the crossing.

Harriet was sitting up, a blanket about her shoulders. She had not shown any sign of coming out of shock. She sat with her knees pulled up and arms clasped around them, staring ahead with blank eyes and shivering uncontrollably, just as she had on the river bank. Lydia sat beside her, holding a steaming mug to her sister's lips, coaxing her to take a sip. Lydia flashed a worried glance toward Carn.

"Is there anything we can do for her, Captain Tregale? She doesn't respond to anything I say—"

"Keep her warm and get as much hot liquid down her as possible. She could be better in the morning, or it might take days. No one can do more than you're doing, Lydia."

No sense telling her the full truth, he thought. He knew Harriet was in deep shock. She was wet and cold, and with the storm blowing outside, there was little hope conditions would improve. Martin had told him Harriet could stay in shock for weeks possibly even months.

Carn turned his attention to Annie Kimberley, lying awake beside her husband. George was wrapped tightly in his blankets, and Annie watched her husband with a worried look on her face. She smiled up at Carn, however.

"You look cold and wet, Captain Tregale," she said.

"Aren't we all," Carn said quietly. "How is George doing?"

"He's sleeping now, thank you. Seems to be peaceful enough, and he's stopped shivering. The crossing really wore him out."

"Did he get something hot inside him?"

"Just a few bites of food, but he had three cups of tea."

"That should do it," Carn said, grinning. "Let someone know if either one of you need anything."

The flap to the tent opened and Alfred Cunningham and his son ducked inside. A cold blast of wind followed them in before the tent flap closed again.

"It's freezing out there," Alfred gasped, banging his hands against his ribs. "Never been that cold in England."

"How are the repairs going?" Tregale asked.

"Done everything that could be done," Alfred grunted. He sat down wearily next to Esther, who looked tired and cold and unhappy. "Fewer problems than I expected. Some loose wheels, several spokes that needed replacing. Only two axles that broke. The carts fared better than the rest of us, I'd say."

Aaron had crossed to Lydia and her sister, stepping over stretched-out forms. He dropped to his knees and took her hand, looking at Harriet.

"No change, I see." His eyes flitted lovingly over Lydia's face. "Have you eaten? You must care for yourself as well as Harriet, you know."

Lydia sighed, putting down the mug she had been using to try to get her sister to drink. "You look tired, Aaron—and you're shivering to death." She held out her arms, and Aaron embraced her, letting his head lie on her shoulder. For the moment, Lydia let her thoughts drift from her sister.

Carn looked at the Tate family, all crowded close together on the far side of the tent. Willie was examining the outstretched feet of Teddie and Freddie. "Is there a problem? It isn't frostbite, is it?"

"Not yet," Willie answered, "but they've both lost their soles, in a manner of speaking."

"The soles of their shoes?"

"Ripped right off by the current, both feet, the both of them."

"They were already half off," Freddie said defensively. "We didn't know they were gone until we started walking after we got out of the river."

Maude was frowning. "You'll have to do something, Willie. They can't go barefoot in this weather."

"Well, I don't know what, mother," Willie said tartly. "If they don't have shoes to wear, they can't wear them, can they?"

"They still have the tops—"

"Well, maybe they can turn them upside down then."

"No reason for a smart mouth, Willie," Maude snapped.

Carn offered a suggestion. "Willie, why don't you cut out soles from one of the buffalo robes? Make them big enough to wrap around the tops and tie them. The hide's thick enough to give some protection from the cold, at least."

"You should have thought of that, Willie," Maude said, casting an appreciative look at Carn. "We'll do that, Captain Tregale."

"And cut some for me too," Beryl added. She lifted up one of her feet and they could see the sole hanging loosely by only a few threads. "The other one's just as bad. They wore out in the water."

Maggie, cuddling on her mother's lap with young Dolly, stuck out both of her feet, a beaming smile on her face. "Me and Dolly have new shoes. We didn't even get them wet."

Carn knew that the Tates were not the only family facing the specter of going barefoot. In every group he had checked, Carn had heard and seen the toll on footwear that the river crossing had caused. Worn stitching had ripped apart under the force of the current and many emigrants were in the position of having nothing to put on their feet. It was a matter of grave concern, for there was a serious danger of frostbite for anyone forced to walk with bare feet along a frozen trail.

Next to the Tate family, Carn saw Art Smith rolled up in his blanket. He had his eyes closed, and even through the coverings, Carn could see him shivering. Art had exhausted himself, so Carn didn't disturb him.

Sam Williams lay next to Art, also with his eyes closed. He was breathing heavily, and though his body was shivering, perspiration spotted his face. Agatha sat beside him, a heavy shawl wrapped around her shoulders and a cloth in her hand, wiping at the sweat that kept trickling down from his forehead. She looked up at Carn and shrugged her shoulders.

"He's not doing well. He won't be doing any walking in the next few days, I can promise you that. Not unless there's a mighty big miracle."

"Appreciate you caring for him, Agatha. If he's no better in the morning, we'll put him on one of the wagons."

"We're moving on then—"

"At daybreak. We have no other choice."

"What about this storm?"

"Captain Martin thinks it'll pass. It's not time for winter yet."

Agatha snorted. "I've got some arthritis in my left leg that tells me winter's here, time or not."

Carn checked the others in the tent. Derek and Gwen Pitts lay huddled together in their blankets. Jim Wilson was next to them, also wrapped in a blanket, and apparently already asleep, or trying to sleep. Carn remembered Jim was scheduled to go on watch at midnight. Beth sat next to him, a blanket pulled tightly about her shoulders, rocking her baby. Beth's eyes looked sunken, her face haggard. Little Nancy whimpered and twitched uneasily in her mother's arms.

Carn stepped over Sam and Art and dropped to the ground

beside Heather. She was still awake, sitting up, wrapped in a blanket. She looked calm, and she smiled at him.

Heather studied Carn's face, noting the deep lines of fatigue. She knew what a terrible strain he had gone through with the repeated crossings of the freezing river, the repeated backbreaking efforts to free handcarts lodged between rocks. Suddenly a warmth tingled through her that took her breath. She could not explain why, but in this very moment, looking into his face, she knew she loved this man. It was startling, completely unexpected. She had been interested in him, cared for him, even thought of the possibility of loving him. But this emotion that swept through her had no reservations or doubts or expectations. She loved him. It was something she knew down to the core of her being. It was so thrilling, tears sprang into her eyes.

Carn saw them and, of course, misunderstood. He reached over to touch her arm, alarmed. "What's wrong, Heather?"

She could only shake her head. The emotions sweeping through her could not be put into words, not now.

The tears glistening in Heather's eyes had a strange effect on Carn. He was shaken, deep inside. He sensed that nothing was physically wrong with her. No broken bones, no shock, perhaps a few bruises like most everyone else. In fact, a radiance shone in her eyes that he could not explain. She was exhausted, and looked it, yet at this moment she appeared more beautiful to him than she ever had. He felt as if she had reached inside him, warming him, pushing aside the terrible aches and crushing weariness.

Carn could say nothing, strangely did not feel a need for words. Suddenly, there in the crowded tent, unashamed and without even thinking, he took her into his arms. He felt her head against his chest, his hand reaching up to stroke her hair. His heart was thudding heavily, pumping warm blood and emotion throughout his entire body. It was as if they were alone, just two people soaring into that delicious warmth. He reached down and tilted up her face. He kissed her, tenderly, on her brow, on the cheek. Then his lips found hers, and a sweetness swept through him that he had never known. It had nothing to do with passion; it was a fulfillment, a satisfaction that he could not hope to explain, not even to himself.

Tregale had been completely unmindful of the other people in the tent until he became aware of Maggie and Dolly giggling. He looked over, and Maggie pointed a finger at him.

"You kissed Heather!"

Embarrassment washed through him, and now he was uncomfortably aware of the adults in the tent also looking at him, at them.

Heather gave a soft chuckle and settled back on an elbow. She tugged Carn down beside her.

"That's all, folks." She smiled. "I think Captain Tregale deserves some well-earned sleep, like we all do."

"Are you going to kiss him again?" Maggie called out.

Heather looked into Carn's face, giving another smile. "Probably, Maggie," she murmured. "I liked it very much."

Agatha came and threw a blanket over Carn as he stretched out on a buffalo robe. As she tucked the blanket under him, Agatha leaned her face close to his ear, so the others could not hear.

"Took you long enough," she whispered. "Now you hang onto her—even if you have to become a Mormon like the rest of us."

The oil lamp was left on in the tent, turned as low as it could go. Shortly before midnight, someone stuck his head through the door flap and called softly to Jim Wilson. He was sleeping soundly, but Beth was awake, still sitting up holding the baby. She answered, and the man left. She shook her husband gently.

"Time to go on watch, Jim."

After a few moments, he grudgingly threw back the blankets and stood up. Already fully clothed, coat and all, he stretched for a moment, then bent over, shivering. He stepped gingerly over the dimly outlined figures on the floor. His foot struck something hard and he reached down to see what it was.

It was Sam's leg, protruding from the bottom of his blanket.

Jim took it gently, intending to move it back under the blanket, but recoiled in horror. The leg, even through the threadbare socks, was stiff and cold.

Agatha's voice lifted softly from beside Sam. "He's dead, Jim. No need to bother the others—there's nothing anyone can do."

Jim stared down at the silent form, feeling that something should be done but knowing Agatha was right. People desperately needed rest, and Sam Williams was beyond help now. He stepped out of the tent door and abruptly came back inside. His eyes were wide, swiveling from Agatha to the gently rocking outline of his wife.

"There's half a foot of snow out there!"

His voice was louder than he intended, and others stirred. Agatha sat up and put a finger to her lips.

"Quietly, Jim," she whispered. "It's like poor Sam here—the morning is soon enough to deal with it."

The bugle roused the camp before daylight, but in only minutes panic had spread through every tent and wagon as the blanket of snow was discovered. Fortunately, the wind had dropped from the ferocity of the night, but the air was still bitterly cold outside. Snow continued to fall, large flakes adding steadily to the accumulation on the ground.

Carn was among the first up in his tent, and in a low voice, Agatha told him about Sam's passing. He had simply sighed and stopped breathing, she said. Carn roused Alfred and Art and asked them to put Sam's body outside the tent until preparations for his burial could be made. It would be better for the children—and the adults—without the presence of death inside the tent.

Carn left and immediately sought out the other captains, crunching a path between the tents. Half an hour later, he took a grim report to Ed Martin.

"There are fourteen dead in camp," he told him. On top of that, there are forty-three who appear too sick or weak to get out of bed. Most of the dead and sick are men. There's probably a score of the womenfolk still in shock from crossing the river who won't be any help in pulling. We lost a few head of stock too."

Ed blew out a long sigh. "So it's started. First thing is to take care of the dead."

"I've ordered the bodies taken over to the edge of the trees— although I don't know how we're going to bury them. The ground is frozen solid."

"We'll have to make it a mass grave," Martin said. "All we can do is put them together and cover them with snow and whatever else we can find. Someone will come along in the spring and give them a decent burial—if the animals and carrion have left anything to bury."

"Do you want to hold a service?"

"It's better we don't. It will only be hard on the families, seeing how little we can do for the dead. Pass the word that everyone needs to get ready to move out. The captains will have to make adjustments to make sure there are enough to pull carts that are short-handed."

"What about the sick?"

"Do what you have to, Carn. I'm leaving you in charge of getting us back on the trail. I'll take care of the burials."

"Ed, you think the weather will be like this from now on?"

"No way of telling. I'm still hoping this is an early storm that will pass over. If it's not, and winter is here—well, there'll be a lot more dead to bury."

There was a lot of crying over the dead, and more than a little protesting as preparations were made to break camp. When it became known that so many had died during the night, people felt they should stay and bid loved ones and friends farewell with a proper service. The captains, under Carn's direction, made it plain that the handcarts must move on without delay.

New assignments were made for pulling the carts where sickness and death made adjustments necessary. Some of the new teams consisted entirely of women, some had nothing but young boys, and everyone accepted the hard truth that keeping the hand-carts moving would be a lot harder now. To make matters worse, many of the carts would now have the added weight of family members too weak too walk.

Many of the sick were put on wagons but since there were only six, with a small amount of available space between them, far too few could be accommodated. The majority of the sick and invalid were forced to ride on top of the carts or somehow stay on their feet alongside.

Harriet, though still not functioning normally, proved able to walk. Her mind seemed capable of understanding what Lydia told her, that she would have to walk alongside and keep up, or they would have to carry her on the cart. Harriet shook her head firmly when Lydia mentioned that possibility. Though she could not speak, Harriet's eyes conveyed a determination to manage by her-self. Heather and Lydia, along with Derek and Gwen, said they could manage to pull the cart without additional assistance.

Willie Tate was obviously exhausted, his face haggard from strain, but he was determined to keep on pulling with his family. The boys and Beryl now had their feet wrapped in makeshift buf-falo-hide moccasins. Maude seemed a tower of strength as she mothered all five children.

George Kimberley had to be put on the Cunningham cart, for he was unable to walk unassisted. One man, Harry Courtney, was transferred from one of the other handcarts to help the Cun-ninghams pull, for Annie would be able to do little more than keep up, and that only with difficulty.

The Wilsons, along with Agatha and Art, said they could man-age without a replacement for Sam Williams. Art was feeling better after a night's rest, though he looked terribly worn.

With all the assignments and changes made throughout the company, the handcarts again started moving north.

CHAPTER FIFTEEN

RED BUTTES

LATE OCTOBER

The emigrants could not see the trail, hidden as it was under the carpet of snow, but it was not difficult to follow, for they now were traveling along the north bank of the Platte. The wind picked up later that morning and by noon was again howling in cold fury out of the north, gusting the snow into blinding clouds.

The snow kept falling all day, and so did the temperature. Carn guessed it was now close to zero, or below. It made for extreme hardship for the emigrants struggling with the handcarts, especially those who had the extra weight of sick family members, along with the extra burden of caring for their needs and keeping the snow from covering them. People could not help but think of the warm clothing they had been forced to abandon at Deer Creek to lighten loads on the handcarts. That had been only three days ago but already it seemed like a lifetime had passed.

They made ten miles that day and when they arrived at the point where the trail veered away from the river and up toward Sweetwater country, Ed Martin called a halt. The wagons and carts circled raggedly and slowly, for there were many stragglers. There was little fuel to be found for fires, so there were fewer of them, and some people waited hours for their chance to cook a semblance of a meal. Putting up tents in the strong wind was a difficult, tiring task, especially with so many of the men unable to perform their usual chores.

Since Tregale's group was among the first to arrive at the campsite, they had the opportunity of cooking an early meal. The tent went up without too many problems, although clearing the ground for it was a backbreaking task. As soon as the tent was standing, the families crowded inside, grateful to be out of the wind and blowing snow.

Tregale spent another couple of hours talking to the families, visiting with the sick, and getting reports from the captains. He tried to be cheerful and optimistic, but seeing the suffering and hardship of the families made it difficult. Those who had fallen sick after the river crossing certainly had no opportunity during this day of fighting wind and snow to regain their strength or lighten their spirits. Carn could do nothing to dispel their mood. Faces throughout the entire camp reflected despair, fear, and something of even greater concern—an unhealthy gauntness etched by constant hunger.

When the bugle sounded the next morning, Annie was sitting up holding her husband's head on her lap, her fingers stroking his brow. George had died in the night, never waking from the time he laid his head wearily on the blankets. Annie said nothing as they took the still form from her, carrying the body outside.

Another seven people had died that night, and again, after the campsite emptied, Ed Martin stood with the burial party and offered a prayer over the mound of snow and brush.

The pitiful line of handcarts kept moving for another day, losing the battle against the blizzard that continued to howl out of the north, whipping raw, reddened faces. The energy was sapped out of even the strongest and hope died that this was but a passing storm.

People were so exhausted at the end of the day that they made no attempt to set a full camp. Families just halted the handcarts and made do with whatever food could be found for a cold meal. There were few fires, for people were too numbed and tired to gather wood. Some did not even have the strength to put up their tents. Families huddled together beside the carts, wrapped as tightly as

161

they could against the driving snow, and slept. One mother, left alone with her three children by her husband's death the night before, spent the night sitting on a rock, one child on her lap, the others clinging to each side of her.

The blizzard raged on day and night and snow continued to pile up deeper around them. Sometimes they had to go around drifts that had piled up five feet deep or more. Temperatures during the day hovered near zero, and at night fell as low as fifteen below. People dropped in their tracks and had to be lifted up onto the carts. Frostbite became a bitter enemy, for the makeshift coverings many wore simply could not protect them against the coating of snow and ice. Some were so numbed by the cold that they did not notice when the coverings fell of until they saw red marks in the snow from cuts and cracks in their feet. Each morning saw more burials, each day the progress became slower.

By the fourth day, the suffering had become unbearable. Tregale sought out Ed Martin and shouted to make himself heard over the wind.

"They can't go on, Ed!"

Martin nodded wearily. "There's a place called Red Buttes just a mile or so ahead. We'll camp there and wait out the storm."

"There's not a soul won't be pleased to hear that."

Martin put his head close so the wind could not whip away the words. Carn noticed tiny icicles hanging all over his beard. "When everyone's settled, have the captains give you a count of all the food that's left. All the private stores too. We're down almost to the last of everything, I'm afraid. Rations will have to be cut again."

"How long can we hold out?"

"Depends on what's left, and how much livestock we still have. My guess is, there's barely enough for a week at most. Doubt if the flour will last that long, even with cutting rations to four ounces."

"What happens then?"

"If we're lucky, we'll meet up with the rescue teams."

"You telling me that we're expecting help from the valley?"

"I'm saying I believe help is on the way."

"Is that something you're hoping, or do you know something I don't?"

"It's something I feel—something I have faith in."

"Sounds like a mighty big chunk of faith. Why would anyone mount a rescue attempt—they don't know we're in trouble."

"We were in trouble when President Richards couldn't set aside supplies for us at Fort Laramie," Martin said. "He knows we didn't have enough to last all the way. As soon as he reached the valley, he'd tell Brigham Young, and the president would see that food and supplies started back to us."

"You really believe that?"

Martin nodded firmly. "Yes, I do. On top of that, I have something that you don't—not yet."

"What's that?"

"My faith that God hears my prayers. My faith that God intended for these converts to come to the valley and build up Zion. I have faith that God won't abandon us now."

"You're right," Carn muttered. "I not only don't have that kind of faith, I can't even understand it. Although I must say, it's not as foreign to me now as it was back in London."

"Do you say your prayers, Carn?"

"I haven't for most of my grown life," Carn said quietly. "But I prayed after I lost Elsie and the baby, and I've prayed on this journey, to tell the truth. I'm not sure who I prayed to, though, or if anyone heard them."

"So why did you pray at all?"

"A need I felt inside, I suppose. I think Heather is responsible for the few prayers I've said on the trail. It's a different need with her—I honestly want to know what she feels about this Mormon religion that I don't."

"Well, take some advice from a friend," Ed said, "and don't stop praying now. Pray that I'm right about those rescue teams."

The campsite at Red Buttes was a small, barren plateau

beneath high cliffs that offered little shelter from the wind. Scattered stands of cottonwoods dotted the plateau, promising at least some firewood, but mostly the site was nothing more than sandy shale and clumps of greasewood, a wide spot along the trail. However, to the exhausted emigrants who pulled their handcarts into a ragged circle below the cliffs, it was as welcome a sight as the grassy meadowland at Deer Creek.

In the four days since crossing the Platte River, they had traveled only sixteen miles, and ten of those had been on the first day. The unrelenting storm had been a savage foe, and no energy was left to fight it.

The Hodgett wagons caught up and made camp that same afternoon alongside the handcarts. The Hunt wagon train, Captain Hodgett told Ed Martin, was camped twelve miles back, having traveled less than four miles from the Platte.

Getting the camp set up consumed painful hours. Men went from tent to tent to hold up canvas and push poles into place, summoning all the strength they had to pound stakes into the frozen ground. When a tent was up, families collapsed wearily inside, needing rest and shelter before even thinking of what could be found to scrape together a meal.

Tregale took a detail of men to gather wood for fires. His metal hook was put to good use, snagging and pulling out limbs that defied the grip of numb, weakened hands, and yanking out stubborn clumps of greasewood. They brought back a sizeable amount of wood and brush, and soon fires crackled throughout the camp.

In their tent, the Tate twins were in agony. Both had put their feet close to the fire outside, the heat at first feeling good against the frost-covered skin. When Maude and Willie took the boys inside and rubbed their feet and legs vigorously, the returning circulation brought screams of pain from them. Beryl was suffering too, but not as badly as her brothers. That was probably because the wrapping of buffalo hide had gone around what was left of her shoes, holding them together, and her feet had not been exposed so completely. Both Maggie and Dolly whimpered from being so cold, and they had to endure brisk rubdowns too, but their new shoes and the fact they had ridden bundled up on top of the cart saved them from more serious consequences. Neither parent could yet feel their own feet, but they had more urgent things to take care of before worrying about that.

The families in the tent talked it over and decided to go all out in preparing a meal that night. Bodies needed all the strength and nourishment they could get, for no one had eaten a decent meal in the past four days. Maude and Agatha braved the blowing snow and went together to the wagon for the daily ration of flour. They found no lines but were dismayed upon being told that the flour ration had been cut to four ounces for all adults. They drew the ration for everyone in the tent and hurried back through the snow.

A couple of hours later they all sat in the tent and devoured helpings of hot dumplings, made from the combined rations of flour. There was a stew of rice and boiled meat, some hard biscuits, and cup after cup of steaming hot tea. Maude even brought out a tin of preserves she had been hoarding, and it made the biscuits taste delicious. To top it off, there were slices of dried apple, issued by the wagon master along with the flour rations. The dried apples had a pleasant flavor, given enough chewing. Altogether, each person did not have much food, but probably as much as gaunt stomachs could handle at one sitting. For everyone, the meal was as deeply satisfying as a Christmas feast.

Carn missed the meal, though Heather saved him a plate of food. Maude and Agatha took turns keeping a kettle of hot water full to pour over the tea leaves, going outside to fetch fresh snow for the kettle when needed. Lydia fed spoonfuls of food to her sister, and everyone was pleased to see Harriet eating. Harriet still had not spoken since her rescue from the river, but she had kept up through these past days of frozen torture, walking by herself beside the handcart. She seemed to know what needed to be done but was incapable of expressing herself.

After returning with the firewood, Tregale met with each of the captains and the wagon masters, explaining what needed to be done. Each of the captains was to meet with his subcaptains and take an inventory of all the food in camp, getting back to Tregale with the tallies first thing in the morning.

Carn finally returned to the tent and gratefully took the plate of food Heather had saved for him. The dumplings were cold and the meat stew tepid, but that didn't stop him from savoring every mouthful. He couldn't get enough hot tea inside him, not even noticing how weak it had become after so many replenishings.

Esther Cunningham voiced the question that was on everyone's mind. "Is it true we'll be waiting here until the storm passes, Brother Tregale?"

Tregale stopped chewing on an apple slice long enough to answer. "That's true, Esther. We'll not be fighting blizzards tomorrow. We can all get some rest."

There were exclamations of relief from all around the tent. A smile came to the face of Annie Kimberley, who for the past two days had been gripped by a worsening fever

"I wasn't sure these old legs could hold up another day," she said. "Don't anyone mind me if I sleep the whole day."

"You'll probably have lots of company," Tregale said, grinning. "We're all played out. I'm hoping to do some extra sleeping myself."

Perhaps no one was more relieved at the news than Beth Wilson. She looked terrible, eyes sunken into deep, dark circles, cheeks drawn into tight lines. She was cradling little Nancy in her arms, the baby lost inside the blankets. "Will there be milk for the babies?" she asked.

"If the milchers have anything to give, the babies will get every drop," Carn promised. "The cows have strayed, I'm told, but they'll be rounded up first thing in the morning. Art, you had the last sight of them—is there milk to be taken?"

"Not much," Art said, "but we should get some, at least. We

166

know where they are, over in the cottonwoods, so rounding them up will be easy. If there's milk to be had, Sister Wilson, I'll see that little Nancy gets her share."

Agatha had another question for him. "The flour ration has been cut to four ounces. Does that mean we're running out of food?"

Now was as good a time as any, Tregale decided, to let everyone know the seriousness of the situation. "We're taking an inventory of all the food in camp. It may be that we only have enough for another week."

His announcement was greeted with troubled silence. After a time, Alfred Cunningham cleared his throat. "Does this mean we can't go on even after the storm?"

"We can, but we can't get far," Tregale answered honestly. "One of the questions we have to decide is whether to keep going, or wait here until help arrives."

"Are we expecting help?" Alfred asked, his voice doubtful. "How will anyone know we're in trouble? We aren't expected in the valley for another couple of weeks, at best. They can't know about the weather we've run into. They can't even know how far we've come. Even then, there are three or four hundred miles of mountains and snow between them and us."

Carn tried to sound reassuring. "Captain Martin is convinced help is on the way. He's expecting to meet up with rescue wagons within the week, two weeks at the outside."

"I have the same question as Alfred," Maude said. "How would they know we need help?"

"Franklin Richards. He knew we were expecting fresh supplies at Fort Laramie, but there was none to set aside for us. He'd tell Brigham Young as soon as he reached the valley, and the president would send aid without delay. That would mean rescue teams left Salt Lake weeks ago. That's what Captain Martin believes—and he believes it strongly."

"Makes sense to me," Willie Tate muttered. "The Saints in the valley would come out to help if they thought we were in trouble."

"Then we have something to pray for, don't we," Annie said, her voice soft but her eyes shining. "I've been praying that God would not desert us, even though I've lost my George. I know Captain Martin has a strong faith and stays close to the Spirit. If he believes help is on the way, I believe it too."

"Well, we just have to hang on until it gets here," Carn told them quietly. "If all of you have faith we'll be rescued, then that's the way it will be."

"What about you, Captain Tregale?" Esther Cunningham asked. "Do you believe rescue teams are coming?"

Tregale hesitated, not so much because he didn't know what to say, but because he suddenly felt a strange rush inside him. It was a warmth, a flooding through him that he had never felt before. He looked over at Heather, saw her staring at him with an intense expression, waiting for his answer. Without any reason or logic behind it, he realized there was a certainty in his heart.

"I believe they're coming," he said slowly. "I'm not a Mormon, and I don't understand your faith in God, but yes—something makes me sure that help is on the way."

Heather rose to her feet and crossed to him. She put her arms around him, tears running down her face, and kissed him lightly on the cheek, whispering in his ear.

"I love you, Carn Tregale. And you may be closer to being a Mormon than you think—"

The next morning there was no bugle and people slept in, bodies badly in need of the extra rest. Tregale met with the captains, who reported their tallies. The amount wasn't much, but frankly, it was more than Tregale had expected. Sadly, there were another seven deaths that first night at Red Buttes.

Tregale reported to Ed Martin, and the captain scratched at his beard, staring up at a sky still filled with dark and threatening clouds. Snow was falling, but the wind had practically stopped, allowing the flakes to drift slowly to the ground. Over a foot of snow lay underfoot, and while the storm itself had eased, the temperature this morning was still well below zero.

"So what do you think, Carn?" Martin asked. "Should we hole up or stay ready to move on again—"

Carn shrugged. "You convinced me, Ed. There's neither strength nor will to put miles behind us. Let's dig in and stretch the food as far as it will go."

"You believe the rescue wagons will come—?"

"What you said makes sense. I believe it."

Martin blew a cold trail of vapor out of pursed lips, then nodded. "Let's get them settled in. We haven't seen the last of this storm. Get men collecting as much wood as can be found, and make sure the rationing is handled fairly. How are we doing on the sick count?"

"Difficult to tell. Most people haven't stirred yet. But we have a lot of fever and dysentery reported."

"And no medicine to combat either one," Martin said grimly. "The people with dysentery will need the most care. That leaves a body weak and vulnerable."

"How are you holding up?" Carn queried, studying Martin with narrowed eyes. The weight of life or death for nearly six hundred souls rested on this man's shoulders.

"As good as you are," Ed said, grinning, "except I've got two cold hands and you have only one."

Tregale placed a restriction on fires, allowing only one for each company of a hundred. This was a matter of preserving firewood, for only a limited supply was available and there was no telling how long it would have to last. People began scraping and shoveling paths between tents and around fire pits, but when they completed the work, all of them again went back into the comparative warmth of the tents. One thing was noticeably different from camps of a few weeks ago; there were no children out playing, and no sounds of laughter or fun.

Sickness was a deeper cause for concern than expected. Scores of people had contracted fever and hacking coughs. The meal that most had enjoyed the previous night proved a bane for the many who had come down with dysentery. Each group of tents cleared a path for those suffering with it, selecting spots as far from camp as possible. Even those who were not sick looked as if they were, faces pinched and gaunt with hunger that for many was turning to malnutrition.

With Martin's permission, Tregale ordered the slaughter of several of the beef cattle. Most of the animals were near death anyway, having had to forage for days for feed that either didn't exist or was buried under a crusty covering of snow. The captains distributed the meat among the emigrants, but it proved more of a burden than a blessing. The meat, eaten without bread or vegetables, worked harshly on even the stronger systems, while having disastrous effects on those suffering from dysentery. It made no difference if the meat was cooked in stews, left on bones and put in soups, or fried. Only a lucky few found they could digest the tough, lean meat without ill effects.

Early in the afternoon, Art Smith brought some milk in a cup for the Wilson's baby.

"It's not much," Art said apologetically, handing it to Beth. "The cows have nothing to give."

Beth took the cup gratefully. She put it down and went to their bedding, where the baby lay sleeping beside Jim. She leaned over, and suddenly her face blanched. She snatched up the baby and began loosening the blankets, calling to her husband desperately.

"Jim—something's wrong with the baby."

Everyone in the tent swiveled their attention to Beth as Jim sat up, staring at his wife in alarm.

"What's the matter, Beth—?"

"She's not breathing!"

Jim leaped to his feet and tried to take the baby, but Beth

170

would not let go, still tearing at the coverings around Nancy. She put her face down against the baby's head, then cried out again.

"She's dead—my baby's dead!" She started screaming hysterically.

Jim took the baby forcibly from her, lifting Nancy close so he could study her. He could detect the faintest flaring of the baby's nostrils as she breathed.

"She's not dead, Beth—she's not dead." He put a couple of fingers against the baby's brow. "She's got a fever, but Nancy's still breathing."

Agatha crossed quickly and took the baby from Jim. She scrutinized Nancy, putting her own hand onto the baby's head. She looked over at Beth, who stood with both hands pressed against her face, eyes wide with fear.

"Jim's right," Agatha told her. "The child has a high fever."

"What can we do?" Beth cried. "We have to do something—"

"There's no medicine," Agatha said calmly, "and no doctor, so we must do the best we can." She looked over at Art. "How long is that milk from the cow, Art?"

"Just a few minutes. I brought it right over."

"Then there's no need to heat it. Put it into the bottle, Beth, and let's see if we can get some nourishment into this baby."

Beth gave her husband a pleading look. "You need to give her a blessing, Jim. If anything can save her, it's the power of the priesthood."

Agatha held the baby close, gently rocking her. She looked over at Willie Tate, standing beside the door. "Willie, why don't you stand in with him—"

Willie nodded. "I have no consecrated oil, though."

"The two of you can give the child a blessing without it. God will not hold it against her."

The two men held the baby and Jim pronounced a blessing upon his infant daughter, speaking in simple words, with faith, and with authority. When he finished, Jim handed little Nancy to her mother.

"There now," Agatha said matter-of-factly, "the Lord can get on with the healing."

That evening, Annie Kimberley knelt beside her bedding and closed her eyes in prayer. She was sitting back on her heels, and she remained in prayer so long that Maggie crawled over and looked up at her. She stared at Annie, then called out softly to her mother.

"Mother, I think Sister Kimberley is asleep."

Maude glanced up, motioning Maggie away. But ten minutes later, when Annie still had not moved, Maude got up and went to her. She placed a hand gently on Annie's shoulder, not wanting to disturb her but concerned that the older woman had indeed fallen asleep.

Maude knew at first touch that Annie was dead. She had slipped away while talking to her Father in Heaven, no doubt praying for the safety of all of them. The children started to cry and there were tears in most eyes as Willie and Alfred wrapped Annie in a blanket and carried her outside. They took her body to a copse of cottonwoods, placing her with the other dead who lay side by side in two shrouded lines. A guard was stationed with the bodies day and night now, at the order of Ed Martin, making sure vultures or wolves did not molest the dead. Snow had continued to fall heavily and was now almost two feet deep. There was too much of it, and the ground was too hard, to even attempt digging graves. In just these two days at Red Buttes, there were already seventeen dead.

The third day passed slowly, snow falling and the wind continuing to blast the camp with subzero cold. The fourth and fifth days passed with no letup and the lines of dead continued to lengthen. Few people even bothered to get out of bed now and the will to live was slipping away, replaced in many hearts by a certainty that death was inescapable. Hunger was a dreadful pain that never left, causing the young to whimper constantly and parents to suffer two-fold. Many pleaded with Tregale and with Martin to increase the rations, claiming they would starve with such severe limits. The captains could only tell them that they had to make what little food was left last until help arrived. But both Martin and Tregale agreed privately that matters could hardly get worse and they prepared themselves to deal with the day when all food would be gone.

Heavy thoughts like these were what took Tregale to the outskirts of the camp late in the afternoon on that fifth day. Despite the cold and the weakness gnawing inside him, he felt a need to be by himself for a few moments, to try to sort out the options and decisions they would soon have to face. What would happen when the supplies ran out? Should the last remnants of food be given only to the children? What chance of survival would they have without their parents? Should those who were sick and near death be asked to sacrifice so that others might live a day or two longer? They were impossible choices, and Tregale knew the reality would be that the strongest would last the longest, and the others would die in their turn, young and old.

His thoughts shifted to the hopes of rescue that for some was the only thing keeping them clinging to life. In these past five days he had talked many times with Martin about his belief that help had been dispatched and would reach the camp soon. He knew Martin truly believed it, and from that moment in the tent five days ago, Tregale also believed it, deep inside. But the experiences life had dealt him so far, the cynicism accumulated through tragedy and disappointment, the hard reality that nothing in life seemed to happen just because it was a good thing for it to happen made it difficult to understand why he believed it at all.

Heather had told him it was a faith inside that he had come to share with the rest of them, a faith in the reality and goodness of God. But he was unwilling to accept that. It would mean he had tapped into the same wellsprings that fed the rest of them, and he knew that was not so. He still had no understanding of what made these Mormons willing to sacrifice everything and suffer every hardship just to go to an isolated valley high in the Rockies, deliberately separating themselves from the mainstream of life, joining a society so foreign it had been driven from the rest of the American civilization.

He heard footsteps crunching in the snow behind him and turned to find Heather. She was bundled in her coat so that only part of her face showed, barely more than some wisps of hair, two dark eyes, and a bright red nose.

"It's too cold to be out here," he told her, concern in his voice.

She came and put her arm through his, shivering. "That's why I came looking for you. You haven't been back to the tent all day. You probably haven't eaten—"

"Neither have a lot of people," Carn muttered. "Is everyone all right?"

"Little Nancy seems better. She's breathing and eating, at least. Still not over the fever, but she's crying, and they tell me that's a good sign. Art looks poorly, but so do we all."

Carn stared at her, thinking of other things that had passed through his mind these past days in camp. No telling how the days would go from now on, not if the deaths and sickness continued to grow. There were no certainties about anything, he told himself grimly. So the time had come to say things he would otherwise have kept until he had sorted them out more clearly in his mind.

"Heather, some things have been troubling me—matters concerning you and me," he said, searching for the right words. He could see her eyes become suddenly apprehensive. "We have feelings for each other, and we've made that plain enough. It's given me greater pleasure than you'll ever know to think you have a fondness for me."

She started to say something, but Carn shook his head. "I need to say what's on my mind. Once I've said it, you can tell me what you will. I've been honest with you, Heather, that I'm not a Mormon. It's true I've had some confusing feelings of late but I can't claim to have changed. I know how important it is to you that the man you marry be a Mormon like yourself—" Again she tried to interrupt, but he shook her words off. "What I'm trying to tell you, Heather, is that I've come to care for you deeply." He interrupted himself this time, giving an angry shake of his head. "That's not true. It's love I feel for you, Heather. I don't know if I should think less of myself for feeling that way, with so little time passed since I lost my wife, but it's the way it is. I didn't look for it, and I'm not ashamed of it. And I'm not sure if we have days or years ahead of us, so I'm going to say what probably would best be kept for a better time. If we live through this, Heather, I want you to know that I love you and want you to be my wife."

He paused, but this time she couldn't say anything because of the emotions choked up inside her. All she could do was put her arms about him, drawing his face down, reaching her lips up to him.

Despite the freezing temperatures, she felt a tingling sweep through her, warming her down to her toes. He held her tightly, feeling the fire in her, the fire within himself. When the kiss ended, they stood holding each other, unwilling to let the rapture slip away.

"I won't promise you I'll join the Church," he breathed, "because that is something only time and living can tell. But I will promise that no man could love you more or try harder to make you a good husband."

"No woman could ask more," she murmured. "And though what you say was true when I left England, about marrying none but a Mormon, I'm afraid that resolution started slipping away the first day I met you. Mormon or not, Carn Tregale, you're a good man, and I'll be proud to be your wife."

CHAPTER SIXTEEN

RED BUTTES TO GREASEWOOD CREEK
LATE OCTOBER

The sixth day at Red Buttes brought more sickness, more suffering, more deaths.

Tregale found it almost unbearable to visit the families in the tents. Practically everyone had lost a loved one or a friend. Every face was pinched and desperate with hunger; the dark-circled eyes of every child silently pleaded for food and warmth. Despair was everywhere. The reports he received from the captains left little doubt that before many more days passed, the dead would outnumber the living. The toll of sickness and exhaustion, the lack of food, the dwindling hope of rescue forced even the strongest to face the specter of death.

Late in the afternoon, Ed Martin stood among the dead in the cottonwoods outside the camp, staring at two vultures perched on a limb above the lines of stiff, cold bodies. He had yelled at them, waved his arms, thrown rocks at them, but the ugly birds refused to do more than flap their wings, determined not to leave such a carnal feast.

For the past two days, Martin had suffered a fever that was sapping the last of his strength. He fell into spells of dizziness, and he had difficulty keeping his mind focused. Yet he was determined not to let anything interfere with his duties, knowing that others watched him anxiously, drawing their strength from him. He felt

176

his thoughts becoming hazy and fastened his sight on the vultures. It was suddenly very important to him that the two birds stop defying him. Somewhere in his mind there was a connection that if he allowed the birds to assume any kind of victory over him, the fever would do the same.

A shotgun was cradled in Martin's arm, and he raised it, aiming at the two vultures. He fired two blasts. One of the vultures blew apart in an explosion of feathers; the other screeched and flapped frantically into the air, circling overhead. Martin reloaded as fast as he could and fired again. The second bird fell to the ground.

Martin looked around, examining the nearby trees for more of the carrion birds. There was none. He felt pleased. The heavy blasts had cleared his mind. He was in control again, in control of his thinking. And temporarily at least, there was no threat to the unburied dead. He heard footsteps and turned to see Carn Tregale approaching. Tregale looked worried and Martin gave him a weary smile.

"A couple of vultures," Martin explained. "They won't be bothering us now."

Carn was studying him, seeing the flush on his face. "The fever's getting worse, isn't it? You shouldn't be out here on guard detail. There are plenty of others to do that—"

Martin shook his head. "No, there aren't, and you know it. How many men do we have still on their feet?"

"Not many," Carn acknowledged. "I've just finished making the rounds. Every day we lose more to fever and dysentery."

"Eleven have been brought out here this morning, by my count."

"That's right. In the past nine days since crossing the Platte, we've lost fifty-six dead."

Martin sighed deeply and put the butt of the shotgun on the ground. "Is anyone not sick?"

"Could be worse," Carn said. "I'd say about a third are bedridden, another third sick but able to manage. The rest are worn out and near starvation."

Martin stared over the bleak, snow-covered landscape. No snow had fallen since last night and the wind now was little more than a cold whisper. They could not see the high peaks of the Rockies because of the closeness of the cliffs about the camp, but both men knew they were there. Neither one thought of moving on, for conditions would only get worse the higher the trail climbed toward the Continental Divide. Either they would be rescued where they sat, or they would all die. This was not something that needed putting into words; it was a reality they both accepted.

"People believe you, Ed. They believe help will come."

"It's not me they believe in," Martin said quietly. "It's the faith they have in God, the trust they have in Brother Brigham and the Saints in the valley."

Somewhere back in camp, a woman screamed. Both men whirled, shading their eyes against the glare on the snow, trying to see what had happened. They both saw her at the same time, a shawled figure outside one of the tents on the perimeter, pointing an arm to the west. They followed the direction and saw what had brought the scream.

Coming out of a canyon below the cliffs, a half-mile or so away, were three figures on horseback. They apparently saw the camp at the same time, for the horses broke into a gallop. Even at that distance, Carn and Ed could hear the sounds of men starting to whoop and holler.

Every person in camp who could get to his feet ran outside, drawn by that first excited scream and the chorus that followed. By the time the three riders reached camp, a couple hundred or more hysterical emigrants were waiting to greet them.

The three men dismounted, and sobbing, tearful people immediately surrounded them. Hands reached out to touch their coats, to seize their hands, to pat them on backs and shoulders. Some shouted expressions of gratitude, but most could say nothing, words choked by emotion. Some at the back of the crowd simply hugged each other, laughing and crying, from the joy of knowing that God had not forsaken them.

One of the riders spotted Ed Martin and crossed to greet him. Martin recognized Dan Jones, a missionary he had served with for three years in the British Isles. The two men embraced warmly.

"Never thought I'd be so glad to see your ugly face, Dan," Martin said wearily.

"Nor I, yours," Jones replied. He waved at his two companions. "You know Joseph Young, of course, and this here is Abel Garr. Abel is recently back from his mission. He volunteered with the other boys of the valley to come help you folks."

Martin shook hands with Abel Garr, then gave Joseph Young a hug. "I thank God you're here. Couldn't be happier if you boys were angels of the Lord. That's what you are to this company."

Garr had been studying the faces in the crowd around them, seeing the sickness beneath the joy, the lines of near-starvation, the bandaged hands and feet that spoke of frostbite. This was a group of people who all too plainly were barely clinging to the thin edge of survival.

"Looks like we found you none too soon," he said to Martin.

One of the women in the crowd edged closer. She was carrying a child, a heavily bundled girl about two or three years old. Desperation showed on her face as she stared at the newcomers. Her attention fastened on Joseph Young, for she knew he was the son of the Prophet Brigham, seeing him in London.

"Excuse me, Elder Young, but I have three children, and they all desperately need food and warm clothing. Does the fact you elders have arrived mean that more help is close by?"

Young looked troubled. "Not as close as we all wish," he told her gently, "but we left ten wagons filled with food and clothing back at Devil's Gate. The three of us left the rescue party yesterday to try to locate you people."

"How far is Devil's Gate?" the woman asked tremulously.

Young hesitated, glancing over at Martin. He didn't want to give the poor woman, or the others around her, any discouragement, but they had to face the bad news sometime. "About forty miles or so," he told her. It was actually more, but he could see on her face how crushing even that distance was.

The woman's troubled eyes swiveled to Ed Martin. "How can we do it, Captain Martin—get to this Devil's Gate? My husband is dead, my two sons both have feet that are frostbitten, and my little girl is too weak to walk. We can't go one mile, let alone forty—"

Everyone around her plainly shared the woman's concerns. Many of the joyful smiles slipped away, replaced by a grim awareness that these three rescuers did not signal the end of suffering. Forty miles between themselves and the food and clothing they needed was little more than another agony to deal with.

Martin considered a moment before answering, knowing what had to be said but wanting to say it in a manner that would push past the stone walls of suffering and despair and reach hearts. "We've prayed morning and night that help would come," Martin began, "and the Lord has heard our prayers. He's brought the elders to us with word that there's food and clothing and medicine not forty miles away. I know how we felt when we arrived here in Red Buttes six days ago—none of us could go another foot along the trail. But I tell you now, look at your children, look at your husbands, your wives, your brothers, your sisters, and tell me you won't go another forty miles to save their lives."

He could tell he had reached them, saw it in the looks they gave each other, in the gathering determination that came to their faces. He pointed to Carn Tregale.

"I'm telling Captain Tregale right now to get this company back on the trail first thing in the morning. We've lost many of our friends and loved ones and it won't be an easy task to move out. You'll have to leave some belongings behind, but hauling our children and our sick is more important than pots and pans. We must do whatever it takes to get to Devil's Gate. Our only concern now is saving lives—and we can do that only if we put our shoulders and backs into it. If we help each other, we can make a hundred miles if we have to. Is there anyone here who doubts this is what the Lord intends us to do—?"

A loud series of cries burst forth from the crowd in favor of what he had said. Suddenly there was light in dull eyes, determination in the set of mouths, strength in the fists that rose into the air. Life had been breathed back into people who had resigned themselves to lifelessness.

"Then it's settled," Martin told them. He turned to the three men who had brought them reason to fight and struggle again. "We'll start in the morning for Devil's Gate. I don't know how long it will take us, but we'll crawl on our hands and knees if that's all we can do."

Joseph Young clapped an arm about Martin's shoulders. "We'll push on to find the rest of the wagons. Do you know where they are?"

"Captain Hodgett, who brought his wagons up to join us, believes Captain Hunt and his train are camped about ten or twelve miles back, near the upper crossing of the Platte."

"We'll find them," Dan Jones said, swinging back into his saddle, "then we'll be back to help you folks all we can."

The three riders headed eastward, leaving camp to another round of cheers. That day, the twenty-eighth of October, was marked down by everyone who still had strength to write in their journals.

The emigrant company spent the remaining hours of daylight busily preparing to get back on the trail. People who had been too sick or unwilling to get out of bed now found new vitality and worked eagerly to prepare for an early departure. Tregale met with all the captains and subcaptains and despite a great deal of confusion, they slowly reorganized the camp so that enough people were assigned to each of the handcarts, which now would be carrying mostly sick and infirm. No one minded discarding more personal belongings—the saving of lives was far more important than any material possession.

Later, Martin had the bugler summon everyone so that he could make one more announcement. "You've all worked hard to get things organized," he told them. "There's a big hill we must climb in the morning, called Avenue Hill. It will take all the strength we can muster to top it. Since there's food waiting for us at Devil's Gate, I see no reason not to increase the rations and have a decent meal tonight. I've ordered the wagon masters to issue three-quarters of a pound of flour to everyone. Have a good meal and a good rest. We'll start on those forty miles at five in the morning."

The shouts and cheers that rose into the air were loud enough to frighten away the wolves skulking in the trees near those who would never leave Red Buttes.

The first handcarts started out on the trail close to seven the next morning. People put on extra clothing and discarded the rest to make room on the carts for those who had to be carried. Not one handcart left Red Buttes without bearing someone who could no longer walk. Muscles had stiffened in the six days, and the emigrants groaned and fretted as they began pulling and pushing. Bodies protested the strains and if it had not been for the vision of those wagons waiting ahead of them, few could have got the handcarts rolling. Fortunately, the weather had greatly improved. No new snow had fallen overnight, and the wind, blowing only in occasional gusts, felt almost warm by comparison to the freezing blasts that had battered them since that first dreadful day of winter had struck nine days ago after they crossed the Platte.

Avenue Hill proved to be as formidable as Martin had warned. The lead handcarts of Tregale's group reached it shortly after leaving camp, the hill rising steeply for some five miles ahead of them. The wind had sheered most of the snow from the ground but that soon proved to be a problem. The warmer wind had softened the hard frost, and the wheels and feet quickly worked the ground into slippery mud. Those who followed the lead handcarts soon found themselves in a quagmire that turned the steep slope into a treacherous, backbreaking climb. Before long, the handcarts were scattered over the entire four or five miles of the slope, every foot of progress agonizingly slow.

About two-thirds of the way up the hill, Carn Tregale came across the Wilson's cart. It had stopped, and Jim and Beth and Agatha were gathered around a figure on the ground. Art Smith was kneeling in the mud, head drooped, gulping for breath, pressing a hand against his chest. Tregale dropped to his knees beside him.

"You having pains, Art?"

Art looked up, wincing as pain lanced through his chest. "Had to drop out, Brother Tregale. I told the others to keep going—"

"Nonsense, Art," Agatha said, "you'll not get out of pushing that easy."

Tregale had seen them earlier. They had volunteered to carry the two Tate boys, who could no longer stand on their frozen feet. The twins were watching anxiously from the cart. Tregale put an arm solicitously about Art's shoulders.

"We'll put you on the cart with the boys. It's not much farther to the top—"

Art's lips cracked into what he intended for a smile. "I've gone as far as I can go. I want to thank you, Brother Tregale, for the friendship you've shown to me. Haven't had many friends in my life. You've shown genuine concern, and I appreciate it."

"Hang on, Art. You'll see the valley yet."

The dying man shook his head. "I have no regrets. I'd rather die here in the mud than still be back in England. God knows I tried, at least. I've felt closer to him on this journey than I could have hoped. The gospel is true, Brother Tregale. I give you my testimony of it. I know that stronger than ever, after sharing this time with all the fine Saints in our group. Tell them good-bye for me—"

Art started to reach for Carn's hand but never made it. He gave one final gasp of pain, then slumped forward. Carn caught him before he fell into the mud. He and Jim Wilson gently lifted him onto the cart. The boys pressed back, but by now death was a familiar sight, no longer feared. Tregale placed Art's arms across his chest and closed the eyelids. Nothing more could be done. He looked at the silent group beside the cart.

"I'll take Art's place," Tregale muttered. "Let's get our shoulders into it."

Dan Jones and Abel Garr caught up with the company about noon, while hundreds were still mired on Avenue Hill. Some had simply given up, unable to find the strength to continue. The two men spent the entire afternoon helping those most in need, tying lariats to carts, the horses pulling them to the top of the hill. The suffering the two young men saw that day burned into their memories. They would never forget the pitiful sights of children walking barefoot through the mud and snow, old men pulling carts burdened with the sick, women struggling to push with their backs against a handcart while they clutched crying babies to their breasts. It was bravery and tragedy that had seen no match on the frontier since the first pioneers turned faces westward.

The company camped that night beyond the crest of the hill. Emigrants were so exhausted that most intended not to bother with tents, but a bitter wind sprang up again, freezing the mud on clothes, making it urgent to put up shelter. Making matters worse was the scarcity of fuel, with nothing more than a few scrub brushes to feed the fires. Again rations of flour were increased to three-quarters of a pound, but hardly anyone had strength to prepare it. Joseph Young rode in a couple of hours after camp was made, having stayed to make sure the wagons of the Hunt train got started toward Devil's Gate.

Several more deaths occurred that night, the bodies placed in the morning beside Art Smith, and once more there was a mound beside the trail, a marker for those who had spent the dream before seeing it fulfilled.

At first light, the three riders met with Martin and Tregale.

"I never could have imagined such suffering as I've seen here," Dan Jones said somberly. He looked at the two captains. "Do you think you can get them on the trail again?"

Martin nodded. "The news you've brought has given them strength they didn't have two days ago."

"Well, unless you disagree," Joseph Young said, "I think the best thing for the three of us is to ride to Devil's Gate and get help started out to meet you."

"No doubt in my mind that's what has to be done," Dan Jones agreed. "You still have thirty-six miles between here and Devil's Gate and I don't think these people can make it. If we leave now, the three of us can be at Devil's Gate tonight. This is Thursday, if memory serves me, so the wagons can move out first thing Friday morning. If you make any distance at all, there's a chance you could meet up with them tomorrow, or Saturday."

Martin looked over at Tregale. "What do you think, Carn—can we stay on our feet for another day or two?"

"You say this is Thursday—I've completely lost track of the days. What's the date, anyway?"

"The thirtieth of October," Abel Garr told him.

"It's been over three weeks since we left Salt Lake," Jones breathed, shaking his head. "President Franklin Richards made his report the day we reached the valley, and when general conference opened the next day, Brigham Young immediately appealed from the pulpit for rescue teams. Within twenty-four hours, sixteen wagons loaded with food and clothing were on the way. We had been back only two days before turning around again. I still haven't seen any of my family." Jones caught himself, realizing his musing might sound like complaining. He sighed. "Just talking out loud. Wouldn't have missed being a part of this for anything. Back to the question, Brother Tregale—can you keep these people moving until Friday or Saturday?"

"If it means shortening the time to meet up with the wagons, they'll do it," Tregale said. "Every day that passes, more people die. They'll find the strength to keep going."

They shook hands and shortly after, the three horsemen disappeared up the trail. The bugle had already summoned the company to morning prayers, and Martin explained the situation. The news they would have to haul the handcarts for only two or three days caused great excitement. For those who had calculated how long it might take to travel forty miles at the rate they had gone yesterday, it was a great relief. Among everyone there was a willingness, an eagerness, to keep on the trail. The anticipation of help overcame the protests of mind and body.

They traveled nine miles that day and made camp at a spot called Willow Springs. Everyone wanted to know if they had gone the distance required to make the rendezvous with the wagons the next day, but of course no one could tell for sure. It was still twenty-seven miles to Devil's Gate and no way of knowing how far the heavily loaded wagons might have come toward them, or if they had started on the trail at all. Both Martin and Tregale cautioned people about being too optimistic, preparing them for the possibility of not having help reach them until Saturday. Still, they saw a liveliness and enthusiasm in the camp that night that neither man wanted to dampen.

In the morning, the difference between willing spirits and able bodies became painfully evident. The march of the day before, coming on the heels of the strenuous climb up Avenue Hill, left over two-thirds of the company virtually crippled. Bodies did not want to respond; muscles felt incapable of functioning. Seeing the pitiful attempts to get up onto legs that shook and trembled and threatened to collapse was heartrending. Still, the emigrants were determined to go on, and for many, that determination eventually summoned strength. Those who could not force limbs into motion no matter how hard they tried were placed on the handcarts with the other infirm. Throughout the whole company ran a spirit of camaraderie, a willingness to sustain each other, to take burdens that another could not bear. That closeness lent strength and comfort, especially to parents like Willie and Maude Tate, Jim and Beth Wilson, and scores of others who saw their children worsening and weakening with every passing day.

The company straggled out of Willow Springs Friday morning, stubbornly determined to meet the relief wagons. They forced themselves beyond endurance, fearful they could not start again if they stopped. They ate a noon meal of leftovers as they marched, not even stopping to light fires to heat water, contenting themselves with melted snow to drink. The afternoon wore on, and dusk began to gather in the sky.

A despondency settled over the company. By best calculations, they had traveled a dozen miles or more from Willow Springs and come within fifteen miles of Devil's Gate, yet still they had not sighted the relief wagons. Somehow they kept going, one foot in front of the other, desperately needing their prayers to be answered.

The answer came just before dark. There on the trail ahead loomed a line of wagons, six of them. It was a heart-stopping sight.

Tregale was in the yoke of the lead handcart, beside Heather. Derek and Gwen Pitts were pushing at the rear, and Lydia was walking beside Harriet, holding her hand. When they and the other people first saw the wagons, it was if all their energy suddenly melted away. Everyone stopped at once, whether pulling or pushing or walking. The hard core of will that had kept them going beyond physical abilities could not force another step from anyone. They simply stood, waiting until the wagons closed the distance, too tired and overcome even to express the joy and relief that filled them inside.

The first wagon, pulled by a team of four mules, reined in beside the waiting emigrants. The mules stood with heads drooped, stomachs laboring, breath shooting in cloudy jets from their nostrils. They obviously had been worked hard. A man who was heavily bundled in an overcoat leaned down toward Tregale.

"I'm George Grant," the man on the wagon said. "Seems we've found Captain Martin's handcart company."

Tregale reached up to shake the man's hand. "I'm Captain Tregale, assistant to Captain Martin, who's back somewhere on the trail. The company's stretched out over five miles, at least. Those of us still healthy and able pushed ahead, hoping for this moment. There have been a lot of prayers cast to heaven that we'd meet your wagons before this day passed."

Captain Grant climbed down, looking around at the people standing haggard and exhausted beside their carts. He needed nothing more than one sweeping glance to tell him how close the relief wagons had come to being too late.

"If you're the healthy ones, Captain Tregale," he said somberly, "I hope God is watching closely over the rest of the company."

Tregale could see that the captain was older than most of the missionaries that he'd come in contact with, a man at least in his forties. He guessed that Grant normally was clean shaven, but the man was now wearing a dark, heavy stubble of beard. He looked stern, with an air of authority about him. Like everyone else, the cold had reddened his face. The three express riders had mentioned that Grant, another member of the group of missionaries just returned from England, was in charge of the rescue train. Apparently most of the missionaries who served under Franklin Richards, who were responsible for so many of the converts in the Fourth and Fifth Handcart Companies, had volunteered to join the rescue attempt.

"Might as well make camp here," Grant said. "They call this Greasewood Creek, I believe. We're as relieved to see you people as you are to see these wagons. The teams are played out, and I was afraid we'd lose some of them if we pushed on much farther. Some of the men will help put up tents and gather firewood, and the rest of us will bring up the stragglers. There's food for a good meal, which it appears all of you can use, and plenty of warm clothing."

"You have our gratitude, Captain Grant, as I'm sure Captain Martin will tell you himself. It's been a long and difficult day."

"Brother Jones told me Captain Hodgett is with the handcarts and Captain Hunt's wagons are about twelve miles to the rear—"

"Captain Hodgett has fallen back a ways. His wagons had to wait at the bottom of Avenue Hill a full day until the handcarts made it up. As for Captain Hunt, he seems to march to a slower pace than the rest of us. Wouldn't be surprised if he wasn't any farther than Red Buttes."

"Well, the first concerns are getting everyone into camp and putting a decent meal in their bellies. In the morning, you can move on with the wagons toward Devil's Gate. Me and my assistant, Bob Burton, will go east and hurry up those wagon trains in the rear. Let's all hope the weather continues friendly."

It was late in the night before all the handcarts reached the camp at Greasewood Creek. Most of the latecomers could barely hobble, bodies now torn with weakness and sickness and strains that made every step an agony. The men from the valley did all they could to ease the suffering, putting up tents and preparing a meal of hot bread and stew rich with meat, vegetables, beans, barley, the flavor made all the more delicious by fresh onions, a taste many had not enjoyed since leaving Florence.

The rescuers passed out the warm clothing donated by the Saints in Salt Lake. There were quite a few pairs of shoes, though not nearly enough to fill the need. There were socks, some freshly darned. Patched underwear. Coats, trousers, dresses, shawls, quilts, blankets made from pieces sewn together. Some of the donors had taken clothing off their backs to send to those in greater need. The emigrants accepted all of it gratefully amid the shedding of many tears, for the clothing literally was a gift of life for those left threadbare by grueling months of travel and forced discarding.

That Friday, the last day of October and the first day of rescue, was another marked down in journals.

CHAPTER SEVENTEEN

DEVIL'S GATE

EARLY NOVEMBER

The physical condition of the emigrants was so poor the next day that even with the help of the men in the relief wagons, the struggling column could make only ten miles. They had to camp yet another night without reaching Devil's Gate, though it was only five miles away. Snow had started to fall around noon and was still falling, with over a foot lying on the ground. The snow had to be cleared away in the dark before tents could be put up, and pounding stakes into the frozen earth proved an almost impossible task for men in such weakened condition. While making camp, the company saw Captain Hodgett's wagons trail in to join them. The temperature plummeted, and the night was spent in misery. There were only five deaths, however, and that was considered a blessing.

In the morning, the painful trek began again, and it took almost the full day to travel those final five miles to Devil's Gate. By Sunday night, when the last handcart and wagon straggled in from the trail, there were eighteen inches of new snow, the temperature had fallen to fifteen degrees below zero, and the wind kept increasing in intensity.

Devil's Gate was a deep gorge where the Sweetwater River cut through high cliffs of granite. The cliffs towered some four hundred feet above the river, the narrow channel at the base about a hundred and thirty feet wide, slicing through the mountain for a thousand feet or more until it widened out again beyond the gorge. The spot was bleak and barren, even at the best of times, the cliffs rising out of the broken country around it, a well-known marker for all who traveled this trail east and west.

For a short time, Devil's Gate had served as a way station for the mail carriers between the east and California, but it had been abandoned. All that was left of the station were a few broken-down log houses and parts of a small stockade, now in sad condition. There was little timber, except for a few cedars and clumps of scrubby pines. The spot was unbearably hot in summer, the cliffs locking in the heat, while the wind that howled continuously through the gorge in the winter made the name of Devil's Gate appropriate.

The men from the valley had several roaring fires going. They had collected firewood to prepare for the handcart company's arrival ever since the three express riders had sounded the alarm last Thursday night. The rescuers had also moved the wagons to the way station from the sheltered cove across the Sweetwater where the relief train had camped. They worked feverishly to patch up everything possible in the ramshackle log houses. The cabins soon were filled with the sick and those needing special attention, although the dilapidated structures afforded little more protection than the tents erected around them.

Many in the log cabins were suffering from frostbite on hands or feet or faces. Among these were the Tate boys. One of the men of the rescue team, Seth Barnes, was a veteran of many winters on the trail and knew as much about frostbite as anyone in camp. He examined Fred and Ted while Maude and Willie anxiously looked on. When Barnes unwrapped the crude buffalo moccasins, he found all the toes of both boys black and frozen. He looked up at the parents, shaking his head.

"Pretty well gone, I'm afraid."

"What does that mean?" Maude asked, her face haggard and deeply lined, her voice sharp with concern.

"The frost has killed the toes."

"Killed their toes—what do you mean, killed their toes?"

"Been too long," Barnes told her. "They've been frostbitten too long. The toes are done for."

"What can we do?" Willie asked. He was looking down at his sons, who were listening to the conversation with wide, fearful eyes.

"Need to take them off, before gangrene sets in."

"Take off our toes?" Fred gasped. A look of terror coming to his face. It was mirrored by his brother.

"But they don't hurt," Ted protested. "You can't take off our toes—"

"If we don't," Barnes told them gently, "you could lose your feet, even your legs. You might even die."

"But we won't be able to walk," Fred said, his frightened eyes locking with his brother's. Both boys' heads filled with terrible visions.

"Sure you will," Barnes assured them. "Just need to learn how to balance a little differently. I know lots of men without toes and they can walk or run or ride as good as the next man." He looked up at the parents again. "It's your decision. But the truth is, you don't have a choice, not if you want to save your boys from much greater harm."

"Well, that's it then," Willie muttered. He reached down and took a hand of Ted and Fred in his own hands. "This man knows what has to be done, boys. Better to live with a shorter shoe than have your mother and I bury you out here in the snow."

"Will it hurt much?" Fred asked, his voice now dropped to a low, fearful whisper.

"You won't even know it's done," Barnes said, giving the boys a reassuring pat on their legs. "No feeling left, is there. You boys just hold onto your parents and close your eyes. I'll tell you when to open them, and by then, you'll be on the way to getting better."

Barnes pulled a container of hot water closer. He took a cloth and a bar of castile soap, working up a lather. Then he gently bathed young Ted's left foot. Ted's leg jumped, but only from nervous fear.

Maude patted his cheek. "Just be calm, Ted. If the man says it won't hurt, it won't."

After a few moments of washing, the toes dropped off Ted's foot one by one, hanging loosely by shreds of black skin. Maude started to cry, trying not to let any sound escape to alarm the boys. Barnes reached over with a pair of small scissors and snipped the skin, trimming it close to the foot. He moved quickly to the other feet. In moments, it was done. Barnes scooped up the loose toes and stuffed them into a bag. He produced some bandages from a coat pocket and wrapped the feet.

"All right, boys, you can open your eyes now," he said.

Both Ted and Fred lifted their heads to stare down at their bandaged feet.

"Is it done?" Fred asked fearfully.

"Our toes are gone?" Ted asked.

Barnes patted each boy on the legs again. "You just keep those feet out of the snow. You'll be up and about before you know it."

More than a score received similar treatment that night, some for blackened toes, some for fingers, some for earlobes. Three had to have feet amputated, five lost at least one hand, and one woman lost both her legs below the knees. Those who lost limbs agonized over their losses but drew at least some comfort from the fact that they would have died without the assistance of Seth Barnes and the others like him.

The new storm howled ferociously all the next day and the temperature fell even lower. A thermometer on one of the wagons registered twenty below. That afternoon, George Grant and Bob Burton, who both had returned to Devil's Gate after contacting the Hunt train, held a meeting with Ed Martin, Carn Tregale, and Captain Hodgett. All five men huddled inside Grant's wagon, looking cold and troubled.

193

"If Captain Hunt has kept to the trail," Grant said, "his wagons should arrive tomorrow. Do you agree, Captain Hodgett?"

"No reason not to be here," Hodgett grunted. His face was almost completely concealed, the lower part by a black, bushy beard that circled his features, the rest by a floppy, wide-brimmed hat that sloped down front and back and looked as if it, too, had grown to his head. Tregale could not remember ever seeing Hodgett without that hat on. Hodgett tugged on his beard, stroked it, then nodded reflectively. "Shouldn't be more than a day behind, even at his pace."

"That will make close to a thousand in camp," Burton said. His brows knit together as he made mental calculations. "Supplies won't last long at that rate."

"Do you expect more relief wagons from the valley?" Tregale asked.

"Brother Brigham called for two hundred and fifty, of which our sixteen were the first," Grant answered. "Six of those went back to the valley with the Willie company, the other ten coming on here to Devil's Gate. The later relief wagons were to travel over the mountains in groups, one closely following another, to keep the trail open. Yes, I'm sure there are more wagons on the trail—question is, how far did they get in this weather?"

Burton nodded. "They could be holed up all the way back to South Pass, for all we know. Keeping the trail open over the divide will be no easy task. And it's hopeless for us to start homeward to meet them. Not in this blizzard, through this rough country, with all these sick people on our hands."

"Best thing to do is send an express west," Hodgett said. "They can urge any wagons they meet to press on to our relief—"

"—and get a report of our plight back to President Young," Burton finished.

Grant turned to Ed. "What do you think, Captain Martin?"

"I agree," Martin replied. "If wagons are holed up back on the trail, an express will get them on the move."

"We'll send young Abel Garr and Joseph Young. They've proved they have the stamina, and Joseph will get his father's ear as fast as anyone. I've got a report to President Young half done already. A couple of fresh horses, and the boys can be on their way this afternoon."

"That's decided then," Martin said. "Our concern now is feeding and caring for our people. Brother Burton is right—a thousand souls jammed together here at Devil's Gate will pose serious problems."

"And there's something else to consider," Tregale added. "When the weather does ease and we can start west again, not many will be able to walk, let alone pull a handcart."

"Saving lives is more important than any goods," Grant said. He looked directly at the wagon master. "Would you agree, Captain Hodgett?"

"Not sure what you're getting at, Captain Grant—"

"How many wagons do you and Captain Hunt have?"

"There're thirty-three in my train. Hunt has fifty, I believe."

"Put those with our ten, and there are over ninety wagons. I'm suggesting we unload all the commercial and Church goods and cache everything here at the station. That way, we'll be able to carry the sick and infirm."

Hodgett grabbed a handful of beard again, tugging as he thought. "No quarrel with what you're proposing, Captain Grant. People are more important than goods, to be sure. But Captain Hunt and I have almost four hundred emigrants who have paid for passage on those wagons. And while we're carrying commercial goods, like you say, and goods for the Church, that's not the bulk of it. Mostly we're carrying the goods of the whole season of emigrants—the personal goods and belongings of everyone who's crossed the plains this year. The commercial goods are bought and paid for, and I have a responsibility to deliver them to the rightful owners. More important, there are a lot of poor Mormon families who will lose everything they own if we don't bring their freight back to the valley. I don't know about leaving the goods here at Devil's Gate for several months unprotected—"

"We'll leave some of the boys to winter here. They can make sure the goods are intact when they're picked up in the spring. As for the passengers, I think most will feel we're all in this together."

Hodgett thought about that, tugged his beard a few more times, then the sloped hat began to nod. "I don't see why that wouldn't work. Not sure how Captain Hunt will feel—"

"All he needs to do is look around and see the suffering," Ed Martin said grimly, "and he'll know what choice has to be made."

"I'm still concerned about finding room in the station for everyone and for all those goods from the wagons," Burton interjected. "We don't know how long this storm will last. We might be wintering here, if it gets much worse than it is. If the snow's this bad at Devil's Gate, think what it must be like at South Pass. The trail could be closed until spring."

"Digging in for the winter has its merits," Grant said. "Some of the boys have made this trip a score of times, and no one has seen it worse as early as this. It might be smart to consider not going on until spring."

Martin was wearing a deep frown. "If we don't get them to the valley soon, most of my company won't be alive in the spring. It's only that hope that's keeping them alive."

"That's the truth of it," Tregale added. "We all believe more relief wagons are out on the trail. That's not a matter of faith for me—I trust what you've told me. We must keep going until we reach Salt Lake—even if we have to battle winter weather the rest of the way."

"I admire your spirit, the both of you, and no doubt what you say is true," Grant told them, obviously touched by the sincerity and concerns of the two captains. "We can prepare ourselves to go on when the weather breaks, but for the life of me, I can't see the people in your company getting very far in their condition."

"Having food in their stomachs will do wonders," Martin said. "They've been on starvation rations for weeks."

Tregale glanced around as the wind shook the wagon. "Some decent rest would help too, but they'll not get it here at Devil's Gate. There's no real shelter from the storm, not in the houses or tents. I'm surprised this whole place didn't blow away years ago."

"I have a suggestion, though it's not an easy one," Burton said, looking squarely at Martin and Tregale. "There's a cove against the mountains not two or three miles west of here. We camped there ourselves, until we got word about you people. It's sheltered, and there's plenty of timber. I'm suggesting we move your company, Captain Martin, to the cove. That will empty the houses to provide room for storing the goods from the wagons."

Grant slapped a knee. "You've been inspired, Bob. It's true, Captain Martin. The cove is a far better place to camp than the station."

"You have six wagons in your company," Burton continued. "We can use those, along with some of Captain Hodgett's wagons, to carry the sick and those unable to walk."

"Most of the handcarts can stay here at the station," Grant added. "They won't be needed when we start west again. The infirm can ride in the wagons and the rest can walk alongside. All the baggage, what little will be left, can be hauled in the wagons."

"Probably will need to take a few carts to the cove, though," Burton said. "Enough to carry pots and pans and camp gear. There'll be no room in the wagons for such things, not with all the sick."

Grant nodded quickly in concurrence. "A few carts to the hundred should be enough. What do you think, Captain Martin?"

"Two or three miles, you say," Ed mused. He glanced at Tregale. "We should be able to do that with the help of the wagons, don't you think, Carn?"

Tregale was studying Bob Burton's face. "You said it wasn't an easy solution. There must be something you haven't told us—"

Burton nodded. "To get to the cove, you have to cross the Sweetwater."

"And the river is running high," Grant said solemnly. "It's two feet deep, swift and treacherous. On top of that, there's a lot of ice coming down from the mountains, so it's freezing cold."

"It could be a nightmare getting across," Burton warned, "even with the help of the wagons."

Tregale and Martin exchanged glances, knowing what each was thinking. Martin expressed it to the other men.

"We just went through a similar crossing, on the upper Platte. Captain Hodgett knows what a hell that was—we had fourteen dead that night in our company."

"The Sweetwater is much smaller than the Platte," Grant said. "Not as far across, but there's no doubt it will be miserable. Still, we have to cross it before we pick up the trail west."

Tregale was looking at Burton again. "This cove is worth the effort to get there?"

Burton nodded emphatically. "It has plenty of firewood, which we'll run out of here in a day or two. And it offers far more shelter from the wind and weather than is possible here. If Captain Grant agrees, the rest of us will join you in the cove after the goods are cached."

Tregale glanced again at Ed Martin. "It has to be done sooner or later, Ed. I say let's get the river behind us and have a chance to rest up before hitting the trail again."

Martin looked around the circle of faces, his expression grave. "Our handcart people are worn to the bone. They'll need all the help we can give them—and I suggest we ask God to put his hand to it as well."

The meeting in the wagon concluded and Tregale met with the captains. He explained the plan to move to the hollow across the river and gave them the task of reorganizing the company. There were so many sick, so many who had died, that groups needed to be consolidated into working units again.

The news that the handcart company was to move out in the morning brought mixed reactions from the weary emigrants. Many were concerned about family members they considered too sick or weak to move; quite a few could not imagine summoning strength to battle the cold and snow again even for two or three miles; most trembled in fear at the prospect of crossing yet another icy river. Few understood the necessity of continuing west if any were to survive. However, all had learned to accept the voices of authority, and so, reluctantly, the emigrants prepared to move out. Besides, most were so exhausted it was almost impossible to think for themselves. There were sighs of relief that only a few handcarts would be taken to the new campsite. It began to sink slowly into numbed consciousness that the nightmarish ordeal of pulling the carts up the mountainous trails of snow was nearly over.

When Tregale returned to the tent that evening, he found two new couples already assigned to the group: Evan and Doris Jones and Arthur and Bessie Farr, the young couples who had married the first day at sea aboard the *Horizon*. It was hard to recognize them as the eager, carefree young newlyweds who had stood before Franklin Richards; their faces were gaunt, their eyes dark and deep-set, the excitement that had shone on their faces replaced with sadness and fear. Evan and Doris had seen all four parents die since leaving Fort Laramie; Bessie had suffered a miscarriage, and in addition to the physical stress, she was having difficulty coping with her loss. But all four of the newcomers could walk and pull, and that was what mattered.

With the deaths of George and Annie Kimberley, Sam Williams, and Art Smith, with the Tate boys no longer able to walk and Harriet still in shock, the strength of the group was sadly depleted. However, they had survived better than most other groups. Because of that, they were assigned to haul one of the two dozen handcarts, loaded with heavy kettles and cooking utensils, across the river.

Tregale exchanged greetings with the two couples, checked on the Tate boys' condition, and saw that Harriet was still leaning against her sister, staring blankly ahead. Then he allowed himself to turn his attention to Heather. She was lying down, apparently asleep. Usually Heather was the first to greet him with a hug and a plate of food she had saved for him. But tonight, she lay unmoving.

Agatha saw his concern and patted his arm reassuringly. "She's exhausted and running a little fever. I gave her some hot broth and made her lie down. She'll be all right."

Heather was breathing a little harder than usual, Tregale thought, but not enough to cause alarm. He chatted with the others for a few minutes, answering anxious questions about the move in the morning, then lay down beside Heather. He pulled a robe over his shoulders and immediately fell into deep sleep.

The morning came too quickly. A weary company straggled to the banks of the Sweetwater River, following the muddy and rutted trail along the south bank of the river. It was still bitterly cold, but the snow continued to hold off, and even the wind had dropped considerably. After about half an hour, they finally stopped before the ford. The water rushed past furiously, icy and forbidding.

Gwen Pitts sank to her knees beside the riverbank and buried her face in her hands. Great sobs started shaking her entire body.

"I can't do it!"

Her husband knelt and put his arm around her. "It's all right, Gwen. I'll be with you."

She shook her head violently. "It's not in me, Derek. I can't go into that water. It's just like the Platte all over again."

"It's only a third as far across—" Derek began, but his wife covered up her ears and cut him off.

"I'll not go, Derek. Look at the ice—huge chunks of it. More than the last time."

Derek looked from the river to the rest of the group gathered beside them, torn between his wife's agony and his knowledge that the river had to be crossed. He tried to lift Gwen onto her feet, but she screamed and broke away, cowering even lower against the muddy bank.

Gwen was not alone in her fear. Every man and woman who looked at the jagged chunks of broken ice in the swiftly flowing water felt the same desperation. Hellish memories of crossing the North Platte just a little over two weeks ago raised the same doubts about being able to reach deep enough inside themselves to find the courage to do it all over again.

The wagons had already crossed, leaving deep ruts in the mud where they had struck out into the river. Almost two-hundred-and-forty sick and injured, along with the babies and small children, had been packed into the wagons, more than half of the surviving members of the company. They had used the wagons from the handcart company, all but two of the wagons in the rescue party, and a few of the wagons from Captain Hodgett's train. Beth Wilson had been put on one of the wagons with her baby, along with Harriet, the two Tate boys, and Maggie and Dolly. Maude had not wanted to expose the girls to as much risk as the last time. Carn had been concerned about Heather, but she had insisted she was well enough to walk. There was little choice, really, for every wagon was crowded to overflowing with those who could no longer continue under their own power. Some two hundred emigrants now faced the ordeal of getting themselves, and some two dozen heavily loaded handcarts, across the river.

Tregale had remained at the station to ensure that all was in order, checking with the captains and solving last-minute problems. Ed Martin had gone in the first wagons with George Grant to ready the encampment for the rest of the company. Satisfied he could do no more, Tregale hurried to the river crossing, accompanied by a group of young men from the rescue party who had remained behind with him to help. They arrived to find the pitiful column stalled beside the river, the people in Tregale's group gathered sympathetically about a sobbing Gwen Pitts. One look at the grim, frightened faces told Tregale what had happened.

"I don't blame anyone for not wanting to cross the river," Carn said. "It seems more than mind and body can take. There's no shame in that—everyone here has suffered more than should be expected in a lifetime. But we can't stay here, and there's no food or tents left at the station. So we'll have to help each other—share what strength we have left—and make it across this river together."

Gwen Pitts looked up at him, wiping at her tears. "I really want to do it, Brother Tregale, but my legs go weak at the thought."

One of the men from the rescue party held up a hand. Young George Grant, son of the leader of the rescuers, looked at Tregale. George was barely eighteen but was built sturdily.

"I'll carry her, Captain Tregale. All she'll have to do is hang onto my back."

Two other young men, David Kimball and Al Huntington, friends of George and the same age, promptly raised their hands.

"We can carry some too, Captain Tregale," Al said, speaking for both of them. "It won't be as hard for us as it is for them."

Tregale looked questioningly at Gwen, then at Derek. "Is that all right with the both of you? Derek, you're needed to help pull the handcart. Gwen, seems like these young men have made a generous offer—"

Tears started gushing down Gwen Pitts's cheeks again. She struggled to her feet, helped by her husband. Derek gave her a long hug, then turned to young Grant and shook his hand firmly.

"My thanks to you, Brother Grant. I thought of carrying her myself, but with my own legs as shaky as they are, I doubt if I could have managed it."

Tregale turned to the other emigrants. "These boys will take the lead and show the way. It's easy enough—straight out from here for about five or six steps, then go with the current downstream for about forty or fifty yards, then cut straight across to the north bank. You'll see the wagon ruts on the far side where you're supposed to turn. That way you'll never be in water more than two feet deep.

"Those who can walk, take someone else's hand and form a chain. Keep together and help each other. Sisters, put modesty aside and tie up those skirts. Those of you with handcarts, you'll find the river bottom soft and torn up some by the wagons. Just keep the carts moving. If anyone sees a cart get stuck, lend a hand to get it rolling again."

Tregale looked around, relieved to see the dread and hopelessness displayed in the faces only moments before now being replaced with gritty resolve. "Those who just can't make it, wait here. Someone will come and carry you across. One more piece of advice," Tregale added, flashing a wan smile, "don't forget what happened crossing the Platte. Take off your shoes and socks and carry them around your neck. That way they won't get ruined and ripped apart."

Minutes later, the crossing began. Fear showed on every face as people stepped into the icy water, but the tight grip of each other's hand lent the needed strength. When a chunk of ice rammed into a shin, there were hands steadying hands. When a handcart stalled, people stepped up to put a shoulder behind it. It was a magnificent moment of desperate people reaching out to help each other accomplish a grueling task that few could have done by themselves.

Tregale remained on the south bank, making sure all who arrived at the crossing knew what was required. He had watched anxiously until Heather had safely crossed, then found himself completely absorbed in keeping the faltering human chain splashing across the river. Several in the rescue party volunteered to carry people on their backs, but the three teens were the ones who returned again and again to pick up the women and men who simply did not have the strength to take their place in the chain. Tregale never before had seen such an outpouring of heroism and selflessness as the three young men displayed that day. Certainly there had been nothing to match it on the snowy battlefields of the Crimea, and that had been a time for heroes.

CHAPTER EIGHTEEN

MARTIN'S HOLLOW
EARLY NOVEMBER

It took almost the whole day Tuesday for the handcart company to move from the station at Devil's Gate to the curving, sheltered hollow beneath the huge granite cliff that rose a half mile north of the Sweetwater. The wagons had been pulled into protective buffers around the cluster of tents that the rescue teams put up in readiness for the soaked and shivering emigrants. A foot of snow was on the ground, hard packed and crusted by the wind, and this had to be scraped away before any of the tents could be raised. The men from the wagons had worked hard getting the camp in order. A dozen or more fires had been started in preparation for the evening meal. There were sagebrush and plenty of cedars, and pine trees near the hollow, but cutting and hauling wood for the fires was no easy task. Still, when the first river-soaked emigrants limped into the hollow, they were greeted with hot food to warm the insides and hot fires to dry the outsides.

People retired early, but they were not to have a night of rest. The wind picked up in intensity and began gusting ferociously. Shortly after midnight, a tremendous blast of wind tore through the hollow and leveled practically every tent. Confusion and panic swept the camp as people found themselves buried under collapsed canvas or rolling helplessly out in the snow. Then began a desperate struggle to set up the tents again and get frightened, bewildered people under shelter before they froze in the subzero temperatures. Even the men from the rescue team found their endurance tested to the limit before order was restored.

Little was done the next day except to pound the tent stakes deeper so such a disaster would not happen again, and to prepare a rough grave for the nine people who had died during the night.

On Thursday, the remainder of the wagons from the Hodgett train, along with Captain Hunt's wagons, arrived at the camp, which by now had become known as Martin's Hollow. When the two wagon trains had started west from Florence months ago, Captain Hodgett's group had thirty-three wagons and some hundred and eighty-five passengers, while the Hunt train had comprised fifty wagons and two hundred emigrants. All were families who had paid full fare and had not needed the Perpetual Emigration Fund assistance program. The wagon trains had experienced some deaths, but the two units had in large part been spared the cruel physical hardships suffered by those pulling handcarts.

The wagons arrived late in the day, and stories quickly spread of disputes back at Devil's Gate between Captain Grant and the wagon masters, particularly Captain Hunt. It seemed Captain Hunt had been reluctant to agree to caching the goods of his train until the spring. His concerns were just, it was said, and largely the same as Captain Hodgett had raised earlier. The goods and belongings of the entire season's emigrants from Europe were in those wagons, along with a sizeable contract for commercial goods and Church items. Captain Hunt had expressed real concern that no matter how well the goods were protected from thievery, he would lose most of the cache to weather during the long winter months. Hunt had argued that the broken-down houses at the abandoned way station would not offer sufficient protection, and that after the snow was gone, little would be worth bringing to the valley.

In the end, it came down to Captain Grant's insistence that saving lives was the most important concern for everyone, and that could be done only if the wagons assisted the almost helpless handcart emigrants on to the valley. No one could dispute that the emaciated, exhausted company could not travel another mile without the help of both wagon trains.

The decision was made. The wagons were emptied of their goods and sent on across the river. Captain Grant remained at Devil's Gate with some of his men and drovers to complete the caching of the goods and decide who would remain at Devil's Gate through the winter.

The next day, Friday, Ed Martin decided he needed to return to Devil's Gate and confer with Captain Grant. When he told Captain Hodgett and Captain Hunt, they decided to accompany him. Just as the three men were preparing to leave—later in the afternoon than they had intended—snow started to fall. Within a few minutes, it was snowing heavily and the wind had picked up.

Tregale, who was to remain with the company, gave Martin a worried word of caution. "Looks like it's getting nasty out there, Ed. You only have a couple more hours of daylight."

"Hard to get lost," Martin said. "It's half a mile to the Sweetwater, then upriver to the way station."

"Well, just in case," Carn told him, "if something happens, light a fire. We'll watch for it."

Martin grinned. "You've turned into a regular mother hen. Don't forget that between me and Hunt and Hodgett, we've got almost as much time on the trail as you've got years."

"And don't you forget what you told me about whiteouts," Tregale retorted. "Even grizzlies can get lost in one of those, you said. And the wind around here can blow pretty hard, if you remember a couple of nights ago."

The three captains started on foot toward the river. Saddling up horses for the short distance had been tempting, but they already had lost most of the animals to cold and lack of feed. The few horses left were foraging for what little nourishment they could find in the foliage scattered at the base of the cliffs, and they would soon be needed to round up the livestock that had also wandered in a search for food. Within minutes, the three men disappeared from sight in the swirling snowstorm.

The wind kept rising, whirling the snow into obscuring clouds. The three men quickly lost all visual connection with their surroundings and they had to stay shoulder to shoulder to keep sight of each other. They headed south toward the river, but after almost an hour had passed, they realized something was wrong.

Martin leaned his head close to the others, shouting to make himself heard over the storm. "We should have reached the river by now."

Hodgett's floppy hat nodded in agreement. "Wind must have blown us off."

Captain Hunt took a quick glance around, could see nothing but a world of white. Hunt was a thin-faced man, with hawkish eyes under bushy eyebrows, the normally close-cropped black beard circling his features now crusted white with snow and ice. "Wind's coming out of the northeast. I'd say we must be heading west, instead of south."

"Only thing I can tell is up from down," Hodgett yelled.

"So we need to backtrack," Martin shouted, "get the wind in our face for a while."

"Sounds right to me," Hunt said. "Keep it a little on the left side and we should hit the river."

"Need to keep moving, whatever." Hodgett gave his hat another tug to keep it firmly on his head. The large front and back rims were flopping furiously in the wind. "It's getting colder. We'll freeze in our tracks if we ain't careful."

Another hour passed and darkness began to close in on the whiteness. The three men realized with sinking finality that they were lost. Not only that, they were exhausted. Every step had become a terrible effort, partly because of physical strain but increasingly because bodies protested the cold numbness penetrating deeper and deeper into their bones.

Suddenly something loomed ahead, something large and black

that reached up into the sky. They stopped and peered through the swirling wall of snowflakes, trying to make it out.

Hodgett was the first to realize what it was. "It's the cliff," he gasped. "We're back against the cliff."

The other two realized he was right. They had wandered around in a circle, coming back to the foot of the cliff. They could see or hear nothing of the camp, but it could not be too far away.

"All we have to do is stay close to the foot, and we'll run into the camp," Hunt said, shielding the words from the wind.

Martin sank wearily onto his haunches. His whole body was simultaneously freezing and burning. His head swam dizzily and he felt as though he was going to faint. "I don't think I can make it," he gasped. "You'd better go on without me."

Hodgett leaned over, studying Martin's face. He could tell that the captain was at the end of his rope. He straightened and put his head close to Hunt. "You go on," he shouted. "I'll stay with Captain Martin."

Hunt looked at the cliff looming darkly above them. "Got a problem with that," Hunt shouted back. "Are we upriver or down-river from camp?"

The bushy face under the hat nodded. "That's a problem, right enough. Don't think I'm up to betting my life on it, either way."

Hunt suddenly pointed ahead to a dark cluster at the foot of the cliff. All three studied the spot, then Hodgett literally pulled Martin onto his feet. "Looks like we got the makings of a fire," Hodgett said. "Let's get ourselves warmed up."

What Hunt had spotted was a cluster of sage and tumbleweeds driven by the wind into a crevice at the base of the cliff. With Hodgett supporting Martin, the captains stumbled forward. They found an accumulation of brush jammed in the crack of granite, piled above their heads. A number of small branches lay scattered around, apparently also blown to the spot. What was more impor-tant, the crevice was deep, reaching into the cliff at least three or four feet. That meant they had a good chance of finding brush dry enough to start a fire.

Hodgett let go of Martin, and the handcart captain again sank to his knees. He looked up at the other two men.

"This would be a bad time to discover none of us had any matches," Martin said, not making any attempt at humor.

"Don't worry about that," Hodgett replied. "Always carry a few, in case of need."

"Me, too," Hunt added, digging in his coat pockets. He nodded as his fingers touched a match box, but there was a note of concern as he added, "The box feels a mite wet."

Hunt and Hodgett proceeded to pull some of the brush free, exclaiming in pleasure as they felt dry weeds crumble in their hands. They scooped out a pile onto the snow in front of the crevice, but even as they tried to protect it with their hands, the wind scattered it. Four times the wind blew the piles apart, no matter what they tried. Finally, Hodgett pulled off his hat. It was the first time any of them had seen him without it and the first time they knew that Hodgett was bald.

Hodgett held the hat upside down, close to his body. He shouted over at Hunt, "Stick the wood in here. Need to dry this thing out anyways."

When the hat was filled with dry brush, Hunt took out his matches and tried to strike a flame. One after another the matches sparked, then fizzled. They were too damp from snow that had been driven into the coat pockets.

"This is my last one," Hunt told them, leaning close to Hodgett to block out the wind. He struck it carefully, but again there was nothing but a momentary fizzle of flame. Hunt tossed the match away with a snort of disgust. "You said you had some, Bill. Hope they're dryer'n mine."

Hodgett handed the hat over to Hunt, protecting the dry brush by bending over the brim. Then he unbuttoned his coat and reached inside to his shirt pocket. In a few seconds he gave the other two men a nod of satisfaction. "Only half a dozen," he told them, "but they're dry. Three trailwise coots like us should be able to get a fire out of that."

They almost didn't. Moments later, Hodgett had also come to the last match. "All right, let's the three of us cuddle together like we was in love. We got to block that wind somehow."

This time, Hodgett burrowed down almost to the bottom of the brush in his hat. The other two pressed tightly together, backs to the wind, spreading their coats and holding the hat close against them. Hodgett struck the last match with his thumbnail, keeping his whole hand down in the hat. The match sputtered into flame, guttered for a soul-tearing moment, then flared again. The brush next to it glowed, then burst into flame. The three men would have yelled with relief, but each was afraid to do anything that might cause the tiny flames to die. In another second, Hodgett's hat had a full-blown fire inside it.

Quickly, Hodgett thrust his hat a full arm's length into the brush inside the crevice. Just when it seemed he had decided to sacrifice his precious headpiece, he upended the flaming contents onto the dried weeds. A rush of sparks and flames and yellow tongues started licking up through the pile of tumbleweeds. This time all three men vented the yells they had held back before.

Minutes later, flames were roaring ten feet into the air, funneled by the wind up through the crevice. Both Hodgett and Hunt scrambled to gather scattered limbs. Martin simply did not have any strength left in his legs—all he could do was edge back from the heat of the fire.

The flames eventually burned out the debris in the crevice, but the fire had been hot enough to start some of the larger, wetter limbs burning. Now it became a matter of keeping the fire lit despite the wind and blowing snow.

The three men squatted beside the fire, shielding it as best they could with their bodies, gratefully absorbing the heat. Hodgett removed his hat again and examined it, peering inside, then turning it over in his hands. He tugged it firmly back onto his head, flipping the brim a couple of times. A satisfied smile broke out on his lips.

"Through fire and flood, it don't look none the worse for wear."

"It couldn't look worse, no matter what happened to it," Martin said, managing the semblance of a grin.

They huddled in front of the fire for another ten or fifteen minutes without speaking, for it was difficult to make any words heard over the howling of the storm. They fed limbs into the flames, but the blaze sank lower, losing the battle with the wet wood.

"Doubt if we'll keep it going much longer," Hodgett said, finally breaking the silence. A gust of wind blasted their backs, and snow swirled up in a cloud over the fire. "I don't see this blizzard lettin' up in the next few minutes."

"You think maybe we should scout a ways while we still got the fire?" Hunt asked. "You and me could go opposite directions and see if we cut sign of the camp. Captain Martin can keep the fire going as a marker to guide us back. Even if it goes out, all we have to do is stay by the cliff."

"Which way you figure the camp is?" Hodgett asked.

"To the right of us."

Hodgett shook his head. "My gut tells me opposite, but since we'll have both sides of the coin covered, it's worth a try. Let's say no more than half an hour out, then we turn back."

Martin had been studying the crevice where the fire burned. "If it comes to it, we can crowd in that crack for the night. Should keep us protected some, and the coals should keep our pants warm through most of it."

Just as Hodgett and Hunt got to their feet, shapes emerged from the darkness. They came from the left, a half dozen of them, from the direction Hodgett had been about to scout.

"Thought you three were going to Devil's Gate," Tregale shouted at the men beside the fire. As he reached them, he put his hands toward the heat. "Nice fire you got here."

"How far did we get?" Hodgett asked.

"About a half mile due east of camp," Tregale replied. "Saw your fire and figured you could use some help." He looked down at Martin, saw that something was wrong. "You all right, Ed?"

Martin shook his head wearily. "Played out, Carn. Can't seem to move my legs much."

"Some of you men need to give him a hand," Hunt said. "And consider yourselves lucky you're not doing the same for Hodgett and me. That's about as trying a walk as I hope to take in this life."

Martin reached up and clasped Tregale's hand. "Thank you. Seems like we needed a mother hen after all."

Hodgett tugged the brim of his hat. "Don't know about you folks, but I'm for getting back to camp. My belly's craving a hot drink—"

The weather was much improved Saturday morning. The snow stopped falling and the wind dropped again, although it continued to gust occasionally through Martin's Hollow. The sun came out, a rare sight these past weeks, and people perked up. Early that morning, Captain Grant and another member of the rescue party, Charles Decker, rode into camp. They immediately went into conference with Ed and Carn and the two wagon masters, meeting in Hodgett's wagon.

"No need to tell any of you how serious the situation is," Grant began. "The food we brought won't last but a few days more, and something seems to have happened to the teams that should have been close behind us."

"Probably got weathered in," Decker muttered. He was a small man, lean and hardened, with skin that looked as though it had turned to leather years ago. Decker had been a mail carrier on the California-to-Iowa run and had spent much of his life either in the saddle or cracking a whip over a team of mules. "I've crossed this trail at least fifty times, and I've never seen an earlier winter, or a harder one. Never seen a group of people suffer so much, either. I suspect those relief wagons are holed up at South Pass—if they haven't turned back already."

"Well, it's obvious we have to do something," Grant said heavily. "We're losing stock every day, both cattle and horses. People are dying. And a lot more are going to die unless we get some relief."

"What do you suggest we do?" Martin asked. A night's sleep had brought some strength back into his legs and he could move around again under his own power, but he still felt weak and wobbly in the knees. "Won't the boys in the express get help started toward us?"

"Not sure if we can count on that," Grant replied. "Like Charlie said, haven't seen this much snow so early in any of our memories. Could be the pass is closed, like we talked about a few days ago. If it is, there's not much anyone can do about getting teams through."

"And if we stay here," Martin said grimly, "the food runs out, and we all starve."

Grant sighed deeply and scrubbed at his beard. "That's hard to hear, but it's the truth."

"So we move on," Martin said quietly. "In the back of my mind, I've been hoping that more wagons would reach us. But it's not going to happen, so we do like we talked about—keep on the trail till help does come."

"The wagons don't have room enough to carry your whole company," Hunt cautioned. "Hodgett and me still have four hundred of our own people to care for."

"Like we discussed back at the station," Martin said. "We put the sick in the wagons and the rest walk. At least no one will have to pull a handcart."

Charlie Decker looked over at the two wagon masters. "Your ox teams will break trail better'n our mules. It's best if one or both of you head out first."

"I got no problem with that," Hodgett said. "My stock is pretty well wore out but I agree they'll break a path better than any mules."

Hunt was more grudging. His thin face looked worried. "Wouldn't want my teams on point the whole way. Too hard on them. The mules'll have to take their turn—"

"I'll blaze trail when we head out," Hodgett interrupted. "You can bring your teams up later, John, and we'll trade the lead somewhere up the trail. The mules can take their turn if needed."

Martin hesitated, then offered one more suggestion. "I think it best not to split up the companies any more than necessary. Both you wagon masters have empty wagons. Instead of each group taking some of our sick, how about if we took those wagons and put them with the six we have and Captain Grant's wagons, and keep all the handcart people together? That way, none of the companies are disturbed. My people have come to know and succor each other through all the hardships, and I think we'll need to squeeze out every drop of succor we can in the days ahead."

Grant looked at the wagon masters. "Sounds like a reasonable suggestion to me. Either of you have any trouble with that?"

Both Hodgett and Hunt thought for a moment, then shook their heads. "That'd be best for our people too," Hodgett said.

Hunt agreed. "They'd rather keep to themselves than take in strangers, I suspect. Especially sick ones."

Grant looked pleased. "Well, then, let's set a time for departure. This is Saturday, Captain Martin. When can your people be ready?"

Martin glanced quizzically at Tregale. "You can answer that better than I can, Carn."

"Sunday morning, if we can get the wagons today."

"How about you other men—Sunday all right with you?"

Captain Hodgett was scratching at his beard again. "We can let you have the wagons this morning. No reason we can't be ready to move out Sunday."

"You can have our wagons too," Hunt said, "but I don't know

about moving out tomorrow morning. Not all my goods are properly stowed back at the station. Can't leave before that's done."

"Our wagons are ready," Decker said. "Sooner we start for South Pass, better off we'll all be."

Grant stood up. "Let's leave it at that. Captain Tregale, we'll hold you to your word. Sunday morning, you start your people west, accompanied by our wagons and those of Captain Hodgett and Captain Hunt. Charlie, I'll leave you here to work out details with Captain Martin and Captain Tregale. Whatever stock is still alive will have to be rounded up today. Captain Hunt and I will ride back to the station and move the storage part along. I'd like to think we can be on the trail behind you that same afternoon, but certainly no later than Monday. We'll catch up as soon as we can."

"Have you decided who's staying to guard the goods?" Hodgett asked.

"Dan Jones was put in charge yesterday. He's got a party of fifteen volunteers to stay with him. They'll need our prayers because I don't know how they'll survive the next four months."

CHAPTER NINETEEN

MARTIN'S HOLLOW
TO THREE CROSSINGS
MID-NOVEMBER

Maude Tate looked pleadingly at Carn Tregale, her hollowed eyes dark with concern. She was kneeling on the ground beside her husband. It was barely past seven on Sunday morning, but breakfast, what little there had been, was already cleared. The tent was broken down and folded nearby, waiting to be loaded onto a wagon. Tregale had stopped by to make sure all was well with his group, especially to check on how Heather was feeling. Maude, her two daughters clinging to her side, called to him.

"Willie doesn't have the strength to walk, Brother Tregale. Is there a place on the wagons for him? I can't lose him now—we've gone through too much for that, and the children need him."

Tregale dropped down beside Willie, giving him a smile as he took in the deep-sunken cheeks, the droplets of perspiration on his forehead. He put a hand to Willie's brow and could feel the fever.

"Willie, I know you're sick," Tregale said, patting him gently on the shoulder. "I've come to love all of you like my own family— you're all the family I have, come down to it. But I might not be able to put you on a wagon. There are just too many old folks and children who can't put another foot forward. If it comes to that, can you just hang onto a wagon and let it be your strength?"

Willie nodded bravely. "Sounds a whole lot better than what we've been doing. Are we really leaving all the handcarts behind?"

216

"The most you'll have to pull is your own weight," Tregale assured him.

Willie flashed a quick smile. "Then I'm glad there's about forty pounds less of me than when we left Liverpool."

Tregale glanced at Maude, could see that she was still desperately concerned. "You watch him close, Maude. If he can't stay on his feet, we'll find a place somewhere. But the wagons are overloaded, and the teams are as near dropping as we are. If we lose more stock, we have to abandon wagons. We'll take it slow—most of the company doesn't feel much better than Willie does." He looked over at the girls. There were no smiles, just big, sad eyes. They had ridden in the wagons crossing the Sweetwater, but now they would have to walk with their parents. "You girls going to help take care of your daddy?"

Little Dolly nodded, leaning closer to her mother, but Maggie blurted out an angry question:

"Why can't we ride in the wagons? I don't want to walk anymore."

"I wish you didn't have to, Maggie," Carn said quietly. "I wish nobody had to walk one step farther. But the wagons don't have enough room for everyone."

"There was room when we crossed the river. A lot of people have died since then, so there should be more room than ever."

Maude quickly put a hand over her daughter's mouth. "That's a terrible thing to say, Maggie—"

Maggie shook her head free. "But it's true, momma. There was room before—"

Tregale pulled her close to him, sat her on his bent knee. "More people have gotten sick since then, Maggie. If you remember, you were all jammed up tight together inside those wagons. That's fine just from the river to here, but people couldn't travel all day like that. There are a lot of sick men and women and children who have to stretch out, who can't even sit up. And there're people like your brothers who've lost toes and can't walk at all. They

217

have to be cared for, all of them, or they'll die. That's why some of us have to walk, even though we're tired and not feeling well, like your daddy. We just can't all ride in the wagons, Maggie, not now. But I promise you this—we'll meet some more wagons on the trail very soon, and when we do, you and Dolly and your daddy can ride for sure."

A little smile broke over Maggie's wan, pale face. "When will the wagons come, Brother Tregale?"

"Soon, Maggie. Very soon."

Tregale crossed to where Heather was sitting in the snow. She had been leaning her head wearily on her pulled-up knees before Tregale arrived but had listened attentively as he tried to comfort Maggie. Now she gave him a big smile and took his hand.

"You're going to make a wonderful father."

Carn squatted beside her. "If I do, it'll be because you'll give me wonderful children. How are you feeling—are you up to walking again?"

"If Willie can do it," Heather smiled, "I can too. We'll hang onto the same wagon."

Tregale reached out and felt her forehead. She still had a touch of fever. "Don't push too hard. Maude said it well—we've gone through too much to lose each other now."

"I don't know how you can love me looking the mess I do. I'm sure I'd faint dead away if I saw myself in a mirror."

"I see you, and I get warmed clear to my heart. No one ever looked more beautiful." He leaned close and kissed her on the forehead. "You have to make it through this, Heather Lee. I have a hunger for life that I never thought I'd have again. This might be a strange time to say it, but I know there are good things in store for us. I feel it inside, like bright sunlight. So don't you do anything foolish."

Tregale spent the entire morning going from group to group, making painful decisions as to who should ride and who must walk. The truth of what he had told Maggie was evident; everyone in the company was exhausted and most were sick. Again and again Tregale felt the weight of telling people that they had to reach down inside themselves one more time and find the strength to drag themselves through the snow again. The only good thing about the morning was seeing the people's relief as they realized they would no longer have to pull handcarts.

By midmorning, the early clouds had blown away and the sun was shining. It served to warm things up somewhat, although it was more in the mind than in reality. Tents, cooking utensils, and camp gear were loaded, and the sick made as comfortable as possible. At eleven o'clock, the company started moving out of Martin's Hollow. There were now thirty-six wagons, including the ten mule-drawn teams of the rescue party, all filled with the weakest members of the handcart company. The rest of the emigrants, a little under two hundred, trailed alongside or held onto ropes and tailgates, stumbling and faltering, helping each other keep up with the creaking, jolting wagons.

With so many ox-teams in the lead, Hodgett waited until all of the handcart company was on the trail, then fell in behind with his wagons. By three o'clock that afternoon, only the wagons of the Hunt train remained in the hollow.

Ed Martin kept the bedraggled line moving westward as long as daylight held. Progress was slow, and the suffering was painful to see, but the company had to put every mile possible behind them. Those riding in the wagons found the going much more uncomfortable than expected: every turn of the wheels brought jarring and bumping that bruised bodies against the hard flooring, tossing them about, and making them hold onto anything not loose. Many began to wish they were well enough to walk.

For some reason, Hodgett's wagons fell behind and by evening trailed at least two miles back. The handcart company camped that night in a grove of quaking aspen, in a ravine just off from the main trail. The ablest bodies pitched tents for those outside the wagons and prepared the evening meal. The emigrants quickly fell asleep, the last thought on many a person's mind that they could not survive another day like the one they had just endured, no matter what the cost.

During the night, the temperature fell to numbing depths and when the bugle awakened the camp on Monday morning, there were sixteen who had gone to a new life. The deaths were the greatest toll for any single night of the journey, and the pall of despair that settled over the company could not be dispelled.

Though mind and bodies rebelled, the company could do nothing but go on. No one wanted to spend another night in the ravine, even if Martin had been willing to let them. So the line of wagons, with their human baggage clinging desperately to each one, once more wound its way upward through the crusted snow and hard-packed drifts toward South Pass, the summit of the Rockies that marked the Continental Divide. No one wanted to think about the fact that once there, they still had three hundred miles to go. All thoughts instead were fastened on the desperate hope that at South Pass they would find more wagons and their stubborn struggle for survival would be rewarded.

Again they traveled until the sun was ready to dip behind the craggy mountain peaks. Finally Martin passed the signal to circle the wagons for the night. The Hodgett train was still behind, out of sight.

Tents were dragged out of the wagons and firewood gathered. Wood was scarce, but they found enough to start a few fires. As pans and kettles were being set out, someone screeched wildly and pointed into the west. There, about a half mile away, two horsemen could be seen approaching.

People crowded excitedly to the edge of camp, everything else unimportant. The horses were galloping toward them and it became apparent there was only one rider. The second animal was roped behind, evidently a packhorse. Still, whether one or many, the sight of any stranger sent hopes soaring.

Ed Martin and Carn Tregale were standing in the forefront of the crowd, beside Charlie Decker. Charlie shaded his eyes against the glare of the sinking sun, trying to identify the rider. Suddenly he gave a pleased shout.

"That's Eph Hanks," he said, "and if I can trust these old eyes, that's fresh meat he's packing."

Decker gave another wild yell and waved his hat in the air, taking a few steps forward. The rider swerved toward him and moments later reined in the horses amid clouds of steam and blowing nostrils. The grizzled rider swung easily to the ground and he and Decker exchanged pounding bear hugs.

"You're a sight for sore eyes, Eph," Decker said, grinning.

"No more'n you," Hanks boomed. "Began to think you boys was cozied up for the winter at Devil's Gate, or even Laramie."

Decker turned to introduce the newcomer to the two men standing beside him. "This is Captain Ed Martin and his trail boss, Captain Carn Tregale. And this here," he said, clapping a hand on his friend's shoulder, "is Eph Hanks, one of the best scouts anywhere west of the Missouri. Between Eph and me, we've turned over just about every rock between Florence and the whole of California."

Hanks was looking around, soberly taking in the gaunt faces of the crowd. "Looks like these folks been having a rough time."

"Never seen anybody worse," Charlie muttered. His glance slid to the two horses and the long strips of red meat draped across both animals. "Looks like you run into some buffalo—"

"Cut a small herd this morning. Got me a cow and dressed it out. Thought if I ran into you people, some might appreciate a taste of fresh meat."

A small hand reached up and tugged on Eph Hanks's long, buffalo-skin coat. The scout glanced down and saw a boy, about seven or eight, gazing at him with wide eyes. He was holding the hand of a little girl, a year or two younger. The boy pointed toward the pack horse.

"Mister, can me and my sister have a piece of that meat?"

Hanks stooped down, looking the boy squarely in the face. "That look good to you, does it, boy?"

He nodded. "Sure does, mister, but I need it mostly for my dad. He's sick."

Another boy nearby, about twelve, spoke up quickly, "Could we have some too, mister? My whole family is starved—"

The scout stood up, took out a long hunting knife, and sliced two large pieces from one of the strips. He handed a piece to each of the two boys and they scurried back into the crowd. That brought a loud chorus of requests from other people. Hanks started handing out pieces, then looked over at Ed Martin. "How you want to handle this, Captain?"

"Well, it should be turned over to the group captains, I suppose. They'll see it gets shared fairly."

The captains came forward and took charge of distributing the meat. The center of activity quickly shifted to where the captains began to hand out portions for each wagon and each family.

"The big question, Eph," Charlie Decker said, turning again to his friend, "is where are the rest of the wagons? We thought there'd be a couple hundred on the trail by now. As you can see, the food we brought is already gone."

Eph Hanks shook his head angrily. "Gets me to boiling just thinking about it, Charlie. A lot of wagons were stacked up at South Pass, but most turned back a few days ago."

Decker couldn't believe his ears. "Turned back!" he exploded. "What in hellfire damnation made them do that?"

Hanks shrugged. "Most got to believing you people in the handcarts were either holed up somewhere for the winter—or already dead."

"Even if we were holed up, they knew we'd need more supplies," Ed Martin grated angrily. "And even if they thought we were all dead, how could they turn back without knowing for sure?"

"Told 'em the same things," Hanks grunted. "They knowed

how I felt about it. I left my wagon at South Pass—couldn't get it through by myself—and came on looking for you."

"Did all the rest turn back?" Charlie asked, disbelief still in his voice.

"Nope. Redick Allred and some of the others felt like I did—we had to be sure what happened 'fore turning around and going back to the valley. Heard what the boys of the express had to say— young Joseph and the Garr lad—and I was convinced you'd keep on the trail."

Relief flooded through Ed Martin. "So there are wagons still waiting at South Pass?"

Hanks nodded. "Allred and those who stayed with him won't turn back until they get final word, from me or someone else."

"Can they get over the pass?" Decker asked.

"Have to work at it, but once they have reason to try, they can get through."

Charlie Decker looked at Ed Martin. "I say we get an express headed out tonight. I've got boys who know the trail and can travel fast, even in the dark. They'll be at South Pass by morning."

"Get them started, Charlie," Ed told him. "Maybe we'll live through this after all."

At Ed Martin's request, Hanks made a round of the sick in the wagons. Eph Hanks was an old hand at trail medicine, particularly when it came to gunshot wounds, snakebites, frostbite, and fever. He had learned by hard experience, some from friendly Indians, and some from others like himself who spent much of their lives apart from civilization. He had probed for many a spent bullet, cauterized or sewn up many a wound. He carried a pouch filled with strange-smelling powders mixed from roots, herbs, and dead insects. If you were sick and Eph Hanks gave you something to drink, you were smart to gulp it down quick no matter how foul it might look or taste.

When people were told this was the man who supplied the fresh meat for supper, he was warmly welcomed and thanked. The scout treated a few for frostbite that had turned dangerous, washing and treating blackened skin, clipping off parts of the flesh that were already touched with gangrene. At these times he was gentle and understanding. He checked the Tate boys, saw that a good job had been done, and joked with them about how soon they'd be running races.

Tregale accompanied Hanks to the tent when he looked at Willie and Heather. He watched anxiously as the man checked their fevers. Maude was down on her knees beside her husband, looking anxiously from Willie to Eph Hanks and back again. Agatha was hovering nearby, unable to conceal her distrust of this mountain-man healer. He sensed it and turned to her with a scowl.

"You done much doctoring, lady?"

Agatha returned the scowl. "Done my share."

"So what sets you apart from the next person?"

"Common sense," Agatha snapped. "I don't get wrapped in no silly emotions, and I don't pretend to know things I don't."

Surprisingly, a big grin spread across Eph Hanks's face, or what could be seen of it through the beard. "I like that." He nodded several times, still grinning. He reached into a leather carrying bag hanging from his side and pulled out a small pouch. Opening it, he held it out for Agatha to inspect. "You don't know what's in there," he told her, his voice no longer challenging. "It's a mix of things you probably never even heard of. But you put a pinch or two of that into a cup of hot broth, and both these people will be chomping the bit by morning. An old Indian medicine man passed it on to me, and I'm living proof it works. What does your common sense tell you about that?"

Agatha looked into the pouch, frowned, then looked up at the scout. "Not sure about you, but I'm willing to trust that medicine man."

The grin again flashed across Eph Hanks's face. "Got any hot broth left from supper?"

"No broth," Agatha replied. "All we got is some warm tea—"

"That'll do," Hanks said. Agatha didn't move, still a little uncertain. The scout waved a hand impatiently. "So get it, woman."

In the center of the tent, there was a metal teapot balanced on top of a smooth, round stone. The stone had been placed in the fire outside the tent and later brought inside to provide some measure of warmth and to keep the teapot warm. It was a trick learned in England: a warm brick taken from the hearth, wrapped in cloth, and put under the bed covers to take off the damp chill at bedtime. Agatha frostily picked up the teapot while Maude and Heather quickly wiped out some cups.

Agatha poured tea into the cups. Hanks took a pinch of powdery substance from the pouch, dropping it into Heather's outstretched cup.

"Just give it a stir with your finger," Eph instructed, "then down with the whole lot. You'll probably get a mite sleepy, but you'll feel as good as new in the morning."

He repeated the process with Maude and she helped Willie get the liquid down. Willie raised a hand to the scout. "My gratitude to you, sir. Do you think this potion might help me grow a beard as proud as yours?"

Hanks chuckled. "Don't know about that. It will grow wings on your feet, though."

The scout turned to leave, then saw Harriet Hilliger sitting beside her sister. Hanks crossed and squatted down in front of Harriet, peering closely into the blank eyes. He looked at Lydia.

"She your sister?"

Lydia nodded.

"How long she been like this?"

"Almost four weeks, ever since we crossed the Platte River."

"The cold and the river did this to her—?"

Lydia nodded again. "She hasn't been herself since. Hasn't spoken a word to anyone."

Eph Hanks peered again into Harriet's eyes. It was as if Harriet didn't even see the bearded face so close in front of her. The scout leaned back. "I've seen this before, among Indians and whites. Some shock or pain or great suffering makes a person hide inside themselves. There's a way to maybe bring her out of it, but I'll have to cause her a little hurt."

"How much hurt?"

"Hardly none. But there's no guarantee it will bring her back to normal, even then."

"Is there any risk she'll get worse?"

Hanks shrugged. "Can't say. Never seen it happen that way. Seems like she's blanked everything out already."

Lydia looked up at Carn. "What do you think, Brother Tregale?"

"She's your sister, Lydia," Tregale answered, "but if it was up to me, I'd want her back. Doesn't seem there's much risk involved, and I trust Eph Hanks knows what he's doing."

Lydia looked back at the scout, her eyes searching the bearded face for a long moment. Then tears formed in the corners of her eyes. "Bring her back, Brother Hanks. We'll both be in your debt."

"Ain't much to it, really," Hanks grunted. "Slip her arm out of that coat."

Lydia pulled one of Harriet's arms out of the coat she had worn day and night for weeks. Hanks reached over and took an inch of the flesh of Harriet's upper arm between his thumb and finger.

"Like I said, this is going to hurt her some, but don't go squeamish on me. It has to hurt if it's going to work."

He started to squeeze the upper arm. The flesh turned chalky white under the pressure. Then Hanks slowly began to twist the pinched flesh. For a moment, Harriet continued to stare at him, no expression on her face, no sign of anything in her eyes. But suddenly her eyes started to twitch and move. Her head dropped to look down at her arm. Eph Hanks kept pinching and twisting. Harriet slowly lifted her other arm and tried to pull Hanks's fingers away. He just kept pinching harder. They could see he had twisted the flesh almost full circle on Harriet's upper arm.

Suddenly Harriet cried out, the first sound that had escaped her since that day at the river. She began clawing at Hanks's fingers, trying to break away from his grip. Tears started to fall down her cheeks. She cried out again, and this time slapped him hard across the face. He didn't seem to notice, just kept on twisting the arm. Now she was hitting him repeatedly.

"You're hurting me," she gasped finally, her voice little more than a whisper, but the words spoken plainly. "Please, let go of my arm—"

A big smile broke across Eph Hanks's face. He released his fingers, reached out, and pulled Harriet against him. She sobbed unrestrainedly and he patted her on the back. "Sorry to do that to you, little lady, but I think it worked."

He released her and Harriet looked around, not even trying to stop the flow of tears, awareness of her surroundings wide in her eyes. She saw Lydia and reached for her. The two of them clung fiercely to each other.

Eph Hanks looked around the tent, saw that every woman in it was crying as they watched the two sisters. The men too were fighting back tears. He turned to Carn Tregale. "Seems like we done it all here. Let's move on."

That night, Tregale had to post additional guards because an unusual number of prairie wolves began prowling the fringes of the camp. He had no real explanation for it; perhaps it was the smell of blood on Eph Hanks's horses, or the lingering smell of cooked buffalo meat hanging over the camp. Throughout most of the night, shots were fired to keep the wolves away from livestock and out of camp.

The company started out again early in the morning and there was a feeling of excitement as people speculated on when they would meet the wagons heading toward them from South Pass. They had seen the express leave shortly after Eph Hanks arrived, and everyone seemed confident that more relief wagons would soon reach them.

Eph Hanks's word proved to be as good as gold—Willie Tate

and Heather Lee both felt remarkably recovered, with no trace of
fever, and much stronger. Harriet was talking a stream with everyone. Apparently she had been aware of much of what had been
going on around her, but she had not been able to break loose
from the terror inside. Every now and then she reached over and
gently rubbed the deep bruise on her upper arm, but she never
uttered a word of complaint.

About ten in the morning, the wagons of Captain Hodgett's
train caught up with the Martin company. Captain Grant and some
other members of the rescue party were with them. Grant and his
men had waited until Monday afternoon when the Hunt wagons
finally rolled out from Martin's Hollow. Then he rode ahead to
catch the Hodgett train and spend the night with them. Hunt had
promised to make all possible speed to catch up with the rest of
the emigrants.

Hodgett and Hanks greeted each other like long-lost friends,
which was the case. Captain Grant swore angrily when he heard
the news of the wagons turning back from South Pass.

"That's the same as putting a gun to all our heads!" he stormed.
"Pure cowardice, that's what it is."

"I feel someone should be made to answer for it," Decker said.
"If it hadn't been Eph telling it, I couldn't have believed any of our
men would cut and run like that."

"You say the express left yesterday—"

Decker nodded. "Probably reached South Pass already."

"You can count on Allred and the boys," Eph Hanks rumbled.
"They'll make it through the pass. First wagons should reach us
sometime tomorrow, I expect."

"Well," Grant growled, "that's some welcome news, at least."

"And none too soon," Martin said grimly. "We'll see the last of
the flour and most of the other rations today."

"Don't know how you people have stood it," Charlie Decker
muttered. "Never been anything like it, not in all the treks to
California or Oregon Territory, that I've heard of."

228

The company made it a short day and camped early that evening in a rocky cove above the Sweetwater, near a spot called Three Crossings. The weather was still bitterly cold, but there was no new snow and little wind. They had almost nothing for supper that evening; the lucky ones had a few bites of dried fruit to chew or a hard biscuit to share. Children cried with hunger, and parents desperately tried to comfort them. People kept looking to the west, hoping for a sign of the relief wagons. With darkness, they fell into fitful sleep.

CHAPTER TWENTY

CONTINENTAL DIVIDE
LATE NOVEMBER

The camp was awakened at five o'clock the next morning, not by the bugler but by the arrival of four wagons loaded with flour and supplies. They had left South Pass early the previous day within hours of the word that the handcart emigrants were alive, and they had traveled hard all day and night to reach the camp. The emigrants wept with gratitude as they reached up to receive not just a ration of flour, but life itself.

As if to celebrate the day, which was Wednesday, the twelfth of November, the sun came out warm and bright. The weather stayed good for the next three days. The weary, emaciated emigrants marched slowly along the trail during those days, gaining strength, nursing health back into the sick, snatching some from the very jaws of death.

On the next Saturday, when Tregale completed his rounds, he made his way to Ed Martin. He stood silently for a moment, blinking against the tears forming in his eyes.

"I have a special report to make this morning," he told Ed, his voice quavering, barely held in control. "It gives me deep pleasure to tell you that, for the first time since crossing the North Platte, we have no dead to bury."

Ed looked at him, felt his own emotions surge. The two men clasped each other, letting the significance of those words settle inside them. A night without death. The loss of life had become so

230

much a part of their lives that both men had become hardened, not allowing themselves to be touched, forcing themselves to accept death and burial as just another problem that had to be dealt with daily. Now, for one morning, they did not have to face the dreadful pain of those who had lost a loved one. It brought a relief that was almost as difficult to deal with as death.

"Thank you, God," Martin breathed. He finally broke away and looked at Tregale. "How many have we lost all told? I kept track for a while, but then it was too painful."

"Same for me," Carn muttered. "About a hundred and fifty dead, near as I can figure. Most of those were lost after the Platte."

"A terrible price—"

"A risk everyone knew they were taking."

"No, they didn't," Ed said, shaking his head. "They had no comprehension. Thirteen hundred miles of marching meant nothing to them. They couldn't picture it. To them, it was a walk across the moors, with nothing more to be feared than a twisted ankle. They didn't know we meant it when we talked of dying."

"Don't go taking it on yourself, Ed. Nothing you could have done different."

"I could have held them at Florence, when I knew it was late in the season. I could have wintered at Laramie, when I knew food was running out."

"You did the only thing that made sense, Ed—made a run for the valley. You've heard the others—worst weather in memory. No one could have foreseen that."

"Still, we left a hundred and fifty good people on the trail. It will take a long time for me to live peaceable with that."

"There're over four hundred and fifty who will make it, and they couldn't have done it without you. That's what to keep in your mind, my friend. We all mourn the dead, but there's a lot of thanks owed for the living."

The next day, Sunday, the company met ten more relief wagons. More warm clothing and bedding were distributed among the emigrants, and a sense of well-being began to soak slowly into people who had all but given up any hope of survival. They met more wagons Monday, and more again on Tuesday. Each day they traveled just a few miles, spending most of the time resting and building strength for the final push to the valley once the divide was crossed.

Tuesday morning saw the clouds hanging low and ominous in the sky again, ending the welcome stretch of nearly a week of good weather. It started snowing in the afternoon, about the time the fourth group of relief wagons were sighted. By evening, it was snowing heavily.

As Tregale made his evening rounds, he was struck by the high spirits he found everywhere. The past few days of warm clothing and full, solid meals had lifted most of the emigrants out of their depression. Completing the checks took Carn longer than usual because several groups invited him to join them in prayers of gratitude for their deliverance. Each time, he was struck by the sincerity of the prayer, the real sense that these were children offering thanks to a Father in Heaven who existed as surely as they did themselves. The emigrants poured out their gratitude that lives had been spared, expressed love for those fellow Saints who had given so freely of their goods, and for those who had come to their rescue. And each time they also remembered the dead, not with deep sadness but with a joy and a certainty that these souls were now happy and grateful to be back in the presence of their Father.

The simple, believing faith expressed in the prayers stirred a strange sensation inside Carn. There was no struggle with himself, no sense of some great revelation of truth, not even a feeling of something missing in his life. He realized that the warmth inside came from the love so freely and genuinely extended to him, an acceptance of him as one of them, a fellowship that reached into the heart and made no demands.

It was something that went beyond smiles and handshakes; it was a touching of spirits. That's what made this so different, this emotion that was churning inside him, Tregale realized. These Mormons had reached out and embraced him as one of them, without reservation, though all knew he was not a baptized member of their faith. And then something even more important struck him: he felt a part of them. He was a part of this family, for that was what they were, no matter where they came from or how long they had known each other. They were one big family, united by suffering, warmed by a love for each other, bound by a faith in God. And he, Carn Tregale, had somehow become a part of it all.

When Tregale returned to the tent, emotions churned inside him. He found the entire group there, enjoying slices of fresh bread still warm from the skillet. He looked around and found a mirror of the gaunt but happy faces in the other tents.

Fred and Ted Tate were sitting up, bandages unwrapped, proudly displaying their toeless feet to their sisters. Dolly hid her eyes, crowding her face against her mother, while Maggie stared wide-eyed.

"Will they grow back?" Maggie asked, not able to tear her gaze away. It was the first time she had seen what the frostbite had caused.

"Won't need them," Ted said matter-of-factly. "We'll be able to run faster 'cause our feet won't have so much weight."

"And I'll still be able to beat you," Fred told his brother, a superior smirk on his face.

"You never did beat me," Ted said heatedly. "Not ever. I beat you every time."

"Liar—"

"Liar—"

Maude looked over at her husband. Willie was lying down, but he raised up on one elbow, glaring at his sons.

"I think your mother is right. I'm sure that's black frostbite I see on your tongues." Willie glanced up at Tregale. "Take a look, will you, Brother Tregale? I think we might have to cut them off, along with their toes."

The mouths of Fred and Ted snapped shut. They looked at each other, then slid down and pulled the covers over their heads.

Alfred Cunningham was talking seriously to his son. Aaron was nodding, trying to listen attentively, though his eyes kept sliding over to Lydia. Alfred called out to Tregale. "Don't you agree it will be a land of opportunity in the valley, Brother Tregale."

"Don't know much about it," Tregale replied, "but with all the people flocking there from around the world, and all the growth that will be happening, seems as though there'll be a great need for carpentry skills."

"That's what I've been telling Aaron," Alfred said eagerly. "Cunningham and Son. We'll be on our feet and prospering in no time."

Aaron smiled, looking across at his betrothed. "The first house we'll build will be for Lydia and me." He saw the little frown of concern that flashed across Harriet's face and quickly added, "There'll be plenty of room for you, Harriet, though you'll most likely have a husband of your own before a summer has passed."

"The first house will be for your mother and me," Alfred corrected. "I don't think your mother will want to spend another winter under canvas."

"I don't want to spend this one, either," Esther said tartly. "You'd better get busy building something as soon as we reach the valley. Aaron can add a room or two as he chooses, until his means catch up with his dreams."

Jim Wilson broke into the conversation. "I heard Captain Grant say President Young has given orders that all of us handcart people are to be taken into homes as soon as we arrive. Beth and I will be grateful for that, having a roof over our heads to protect little Nancy, until we can strike out on our own."

"I know we've a long way yet before we reach the valley," Derek Pitts said, "but since we all seem of the same mind to look ahead, I want all of you to know how much Gwen and I appreciate the help and the love you've shown to us. You'll all be dear to us the rest of our lives."

"That's true," Gwen said quickly. "You will always be family to us, and welcome in our home. I expect it won't be very grand, not for a few years at least, so if you all visit at the same time, expect it to be a little crowded."

"No more than this tent," Derek said, grinning. "This has served well as home and shelter to all of us for what seems to me half our lives—"

Agatha was on her way to the teakettle when Tregale reached out and stopped her. "What about you, Agatha?" Carn asked. "You've been mother and friend to us all these months. What are your plans for the future?"

Agatha looked uncomfortable. "Got no plans," she muttered, starting again for the kettle.

Tregale put his arm firmly around her shoulders. "No sense trying to brush us out of your life, Agatha," he said softly. "You've won a spot in all our hearts. We all owe you a debt. You've been the glue that held us together, when each one would have fallen apart. Like it or not, Agatha, we all love you."

"That's nonsense," Agatha said, trying to make her voice sharp but failing miserably. "You've all gone daft. No sense talking about such things while there're all those mountains ahead of us. Time enough to get maudlin when we're safe in the valley."

"All well and good," Tregale said, grinning and keeping his arm about her, "but you're begging the question. What do you plan to do once you reach the valley?"

"Like I said, I don't have any plans."

"Agatha, if I've learned one thing about you," Carn said, "it's the fact that you always look ahead. You won't convince any of us you had nothing in mind when you decided to make this trip."

Heather stood up and joined Agatha too, putting an arm about her waist. "Come on, Agatha. You can't ever not be a part of our lives, especially for Carn and me. If you truly have no plans, then come and live with us."

Agatha heaved a deep sigh. "Very well, I see you're all determined to put your nose into my business. As a matter of fact, I do have something in mind. It's not exactly what I thought back in England, but it's what I've decided."

Everyone waited, but Agatha said no more. Willie raised both arms in frustration.

"You can't leave us there, Agatha—"

"I have a plan for my life," Agatha snapped. "That's enough said."

"No, it's not," Maude said, getting to her feet. "We love you, Agatha, but you'll get no rest until you tell us."

Agatha looked around the tent, saw the smiles and the love. She felt Carn's arm tighten about her shoulders and suddenly her eyes moistened.

"Very well, if you must know," she muttered, her voice so low it almost couldn't be heard, "I'm planning to get married."

The news shocked everyone. Willie was frowning, as if he hadn't heard right.

"Did you say you was going to get married?"

Heather gave her a hug. "That's wonderful, Agatha. That's absolutely wonderful—"

"Have you picked the lucky man?" Tregale asked.

Agatha curtly shook her head. "Haven't seen one worth having. But you people are to blame for putting such foolishness in my head. We've been a family these past months, a close one. Frankly, it got so I couldn't bear the thought of being alone again. So I'm going to find a man when I get to the valley and get married. Might even be one of those polygamous wives I hear about. Are you happy now you've pried open my private thoughts?"

The tent flap opened and Ed Martin entered, brushing snow-flakes off his coat. He looked around, saw the grins and beaming faces, and broke into a smile himself. "Seems like this is a cheery place—"

Freddie Tate poked his head out from under the blankets. "Agatha just told us—"

"Hush!" Agatha cut him off, pointing a finger threateningly at him. "One more word, and I'll be doing that operation your daddy was talking about."

Freddie ducked back under the covers.

"Looks as if it's still snowing out there," Tregale said.

Martin nodded. "Piling up, I'm afraid. Won't make it any easier on the trail." His face broke into another smile. "But that's what I came to tell you folks. With these wagons that joined us this afternoon, there's room enough for everyone to ride. No one needs to walk one more step."

A cheer broke from every throat. Those who were standing hugged each other. Some began to cry again.

"That's good to hear, Captain Martin," Maude Tate said. "It's got harder and harder to put a foot forward, even without the handcarts."

"Thought you'd like to know," Martin said, teeth showing in the broadest grin he'd managed since starting out on the trail. "And none of us should go hungry, either. I'm told there're more relief wagons almost every mile between here and the valley."

Tregale crossed and clapped a hand on Martin's shoulder. He looked about the tent, and a grin creased his face. "If Ed hadn't dropped in, I was going to fetch him. There's something you should know about this man who's kept us going through hell. Today is Ed's birthday—"

Congratulations poured from the people in the tent, embarrassing Martin. He punched Carn on the shoulder. "No need to tell people—"

"How old are you, Captain Martin?" Maggie Tate asked.

"Well, Maggie, if anyone but you had asked, I'd have sent them out looking for strays. But since it's you, I'll tell you. I'm thirty-eight."

Maggie's eyes widened. "You're old!"

"Shush, Maggie," her mother cried. "That's rude."

Martin grinned. "Not as old as I feel, Maggie. I'm grateful for that."

Tregale took Heather's hand, pulling her close to him. He looked around the tent and the noise quieted, for it was plain Carn was about to say something important

"The words have been said that express how we feel about each other," he began, "but there are a few things more I'd like to say, and this seems the right time to say them. First, thank you for taking a stranger not of your faith into your hearts. It came at a time when I had suffered a great loss, and I was pretty much lost myself. There are no words to thank my friend, Ed Martin, for his help and encouragement. Ed was the one who talked me into coming to America, and though it's been misery these past weeks, I've found more than I ever hoped for."

Carn looked at Heather and held her hand tightly. The others saw his mouth tremble for a moment as he tried to keep feelings under control.

"This young lady at my side has put meaning into life, has lightened my heart and refreshed my soul. Until I met her, I wasn't sure I had a soul, nor did I care much one way or the other. But she has stirred something within me I cannot explain. I look at her, and somehow I know there is a God who cares for us. The feeling inside me reaches beyond the here and now and tells me there is more. I don't pretend to understand what has happened inside me, and frankly, I'm amazed I've been able to express what I have. All I really know is that I want this woman to be my wife."

Heather circled him with her arms and held him, tears running down freely. It was enough to set off every other woman in the tent. Heather finally released him and Tregale put his good arm round her waist.

"You people are all a part of what has happened. Our life together, however long it lasts through this life and the next, will always be tied to this experience we've shared as friends—and as family. Things will be different from now—we've seen the worst. We should reach the valley in another ten or twelve days, and no telling what will happen to us after that. We'll all scatter every which way, probably. I haven't said anything to Heather about this, but I can't think of a finer group of friends to be at our wedding, nor a man I would rather have perform the ceremony, than are gathered right here in this tent."

Heather looked up at him, eyes wide. "Are you proposing what I think you are—?"

"I would be most honored if you would marry me, Heather, right here and now. That way, this part of our life, the part that brought us together, will never go dim in our memories."

Heather put both arms around him and kissed him hard. "I thank God for bringing you to me, Carn Tregale. I'll be most honored to marry you, here and now."

The Fifth Handcart Company, those who had survived, arrived in the Salt Lake valley shortly before noon on Sunday, the thirtieth of November, ending a journey that had begun six months earlier.

No company had ever seen so much suffering and death in all the annals of the westward flow along the American frontier.

No company ever welcomed their arrival in Zion more gratefully, nor felt as deep a joy in life itself.

ABOUT THE AUTHOR

John McRae was educated in British private schools, then served aboard a destroyer in the Pacific theater during World War II.

As a writer and producer of trade and educational films and television commercials, Mr. McRae has frequently been honored for his accomplishments. His work has won such prestigious awards as an Emmy, a New York Art Directors award, and several Telly awards. Two of his educational films have been widely used in U.S. schools.

Prior to moving into advertising and filmmaking, he worked for fourteen years as a newspaper feature writer. He has recently turned to a full-time career as a novelist and screenwriter.

John McRae has served in many callings in The Church of Jesus Christ of Latter-day Saints, including elders quorum president, high priests group instructor, and high councilor.

The westward movement of the Latter-day Saints has long interested him, and his research into the handcart companies culminated in his first published novel, *Fire in the Snow.*

He and his wife, Vicki, live in Kirkland, Washington. They are the parents of seven children.